HIGH PRAISE FOR
THIS DOG FOR HIRE
The Debut Novel in the
Rachel Alexander and Dash Mystery Series

"FIRST-RATE"—*The Plain Dealer* (Cleveland)

"A spirited debut, written with enough flair to make it appealing to more than just dog lovers. And Benjamin writes with wit nearly as sharp as Dash's teeth."
—*Publishers Weekly*

"It's always a pleasure to note the appearance of a first book from a promising writer, especially one as promising as Carol Lea Benjamin."
—*The Washington Times*

"A witty and colorful story; *This Dog for Hire* is great fun."
—*Mostly Murder*

"A refreshingly unique reading experience."
—*The Midwest Book Review*

"Carol Lea Benjamin is as good at writing mysteries as she is at writing about dogs. The writing is as gritty and edgy as the location, with a good dollop of humor thrown in."
—Laurien Berenson, author of *Underdog*

Dell Books by Carol Lea Benjamin

THIS DOG FOR HIRE
THE DOG WHO KNEW TOO MUCH

THE DOG WHO KNEW TOO MUCH

A Rachel Alexander and Dash Mystery

CAROL LEA BENJAMIN

A DELL BOOK

Published by
Dell Publishing
a division of
Bantam Doubleday Dell Publishing Group, Inc.
1540 Broadway
New York, New York 10036

The trademark Dell® is registered in the U.S. Patent and
Trademark Office.

ISBN-13: 978-0-440-22637-6

ISBN-10: 0-440-22637-6

Reprinted by arrangement with Walker and Company

Printed in the United States of America

Published simultaneously in Canada

October 1998

10 9 8 7 6 5 4 3 2

WCD

For Noah Kahn
I love you, Dad.

The author wishes to thank

The school of T'ai Chi Chuan, New York City, especially Pat Gorman for her giving nature and extraordinary ability to teach and inspire, George Fletcher for the lovely way he grew along with his students, and Jackie Harris, classmate and friend

For the generous sharing of information and insights, Joel McMains, former deputy sheriff; George Axler, graphologist; Larry Berg, cynologist; Detectives Joseph Barker, Daniel O'Connell, and Bob Moller of the Sixth Precinct; Barbara Jaye Wilson, fellow mystery writer; and Beth Adelman, whose interests and talents coincided in the most serendipitous way with the needs of this book

Mystery Writers of America, Private Eye Writers of America, Sisters in Crime, the Authors Guild, and the Dog Writers Association of America, professional organizations that help writers be considerably more savvy in a dog-eat-dog world

Gail Hochman and Marianne Merola at Brandt & Brandt

Michael Seidman, maven d'editing

My friends and family, especially my sister Mimi and Stephen Lennard, my sweetheart

And Dexter and Flash, because if there's Zen at the top of the mountain, some dog brought it there

1

If You Weren't Careful

DASHIELL STOOD MOTIONLESS on the dark, wet sand, his eyes cemented to the driftwood log I held up over my head. Just before I moved to send it spinning over him and into the ocean, as if he were able to read my mind, he turned to mark its fall; then, all speed and power, he ran flat out into the surf. Looking beyond him at the vast, gray-blue Atlantic Ocean, flattened under a bright spring sky, I remembered myself as a child playing fetch on this very beach with some other dog, now long gone.

I used to come to my aunt Ceil's house in Sea Gate, the gated community just beyond Coney Island, when I was a kid. I would race for the water the minute we hit the beach, shedding flip-flops and T-shirt as I ran, staying in until Beatrice, my mother, standing on the shore about where Dashiell stood a moment ago, hands on her hips, a line showing over the center bridge of her sunglasses, would shout to me that my lips were turning blue, and why didn't I come out and play on the sand like a good girl, as my big sister Lillian had long since done.

"I can't hear you," I'd call back, bobbing like the stick I'd just thrown for Dashiell.

"You'll be the death of me," Beatrice shouted, her voice like the roar of the waves from far away on the shore.

Playing on the hot, gritty sand under my mother's scrutiny held no charm for me. The ocean was the lure—all that power, beauty, mystery, and life. Even death, if you weren't careful. At least that's what Beatrice used to say, as if being careful could do the trick and keep you safe.

Beatrice found the scary side of everything, the don't instead of the do. That's why I grew up looking for trouble, just to defy her. At least that's what my shrink used to say. That sad fact, according to Ida Berkowitz, Ph.D., would explain what I was doing here today, even though my mother, like that pup I had played fetch with when I was a kid, was long gone.

Dashiell was riding a foamy, frigid wave back toward me, the driftwood crosswise in his mouth.

I had hesitated for only the moment it took for the guard to call ahead and make sure I had actually been invited to come to this private and protected community that occupies the point of land where the Atlantic Ocean meets Gravesend Bay. By the time he had lifted the barrier and motioned me to drive in, I knew I had a stop to make before keeping my appointment, for my sake as much as for Dashiell's. I'd headed here, to the deserted beach, so that my partner, the other unlicensed PI with whom I was in business, could dig in the sand, swim in the ocean, and roll in dead fish and used condoms, reminding me as he always did precisely how delicious it was merely to be alive. Soon enough I'd be immersed in less expansive feelings, because it was a case that had brought me to Brooklyn on this cool, clear April day.

Dashiell stood squarely in front of me, holding the stick dead center, eyes locked on mine, water running off his underside and down his legs, his one-track mind on the task at hand.

"Out," I told him. I have a way with words.

He dropped the driftwood heavily into my hand and, hoping for another toss, retreated to where the incoming waves could just reach him, washing over his feet from behind, then swirling in front of his ankles before returning, as eventually we all must, from whence it came. I gave him one last swim, sending the driftwood high and far over the waves, watching him watch it, electrified with pleasure. We saw the splash. Dashiell, the quintessential pit bull, charged forward with sufficient grit, strength, and tenacity to bring the damn ocean to its knees, if need be. Work or play, it was all the same to him. He'd use whatever force he deemed necessary to meet a challenge.

We ran around on the sand to dry off, then headed back to the black Ford Taurus that David and Marsha Jacobs, Aunt Ceil's neighbors and friends, had rented for me so that I could drive here to the quiet community where they had lived for forty-seven years and listen to them tell me about the sudden, unexpected, and violent death of their only child.

2

We Could Hear The
Kettle Whistle

MARSHA JACOBS WAS one of those women who wear stockings and heels even in their own homes. She'd answered the door in a dark gray silk dress, the uneven piece of black grosgrain ribbon that signified a death in the family pinned to her chest. It would leave holes in the silk, I found myself thinking, then silently berated myself for the frivolous thought.

Driving home along the Belt Parkway, I couldn't get the image of Lisa Jacobs's mother out of my mind. For that's what she was, first and foremost, the devoted Jewish mother of a beautiful, blue-eyed, curly-haired thirty-two-year-old who ten days earlier, with no clues to foreshadow the act, had opened one of the oversize windows at the t'ai chi studio where she studied and taught and jumped five stories to her death.

"We want to show you our Lisa," Marsha had said, welcoming me into the living room time forgot. "Come and sit, Rachel. Can I get you some tea?"

"Thank you," I said, feeling chilled by the room and

my wet clothes. Dashiell had body-slammed me several times right before we left the beach, and my leggings felt as if I had been in the ocean, too. I wondered if we'd each get a different pattern of bone china from which to drink our tea, like the cups my mother had collected.

David Jacobs was sitting on one side of the couch, a thick, leatherbound photo album on his lap. He patted the middle seat, and hoping I wouldn't leave a big, wet ass print on their sofa, I sat next to him.

"This has been very hard on her," he said as soon as Marsha had left to make the tea. "She—" he began, but then hesitated. "She's up all night," he whispered, "pacing, pacing. She's driving me *crazy*. She—" he sighed before correcting himself—"we, *we*," he repeated, "would like you to help us, Rachel. We cannot understand what could have possessed Lisa, what made her do this awful thing." He sounded angry. "We don't have a guess. Not a clue."

David placed the album on the coffee table, stood, and went to get his cigarettes from the top of the piano. His suit pulled across his potbelly and hung too loosely around his arms and shoulders, as if he had recently lost a good bit of weight, a supposition that, considering the circumstances, I would not have had to be a detective to make.

"Lisa never complained, never complained. She never spoke of any problems. She was always cheerful, kind, a happy girl. Ach," he said, stopping to light his cigarette, "how could this have happened? We gave her everything."

I could hear Marsha talking to Dashiell in the kitchen, where she'd suggested I stash him, even though he had already stopped dripping by the time we'd arrived. Dashiell's tail tapped out his answer on the tile floor.

"She was studying to be a Zen Buddhist priest, my Lisa," Marsha said, standing in the archway at the rear of the living room. "The study and the t'ai chi gave her peace. Peace. That's what she told her father and me. So why—"

"Sit, Marsha," David said, blowing smoke into the middle of the room. Marsha sat next to me. Now I had their grief on both sides. In our silence we could hear the kettle whistle, and Marsha left again to make the tea.

"Are you cold, Rachel?" David said, as concerned as if *I* were his daughter.

"No, no," I lied, "I'm fine."

"Are you sure? Marsha, bring her a sweater," he shouted in the direction of the kitchen.

"No, thank you, I'm fine. Really."

"It's no trouble," he said, half to himself. "We have plenty of sweaters."

He moved the album closer but didn't open it.

"Ceil said you used to be a dog trainer. Before."

I raised my eyebrows.

David looked at me and puffed on the cigarette, ashes dropping onto his suit pants. "Before your—before you were married." He brushed at his trousers, leaving a dry, gray trail where the ashes had been.

Marsha arrived with the tray and placed it carefully next to the photo album. She handed me a cup with yellow tulips on it and gave David one with purple irises, saving the one with the tiny red rosebuds for herself.

"Marsha—the sweater, the sweater," David said impatiently.

Suddenly I had the eerie feeling I was in some relative's suffocating home. I reached for a cookie. Marsha returned with a navy blue sweater and handed it to David, who handed it to me. I put it over the arm of the sofa.

"So—" David said. "You married again? Your husband approves of this kind of work, de*tec*tive work?"

Marsha was biting a small biscuit. She looked up, curious.

Ceil would have told them I hadn't married again, wouldn't she?

I reached for another cookie. "Lisa was single, wasn't she?" The eighth law of private investigation, according to my erstwhile employer and mentor, Frank Petrie, is, Don't *give* information. *Get* information.

"Lisa never married," her mother said.

"No, marriage wasn't what Lisa wanted," David said.

"Her studies were everything to her." Marsha gathered the crumbs from her silk skirt onto one hand and carefully brushed them off in one corner of the tray.

"The mother has a college degree, too. Did your aunt mention that?"

"*Da*vid." Marsha flapped a hand in his direction.

"Six years she studied, three at night, three full time, at Brooklyn College, competing with all those young hotshots. She got wonderful grades, wonderful."

I smiled at Marsha, and she patted my damp leg.

"She taught school, too. A very intelligent woman. That's who Lisa took after. Her mother. A bachelor's degree. Just like the hotshots."

"Is that how you met, at college?"

"Fourteen years," he said. He took a last puff on the cigarette and put it out. "That's how long we waited for Lisa."

"David, we shouldn't—"

"Rachel needs to know these things, isn't that so, Rachel? She came here to get the facts, so that she could help us. We never thought there would be a baby, not for us. Fourteen years it took."

We sipped tea for a moment in silence. Finally David opened the album. But I had already seen Lisa. Across from us, on the baby grand piano in a standing silver frame, was a photo of a pretty young girl smiling.

"She was an extraordinary child," Marsha told me as David turned the pages, "not average."

I looked at Lisa in her carriage, Lisa in the bath, Lisa sleeping.

"She did everything early, before the books said," Marsha told me, looking at me for approval.

"Everything early," I repeated.

"This was the summer she went to camp," I heard David say, "but we missed her. Marsha kept saying, 'David, we have the beach right here, we have the Atlantic Ocean at our beck and call, why does Lisa have to be in the Adirondacks with all those mosquitoes and no ocean?' So, what else, we went up on visitors' day and brought her home. At the end of July. Slow season. I could take her to the beach every day. No problem. She was some swimmer, that child. Like a fish."

"She was a varsity swimmer," Marsha said, "at Abraham Lincoln High School." She got up and brought over the medals and one of the trophies that sat on the shelves across from the couch.

"She was the valedictorian," David said. "She made a speech on graduation day. Smart. Like her mother. There was nothing that girl couldn't do, if she set her mind to it."

"When did Lisa get interested in t'ai chi?" I asked.

"While she was in college," Marsha said. "Just be-

fore she broke her engagement, the end of her sopho-
more year."

I could feel David tense. Marsha looked into her lap.

"You liked the boy?" I asked.

"He was going to be a dentist," she said, "like his
father."

"Water under the bridge," David said.

Had Ceil told them *I* had been married to a dentist,
that I too had let a professional man go?

"In her third year," Marsha said, "that was when—"

"China, China, she wanted only to go to China. To
study. She was nineteen. What did she know? Imagine,
running to China, a nineteen-year-old kid, alone, on the
other side of the world."

"So, did she go? Did she study in China?"

"Go? Did she go?" David bellowed.

For a moment he looked as if he were on fire, red
smoke swirling about him as his aura turned the color
of his rage.

"You tell me if you'd let a kid like that go off on her
own to a foreign country. What did she know, to do a
dangerous thing like that, by herself? She stayed here. It
was for her own good. Everything we did was for her,
everything."

"She studied here," Marsha said. "At Barnard. Eastern philosophy and Chinese language."

"She spoke Chinese, what else, beautiful, just as good
as if she had lived there, you should have heard her."

"After her postgraduate studies, five years at Colum-
bia on a fellowship, that's when she met Avram, the
director of the school where Lisa worked. She studied
with him since then." Marsha picked up a napkin and
held it to her mouth for a moment. "Avram adored her,
you know. He said Lisa was his best student."

"Then she was here, living here with you?"

"Oh, no. She was at the Printing House," Marsha said. "On Hudson Street. Not far from you. She wanted to be near the school. To walk."

"She wanted the Village, the Village, so, what else, I bought her a condo," David said.

He took his checkbook out of his breast pocket. I began to protest, but his hand went up to stop me.

"It's just that—"

"The police have looked into our Lisa's death," Marsha said as David wrote, "but they're busy with many other things, there's so much crime in the city, so much."

David looked up. "What we need," he said, "it's not really police business, Rachel. They're finished now. But we're not. We're the parents. We have to know what happened, what went on. We need"—he practically bellowed—"to find out why our daughter took her own life."

"David," his wife said, trying to calm him.

"Mr. Jacobs, I—"

"David. Forget this Mr. Jacobs. You could be Lisa's friend, you're so young. You could be my own daughter."

"And call me Marsha, Rachel. We know your aunt so long, we feel we know you, too."

"David. Marsha. To find out something so intimate about a person, it might take a long time. Often the victim's best friend, or her parents, had no idea she was depressed."

"Spend the time, Rachel. We can afford it," David said. "Now tell me your fee, please."

I did. And asked for a thousand in advance.

"Money I have," he said. I heard the sound of a check being torn from a checkbook. "A daughter I don't have, but money I have." He handed me the check. Without looking, I folded it in half and put it into my shirt pocket.

"Even if I do spend the time," I said, "I might not find the answers you're looking for."

"I can't think of anything more important to spend money on than at least *trying* to understand what happened to Lisa. Can you, David?"

But David Jacobs didn't answer his wife's question. He had turned his back to us, and I could see his shoulders trembling. With one hand he removed his bifocals. The other carried an ironed white handkerchief toward his eyes.

"I'll do my best," I heard myself promise. I called Dashiell and heard the jingle of the tags on his collar as he got up.

"We already know that," Marsha said, squeezing my hand.

"I'll have to speak to people—"

"Of course," Marsha said.

"I'll need Lisa's address book, her appointment calendar, and access to her apartment, if possible."

She slid her arm in mine, the way my mother always used to, to walk me out. There was a briefcase on the small table near the door, Marsha lifted it by the handle and gave it to me.

"There are some letters she wrote to us in here, so that you will be able to see for yourself the kind of person she was, how bright, how thoughtful. Her keys are in the zippered pocket. You know the Printing House?"

I nodded.

"Anything else you need, you just ask us."

Despite my willingness to travel as I always did, by foot or subway, David insisted I'd need a car for the duration of the investigation and had already paid a month's rent in advance on the Taurus.

Once out of their house and inside the car, I opened the briefcase and looked inside. There in the pocket, as promised, were Lisa's keys. Her apartment, Marsha had said, was undisturbed. As I was leaving, she'd urged me to go there, where there might be clues, something, anything, that might help me discover what I had to do in order to help her understand what had gone wrong in the perfect life of her perfect child.

Yeah, yeah.

I wondered what Lisa had *really* been like.

I started the car. Then I slipped the check out of my pocket to take a look. It was for three thousand dollars. I had been redefining hand-to-mouth for a month or so. Now if I found myself headed for the poorhouse, I'd be able to go by limo. Driving home, I thought about hiring a cleaning lady. And a gardener.

3

Don't Mention It, He Said

IN THE MORNING, after leaving a message for Avram Ashkenasi asking to see him about Lisa, I headed across the street to the Sixth Precinct to see if my friend Marty Shapiro was around. The officer at the desk said Marty was exercising Elwood and Watson, two of the bomb dogs he worked with. That meant he'd be in the wide alley that ran along the side of the precinct, between Tenth Street and Charles, where the cops parked official vehicles. I found him there, tossing a tennis ball.

"Look at El, Rach," he said as soon as he saw me. "No waistline, and a belly like he swallowed a cantaloupe."

"Too early in the season for melons. More likely it was a box of doughnuts. Maybe you ought to take him to Overeasters Anonymous, on Christopher Street."

Dashiell's nose was welded to Watson's ass.

"I'm taking *him* to Sniff Enders," I said, hooking a thumb toward Dash. He and Watson danced in circles, play-bowed, and began taking turns trying to hump each other.

"No kidding?" Marty said, the tennis ball poised over his head, then flying down the alley, a very overweight Elwood slowly running after it. "Why don't you just change his name to Bruce?"

"Very amusing, Shapiro."

Elwood, the fat yellow Lab, dropped the ball at my feet. I kicked it toward Charles Street.

"Marty, you know anything about the Lisa Jacobs suicide? Her parents have asked me to look into it."

"Look into what?" he asked, surprised.

"Oh, they want to find out what made her depressed enough to go out the window."

"Yeah, right. Good luck on that, kid."

"Why do you say that? I know it'll be difficult, but—"

"Look, Rachel, they're *par*ents. They wanna know it wasn't their fault, you know what I'm saying. Do them a big favor. Spend a few days in the park, catch a few rays, give 'em a call and tell 'em what they need to hear. It's a horrible thing to lose your kid. They don't need guilt on top of it."

"One thing was odd, Marty. They talked to me for ages, but they didn't say much about the incident."

"Not unusual. They don't want to think about it."

"So what was the deal? I heard she did it from the school."

"Maybe her place was too low for a guaranteed success. Maybe she hated her boss, you know, a passive-aggressive last act. Who knows?"

"Are they sure it was suicide?"

"Okay, you want the scene, right?"

I nodded.

He began ticking off the facts on his fingers as he spoke.

"She went out sometime after midnight. No sign of a struggle. The door was locked—"

"Chain on?"

"No chain. Anyone with a key could have locked up on the way out."

"Bingo," I said.

"You New Yorkers, always in such a rush, jumping to conclusions before you got all the facts." He tossed the ball for El, then looked around the alley to make sure we were still alone. "Okay," he continued, "you got a negative scene. No overturned furniture. No burning cigar. No smashed mirrors. No handprint on her back. You following this?"

I nodded.

"No one bent over and let his wallet drop out of his pocket onto the floor for us to find. In fact, there was no nothing."

I nodded again to show I was paying attention.

"You got your locked door, true, without the chain on. You got no one across the street seeing nothing. We checked it out. Maybe that was because the lights were off in the studio. Maybe it was because of the courtyard and all the trees blocking the view. Who knows? Then you got this poor woman coming home from St. Vincent's Hospital, a private duty nurse. She finds the body on the sidewalk. You got the dog upstairs in the studio—"

"Dog? What dog?"

"The victim's. A big Akita. No one's going to bother her with *that* thing around."

"Any big dog would offer a certain amount of visual protection, but—"

"And you got the note."

"Oh," I said, "no one mentioned a note. What did it say?"

" 'I'm sorry. Lisa.' "

All at once the dog was beside the point. True, the Japanese claimed the Akita Inu would protect its master with its very life. But as it turned out, it was only herself Lisa had needed protection from, and hometown hype aside, no dog could do that, not even the national treasure of Japan.

" 'I'm sorry. Lisa'? That's it?"

"What do you want, a memoir? She was depressed, right? She wanted out, so she's out. Young," he said. "And pretty, too. The parents must be real broken up."

"Her father's not eating. Her mother's not sleeping. Their worst nightmare came true."

"So, you're going to put them out of their misery, so to speak. You're going to tell them what good parents they were, right?"

"Right," I said, only half listening. "Where's the dog now?"

"*Now* you sound like the girl I know and love."

"The dog, Marty. Who's got the dog?"

"The guy who owns the school, Ashkenasi, he took her that night. He came to let the detectives in, and when everything was done, he took her home. I don't know where she is now. But if I know you, you'll find out. So good, now you have your work cut out for you."

"Did you secure the scene?"

"No need to put Ashkenasi out of business, Rachel. It was a suicide."

He tossed the ball toward Charles Street and it bounced under one of the police cars. Watson and Dash went to wrestle the ball out from under the car while

Elwood stood by, so dopey looking he might have been drugged.

"Right," I said. "There was a note. Where is that now?"

"In the file, Rach."

"Could I see it, Marty?" I whispered, even though there was no one else around.

"Let me get this straight, you're standing there asking me to break the rules?"

Every cop lives by two rules, Marty had told me the first two hundred times I'd asked for information. Rule one, Keep your mouth shut. Rule two, Never break rule one.

"Just this once," I said. As usual.

He rolled his eyes.

"You're a pain in my butt, did I ever tell you that?"

"You did," I said. "Several times."

"Okay, as long as it's on the record. Wait a minute. Wait right here."

Information you don't *share*, he'd say, drawing out the significant word, can't come back to haunt you.

He opened the side door, the one that led to the kennels. Elwood and Watson ran inside, and then Marty disappeared, too. I waited in the alley, Dashiell at my side. In a few minutes Marty was back, a doughnut box in his hand, Elwood waddling along behind him.

"These are the doughnuts you accused me of feeding Elwood," he said. "Here, take this home and read for yourself. These are *fat free*, Rachel. No way Elwood coulda got fat on these. I think it's his metabolism."

I took the box and looked at Elwood, remembering that not so long ago he was thinner, faster, and *smarter*.

"You might have a point there, Marty. Have you ever had his thyroid function tested? He might be hypothyroid."

"Yeah? Gluck has that, the guy at the desk. Blew up to two-fifty couple of years ago. Slept ten hours a night, sucked caffeine all day, and he was always looking to take a nap. Now he takes his pills, he's just like normal. I'll get El checked out. Thanks, Rach."

"Thank *you*," I said. "For the doughnut box." I gave it a shake. "And the doughnut."

"Don't mention it," he said. Then he whispered, "I mean *really* don't mention it."

I nodded.

"You take care, kid, okay?"

I clipped Dash's leash to his collar and headed back toward Tenth Street. As soon as I had turned the corner onto Hudson, heading south, I read the box, then opened it. There were two things inside. I pocketed the folded piece of paper, ditched the box in the trash basket on the corner, and ate the delectable-looking, full-fat, chocolate-covered doughnut on the way to Lisa's.

4

She'd Called Her Penny

LISA JACOB'S APARTMENT was on the second floor of the Printing House, one of many formerly industrial buildings that had been converted into high-priced condos or co-ops, only in the case of the Printing House, the prices were so high that a lot of the units had failed to sell and were rentals. Not Lisa's. Lisa had wanted the Village, the Village, so her daddy had bought her a condo, one with full-time concierge coverage, maid service, and a gym on the top floor. Lisa's apartment faced east, overlooking Hudson Street and, beyond that, James J. Walker Park, where kids played baseball in the warm weather and dogs played Who's Dominant? from December through March.

Dashiell went crazy smelling the odors left by Lisa's Akita as I walked around trying to get a feel for the place and for the woman who until recently had lived here. Straight across from the door was a wall of enormous windows, serving both the downstairs and the bedroom, up a flight, built as a balcony over the end of the apartment nearest the door and looking down over the living room. The place was painted white, underfurnished, clean, interesting—it looked as if it had been a cheerful place to live. There was a small, colorful rug in the area opposite the kitchen where the dining room table sat, and the *Times,* nearly two weeks old, was lying there as if Lisa had just gone to heat up her coffee. Or more likely, get another hit of herb tea. Over the table, hanging upside down from the ceiling, were dozens of dried bouquets of roses, still fragrant, and on the table was a teal blue vase, empty now. Near the vase were Lisa's appointment calendar and a small address book. I slipped them into my pocket.

The kitchen was small, utilitarian, and neater than mine. No big trick. On the floor, opposite the sink, were two bowls, one obviously licked clean by a large dog with a healthy appetite, the other with a small amount of water still in it. I picked up the water bowl, rinsed it in the sink, then let the water run until it got cold. It was a ceramic dish, cream with a rust-colored dog bone, rimmed in blue, smack in the center. On the outside, in the blue, was written "My Dog." I filled it and put it down for Dashiell. I could hear him drinking as I stood in the center of Lisa's living room and looked around.

On my left there was a wall of books, with photos of Lisa doing t'ai chi tucked between the volumes. All the photos were of Lisa, none of anyone else—not a boyfriend, not even her Akita.

Under the huge windows there was a comfortable-looking black couch, a small glass coffee table, and two black leather chairs. The rest of the room was empty. I tried to imagine Lisa practicing t'ai chi there.

Dashiell was on his way upstairs, his nails clacking on the wooden steps. I followed him up, then sat on

Lisa's double bed. The *Tao-teching* was on the night-stand, with a piece of lavender string as a bookmark. I opened it and began to read. This was enough to make *me* want to end it all.

I had gone through a Zen phase years before, when I was nineteen or twenty. I wore black, studied t'ai chi, and for the hours between lunch and dinner one day became a vegetarian. But aside from an occasional line that made sense to me, most of what I'd read and heard was incomprehensible.

"Mystery of mysteries," it said on the page where Lisa had marked her place. She had not only underlined it but copied it in the margin in her small, neat hand-writing.

How could you come to understand something that couldn't be explained and couldn't be taught? More-over, when you finally thought you had a handle on it, you didn't. Give me a break, I thought, putting the book back on the nightstand. Life is difficult enough without Zen.

But then I picked it up again. Lisa had been reading it. Probably for the hundredth time. Maybe I ought to give it one more shot. I left it on the foot of the bed to remind me to take it home. I would put it on *my* night-stand. Beyond that, I couldn't say.

I looked at Lisa's clothes. Almost everything was black, soft cotton tops and pants you could wear when you practiced or taught t'ai chi. But there were a few cheerful touches in her neat closet, too—a pair of pink high-tops, a pair of red cowboy boots, a sort of patch-work quilted jacket, and silk scarves, lovely ones in nearly every color, long ones, the kind you could wrap around twice, knot, or play with seductively as you leaned close to chat. I pulled out a lavender one and draped it around my neck, smelling Lisa's perfume, which still clung to the fabric.

On the tall oak dresser, there was a wooden jewelry box. I opened it and pawed through Lisa's treasures. I looked in the dresser drawers, too, at her underwear and sweaters. I rifled the nightstands. I checked under the bed. Snooping was my profession, wasn't it?

If Lisa had been depressed, I couldn't see any signs of it. There were no clothes strewn around, no pile of neglected laundry or unpaid bills, no Prozac, Valium, or sleeping pills in the medicine cabinet of the upstairs bathroom. There weren't even dust elephants under her bed. Maybe Daddy had paid for a maid, too.

There was lots of makeup, bubble bath, body lotion, perfume, and some pretty necklaces hanging near the oak-framed mirror opposite the sink. She didn't seem to lack anything. There were even condoms in the nightstand drawer.

Perhaps there had been a sudden descent, something that made her feel she was falling down a bottomless black hole. Or maybe the change had been chemical. I thought about Elwood waddling down the alley.

I walked around the bedroom once more, touching Lisa's things, feeling that there was something missing. Of course. There was no dog bed. I undid the neatly made bed. On the side nearer the stairs, there was black fur on the sheet. The dog had not only slept on the bed, she'd slept under the covers.

Years ago, when I training dogs for a living, I'd had a client named April Anton, a nurse, who had hired me to train a little dog she had rescued from the shelter. She'd called her Penny because the adoption counselor had told her the pup looked like a scent hound, and April, who had always taken advantage of her access to drugs, heard it as "cent hound."

But I never got to finish the course. One evening her brother called to cancel the last lesson. When April hadn't shown up for her shift and hadn't answered the phone, he'd been called. He'd gone to her house to find that his sister had reached the end of her ability to tolerate her troubles. He found her in bed, the cigarette she had been smoking burned down to her fingers, Penny pressed close against her side. After calling 911, he'd called the animal shelter and arranged to have his sister's dog euthanized.

I'd always wondered how she'd been able to desert Penny. Now I found myself wondering how Lisa had been able to leave her dog so unsafe. Lisa's parents hadn't even mentioned her. I wondered where she was and what would become of her. I sat on the bed, picked up the phone, and called Marsha Jacobs.

"Marsha? It's Rachel."

"Yes, dear," she said. "Have you learned something?"

"I'm calling about, um, well, you didn't say and I was wondering, was Lisa seeing anyone recently?"

"There was a young man she mentioned, a Paulie Wilcox. But we never met him, this Paulie person."

That made sense. Barring the use of torture or drugs, who would discuss their love life with their parents or sacrifice an innocent young man by bringing him home for the grand inquisition?

"Do you know if she was still seeing him at the time, um, recently?"

"I don't know for sure."

"Oh, okay, and one other thing I wanted to ask was about the dog, Lisa's Akita."

"Yes?"

I hesitated, afraid of what I might hear. "Where is she now?"

"With Avram, dear. Why? Do you want her?"

For a moment I listened to the sound of Dashiell breathing and the hum of the refrigerator from downstairs.

"I'm sure she's lovely, but I already have a dog."

"Maybe Avram will keep her. She's used to him."

"One other thing, Marsha, about the note, Lisa's note—"

"Her apology?" her mother asked.

"Um. Yes."

Now the silence was on her end of the line. I could hear some muffled conversation, as if the mouthpiece had been covered.

"We didn't mention it—"

"Yes?"

"Because we thought it was personal."

"I see," I said. But I didn't. I thought it was very queer that they hadn't mentioned the note. Then again, they hadn't said much else about the circumstances of the suicide, and Marty hadn't thought that weird at all. Still, I'd ask about the note again, but only when I could see them.

"Well, I'll be in touch, okay, Marsha, and thank you."

"No, thank *you*, dear. We feel so much better that you're helping us."

I put the phone back in its cradle and sat quietly on the edge of Lisa's bed. A film of dust covered the top surfaces of all the furniture. I drew a small Akita head in it with my pointer. The only sounds now were the occasional noises of the traffic outside on Hudson Street, a horn honking or tires screeching because someone was in too big a rush to get to the next red light. Even the comforting smell of dog was no longer detectible by a mere human nose. Lisa's apartment was a lonely place now. It had been deserted.

I pulled the folded piece of paper out of my pocket. It had some chocolate stuck to one side, which I carefully peeled off and ate.

"I'm sorry. Lisa," it said.

There was no date, no To whom it may concern, no By the way, could someone please be kind enough to give my dog a home. Just "I'm sorry. Lisa."

Had Lisa, once upon a time, expected her dog to protect her? Then shouldn't she have protected her dog right back?

What could have made her abandon her dog?

What was it that troubled her so that it didn't seem reparable?

I surfed my mind for a possible explanation, but found none.

There is a Zen saying I had once read. *When you seek it, you cannot find it*. Would I ever understand why Lisa Jacobs had taken her life? Like Zen, it seemed to make no sense at all.

5

I Stood Behind Him

BY LUNCHTIME DASHIELL was shaking his head so much, I had to take him to the veterinarian. He had an ear infection, probably from getting water in his ear while he was swimming. I had neglected to dry his ears.

One guilt attack and one hundred and thirty-two dollars later, we were home and I was making room on the small kitchen counter for the Q-Tips, the ear cleaner, and the otic antibiotic. After listening to my messages, I headed back to Lisa's apartment to watch her t'ai chi tapes, look through her books and papers, listen to her music, and gaze out her windows.

Late that evening, still wearing Lisa's scarf, I walked over to Bank Street T'ai Chi to keep my appointment with Avram Ashkenasi. I took the elevator to five and tied Dashiell's leash to the railing at the top of the stairs, just across from a long, low shelf filled with pairs of black cotton shoes of all sizes, the kind you see for sale in Chinatown, only used. Since this was the top floor, and it was so late the building seemed deserted, I thought it would be safe to leave Dashiell in the hall while I spoke to Lisa's mentor and former employer.

He opened the door, looked us both up and down, then motioned with a sweep of his arm for me to follow him.

"Yes," he said as if I had asked a question. "Bring him, too."

He was a troll—barrel-chested, short waisted, long armed, his meaty hands, red and hairy, hanging at his sides, fat, clumsy, and useless looking, his yellowish white hair long and held in an elastic band, the scraggly ponytail reaching halfway down his back, his stern-looking face half hidden behind an untrimmed white beard.

Santa Claus. In a horror movie.

"Take off your shoes," he commanded before we walked onto the polished wooden floor of the studio.

He was cranky, too.

Most of all, he looked dangerous, like one of those professors the other girls would tell you not to get caught alone with.

Keeping my eyes suspiciously on him, I obeyed, taking off my shoes and leaving them, toes touching the wall, next to another pair, black cotton shoes, small, like mine, not big, as his would be.

He pointed one of his big hands to a spot against the mirrored wall of the studio. "Sit," he said, as if I were his dog. I did.

"You, too," he told Dashiell, who usually obeys no one but me unless I hand over his leash. Dashiell sat, too.

Turning toward the adjacent wall, also mirrored, he began the form, first breathing deeply, then finding shoulder width with his feet.

He raised his too-long arms as if they had been lifted

by a string attached to his wrists. Next the fingers rose, and soon his body began to move, ever so slowly, as if propelled not by his own power but by another force. A weather vane, pushed by the wind.

Legs folded in front of me, Dashiell at my side, I watched as he moved silently through space, strong, smooth, and graceful, his body shifting direction, his arms and hands slicing through the air, decisive, deliberate, and painfully slow, like foreplay. Before my eyes the troll became beautiful, transformed by movement into something almost holy.

When he stopped, I stood, full of questions. I had come, after all, about Lisa.

"Mr. Ashkenasi—"

He stopped me with one finger to his lips. "Now you," he said.

"Look," I said, straightening my back, "I came about Lisa, not to learn t'ai chi. As I told you on the phone—"

"Yes, yes," he said, "you're a friend of the family. You want to know about Lisa. You have many questions to ask."

"A cousin."

"A cousin?"

"Yes. And I've promised my aunt and uncle—"

"Of course you did," he said. "I am going to help you, Rachel. *If* you'll trust me."

It was a question. Though it wasn't spoken as one.

"I—"

He smiled to himself.

"I know. It's asking a great deal of you, an enormous leap of faith on the word of a stranger. But you are asking a great deal, too, Rachel, to try to understand a person who—" He waved his hand in the air. "Has vanished from our midst. But, of course, you knew her, your cousin. So—"

"We weren't close," I said. "It's sad, when you think about it, living in the same city but being so wrapped up in our own lives—"

"That happens, of course."

"The truth is," I said, "I hardly knew her at all. I hadn't seen her since we were kids."

Had I been a wooden puppet, he would have been impaled on my nose by now.

I looked into his pale eyes. He seemed moved to tears.

Damn, I was good.

"You won't learn anything worthwhile about Lisa by asking questions," he said softly, so softly I had to lean closer to hear him. "The police have already done that, Rachel, and what have they learned? If you want to learn about Lisa's life, you must walk in her shoes."

He picked them up, the single pair of shoes that I had placed mine next to, little black cotton shoes with rope soles, like the ones I'd seen in the hall, only these had "Lisa" written in black Magic Marker inside each shoe.

He held them out to me.

I didn't move.

"What can it hurt?" he asked. "You're already wearing her perfume."

When I took the shoes from his hands and lifted one foot, I felt his large hand cup my elbow. I let him support me while I slipped each one on. His hand was as warm as the heart of my fireplace after a fire had been burning all evening.

"They fit," I said.

He smiled.

"Does he need water?" he asked. "Come," he said to Dashiell, "there's a bowl in the office." A moment later I heard the slapping sound of Dash drinking. Good, I thought, he still has the Akita.

The huge windows on the north side of the studio opened out, which must have made it easy to see from the street below from where Lisa had taken her plunge. I wondered which one Lisa had gone out of and exactly what she was thinking at the time. I wondered how I'd possibly find out what made her so desperately unhappy that she had decided to take her own life. Was it in fact a decision? Or might it have been instead a thoughtless, spur-of-the-moment rush to make an end, once and for all, to her pain?

I tried to picture Lisa in pain, but I couldn't. All I could come up with was the lovely, smiling face I had seen on her parents' piano and in their photo album.

Not average, her mother had said.

Avram returned with Dashiell padding along at his side as if they were old friends. He took my hands in both of his.

"I am so glad you came," he said, his eyes filling, as if he would cry. But then he let go of me and stepped onto the polished wooden floor of the studio and faced the mirror again.

"I do not want you to worry about what you look like. Just copy. Come, come, come, stand behind me. One day soon, you will feel what t'ai chi is. I cannot explain it to you any more than I could explain Lisa to you. You will feel it for yourself. And then one day you will feel Lisa."

I stood behind him, heels together, toes to the diagonal, and shifting my body and then my legs and feet, evet so slowly, I found shoulder width. My arms lifted as if a string were tied to my wrists, gently pulling them toward the heavens, and I moved as Avram did, slowly through space, my dog lying at the edge of the tan carpet with only his front paws touching the light oak flooring of the studio.

Each time Avram stopped, I stopped, and we would begin again; sometimes repeating the same few movements over and over again; sometimes Avram would go ahead as I struggled to mimic him, clumsy where he was graceful, shaking where he was steady, struggling where he was authoritative, worried where he was calm.

After a while my legs were burning, especially the few times he spoke, asking me to hold a position while he looked at me. Several times he gently moved me, adjusting the position of an arm, a foot, straightening my spine or wrist, and afterward I felt something like a breeze, but inside, not on my skin, something cool and calming, something moving slowly, something wonderful, and when that happened, I wanted never to stop.

We worked from eleven to three in the morning, and finally Avram stopped and sighed audibly.

"I've forgotten everything already," I said in a panic.

"Go home, Rachel. You're tired. We're both tired. You couldn't possibly hold all the movements in your mind. Your body is learning t'ai chi. Your body will remember for you."

"But when will you—"

"Shh, shh, shh," he said, holding his head as if I had given him a headache. "Are you familiar with the parable of the tiger?"

No, I told him. I shook my head no.

"A man was walking alone in the country, and he came across a tiger. He began to run, but the tiger also ran. It pursued him. Finally he came to the edge of a cliff, and grasping a vine, he attempted to escape from the tiger by climbing down. As he climbed, he looked beneath him. There below him was another tiger, looking up, waiting to devour him."

What was he talking about? He might as well have been speaking Chinese.

"One tiger above, one below. Only the vine saved him. But when he looked back up, he saw two mice, one black, the other white, gnawing away at the vine. That's when he noticed, right in front of him, growing on the side of the cliff, a perfect strawberry. He plucked it and ate it. It was delicious."

He smiled, then shut off the light in the studio.

If the man had something to say, why couldn't he just say it?

"You'll be safe walking home," he said. Again, a question that wasn't one.

"I have Dashiell," I told him.

I slipped into my own shoes and put Lisa's carefully back where they had been, toes pointing to the wall. Everyone else's shoes were relegated to the hall. Only Lisa's shoes had a place of their own inside.

"Tomorrow night classes end at ten. Come at ten thirty. Bring your boy."

"Look," I said, standing in the doorway, "this was interesting, tonight's work. But I didn't come here to learn t'ai chi. I came—"

"First the t'ai chi. Then the questions. And Rachel, next time, don't take the elevator. Walk. It's good for your legs."

Meditation in motion. That's what one of Lisa's books had said t'ai chi was, a kind of Zen for people with ants in their pants. Okay. I had done it. Now what? Where was the brand-new world Zen was supposed to give me? Except for the pain in my knees, nothing had changed.

All the way home everything looked the same, homeless people sleeping in doorways, trash swirling about like tumbleweed when the wind blew, transvestites heading home after a long night, their false laughter echoing in the empty streets.

Where with each step was my connection to the earth? Where with each breath was my connection to the sky?

I unlocked the gate and followed Dashiell down the narrow passageway that led to the garden in which my cottage sat.

Where, I wondered, were the answers to all my questions? Where, in fact, were the questions?

I unlocked the cottage door, but I didn't go inside. Instead I sat on the cold steps in the skeletonlike shadow of the big oak tree, waiting unsuccessfully for enlightenment.

6

I Wondered If It Might
Have Been Lisa

THE NINTH LAW of private investigation says, Keep
moving. This advice is meant to aid the operative during those unfortunate times when he or she is being
shot at by one or more disreputable persons, but as a
law to live by, it can't be beat. I had learned the wisdom
behind it back when I was training disreputable dogs.

Keep an aggressive dog still while you berate him for
his rotten nature and unacceptable behavior, and he'll
have nothing better to do than figure out precisely
which of your many body parts might be the most suc-
culent. But keep a bully moving by walking fast, changing directions, appearing to all but ignore him, and
your unpredictability will consume his mind. It's as effective as if he were a balloon and you had a pin.

Keep moving. It gives you a much better chance of
keeping yourself intact, whether it's bullets or teeth
coming in your direction.

Unfortunately, when I got up late on Thursday morning, moving seemed all but out of the question. I could

barely lift my arms or swing my legs off the bed. With a gait so stiff that if I were a dog the word *euthanasia* would come to my owner's mind, I finally made it to the bathroom and into a hot bath. And much as I would have liked to stay there all day, I decided to obey law number nine. It was time to check out the boyfriend. His phone number was in Lisa's address book. But before I called, I looked through her appointment calendar and found two most curious things.

I reached Paul Wilcox at work. He listened politely to my request and said that if I could come by at one thirty, he could talk to me about my cousin Lisa.

Okay, I do sometimes stretch the truth a bit, but only in order to get the job done. I learned the hard way that revealing my occupation has a silencing effect on people, even those whose worst crime has been finding a quarter in a pay phone and failing to return it to the phone company.

I had time before my appointment, and time was what Dashiell needed. I cleaned and medicated his ear, then headed for the dog run at Washington Square Park. Dashiell needed to spend part of every day just being a dog, and I needed to spend part of every day watching him do exactly that.

It would be nice to imagine the dog run as a fenced outdoor area where dogs can safely run around and play in the fresh air. But this was New York City. There is no fresh air.

As for safety, just as in playgrounds reserved for human children, there's a microcosm of life, and life, my mother would be quick to point out were she here, is lots of things—but safe isn't one of them.

So while Dashiell played, I paid attention. Once I saw that things looked benign, I let my eyes wander, noticing a young man practicing t'ai chi on the grassy area just to the west of the run. I had once seen a young woman practicing there. I wondered if it might have been Lisa.

In China, Avi had told me when we took a break from practicing the form, people always practiced out of doors. Groups of hundreds of people gathered in the early morning, before going to work, and in the evening, on their way home, to do the form in a sea of shared energy. Most Americans practiced alone, as Lisa must have, Lisa who had wanted to go to China but had gone only in her imagination.

I got up, walked to a corner of the run, faced north, and practiced whatever I could remember from years earlier and the night before. An hour later Dash and I headed for the West Village Fitness Club, on Varick Street, a short walk from Lisa's apartment. The Club, as it was called, had a twenty-five-meter indoor pool. I suspected that it was where Paul and Lisa had met.

As I entered the cavernous space, the pool was down a flight of stairs on the left. I could smell the chlorine. The aerobic equipment and weight machines were in a large mirrored room off to the right. The health bar, where Paul Wilcox had said to ask for him, was straight back.

I walked up to the young man who was standing near a display of high colonics making carrot juice and politely waited for him to notice me. To my surprise, he was practically naked, though if I looked half that good, I too might walk around wearing nothing but a tiny orange bikini. He was my height, maybe an inch or two taller, my age, maybe a year or two younger, and looked to be about 155 pounds soaking wet, which he was, his hairless body the color of jasmine tea.

"Would you like a carrot juice?" he asked over the sound of the juicer. His almond-shaped eyes, mysteriously hooded beneath epicanthic folds, were the color of melted bittersweet chocolate.

It was the voice from the telephone. Sounded like Queens. Must be ABC, I thought, American-born Chinese.

"Paul Wilcox?"

"The cousin?"

"Rachel," I said, reaching out my hand.

He didn't take it.

"Funny she never mentioned you," he said, pouring the hideous-looking brown juice into two glasses, "but I can see the family resemblance."

"Yeah?"

Cool, I thought.

"Yeah. It's really strong." He took off his round, metal-rimmed glasses and stared at me. "Your coloring is different. Lisa's was more extreme—whiter skin, darker hair. But you have the same body type, the same-shaped face, the same wild hair."

Apparently the ancient rules of politeness had gotten lost in translation.

He walked around to the front of the counter and stood next to me. "And you're the same height."

He was barefoot.

"The same shoe size, too," I told him.

"So, are you like her in other ways?" he asked, carefully putting his glasses back on.

"Yeah. We were identical cousins."

"Then you speak Chinese?"

"Not a word. How about you?" I asked.

"Not a word," he said. "I'm only half Chinese, in case you were puzzled by the name."

I shrugged one shoulder, as if to say, hey, you wanna be half Chinese, what's it my business.

"An identical cousin," he said. "Another swimmer?"

"Dog paddle. Olympic quality."

"You hide your grief well," he said.

"Thanks. According to the Talmud, the deeper the sorrow, the less tongue it hath." I emphasized the *th*.

"Ah, another scholar in the family. That's just the sort of thing she might have"—he took a swig of juice—"said," he said, studying me.

I studied him right back.

I remembered a trick Ida had shown me, the time she asked me to bring my family album to a therapy session. She had placed her hand over the top half of people's faces, my mother's, my father's, Lili's, and mine, to show their smiling mouths. Then she'd slid her hand down and covered the mouths, exposing the tops of the faces. Without the smile, something else showed. I looked afraid. Lili looked defiant. My mother's eyes looked angry. My father's eyes looked sad beyond belief. Like Paul Wilcox's dark eyes.

He handed me one of the glasses of rust remover and led the way to one of the little bistro tables next to the juice bar.

"My cousin and I weren't close," I confided. "You know how it is."

"For sure."

"Funny, you don't sound half Chinese."

"Born in the USA." He smiled, showing me his dimples. "Flushing."

I skipped all the obvious cheap shots and got down to business. "The reason I called, Paul, is that I was wondering if you could tell me about Lisa. What she was like, you know, as an adult. What might have made her"—suddenly feeling the weight of what I was saying, I lowered my voice—"make the decision she did."

He scratched Dashiell's nose-tackle-sized neck.

"He's huge, your boy," he said. "What does he weigh?"

"Is this where you met my cousin?" I asked.

"What is this all about? Lisa never mentioned you, and I don't mean to be rude, but what's the deal?"

"It's my aunt Marsha." I lowered my eyes. "She's not sleeping well. She needs—we all need—answers. Did you ever meet her, Lisa's mother?"

"No. I never did. Lisa said she wouldn't sic her relatives on a dog." He shook his head. "No offense meant."

"None taken," I told him.

He took another swig of the sludge in his glass. "You're not drinking your juice," he said.

I nodded. He was right. I wasn't drinking it.

"So you never met them?" I asked.

"What's the point of this, Rachel? She's dead." He began looking around as if he were bored.

"Look, I'm sorry to stir things up. But my aunt asked me if I could find out what the hell was going on that made Lisa, you know, kill herself. It's so hard to—"

"Swallow," he said. "Isn't it though? Lots of things in life are difficult to swallow. Don't you find that so, Rachel? Is it Rachel Jacobs?"

"Alexander. That branch of the family. Not the Jacobs branch."

"And the Alexander branch resembles the Jacobs branch."

"Exactly."

"How homogeneous." He drained his glass.

I picked up my glass of juice and set it right down again. If Lisa's boyfriend saw the family resemblance, perhaps the person at the desk would, too. Lisa's membership card to the Club was in one of the pockets of her calendar. Clearly my clever interview technique wasn't winning Paul Wilcox over. Maybe my dog paddle would.

"Did Lisa swim here?" I asked. "Is that how you met?"

Paul was looking away, and for a while he said nothing. "Maybe she got dizzy. It can happen when you exercise. Maybe she went to the window for a little air, and—"

"There was a note," I said softly.

He turned and stared at me. "A *what*?"

"A note."

He covered his face with his hands. They were clean and strong looking, his fingers long and graceful. He moved them to his lap when Dashiell got up and laid his head there.

"What did it—"

" 'I'm sorry. Lisa.' That's all. No one told you?"

" 'I'm sorry. Lisa'?"

I nodded.

Suddenly the top and bottom halves of Paul Wilcox's face were in concert.

"No way," he said, his fist hitting the table so hard the top jumped and then continued to vibrate for another minute. Dashiell backed up a foot and barked until I signaled him to lie down.

"No *fucking* way. Lisa Jacobs never apologized to anyone in her life."

"Is that a fact?" I said, cool as a Borzoi.

"Look, cousin, I found the first news difficult to believe, and now *this*. Give me a break."

He pushed his chair back and got up.

"Wait a minute here," he said, leaning over me, so close I could see his tonsils. "Are you telling me my name was on it?" he whispered. "That it was addressed to me? Is that why you're here?"

"No. Should it have been? Addressed to you?"

He just shook his head.

"Paul, were you and my cousin still going together when this happened?"

"No," he said, pushing the chair back against the table so hard it moved the table closer to me. He began to walk away.

Good, I thought. At least one of us was telling the truth. His name hadn't appeared in Lisa's calendar since January 11.

And that time, it had been crossed out.

"When did you break up?" I asked his back.

But he didn't bother to answer me. Without turning around or saying good-bye, he disappeared down the stairs that led to the pool.

7

How Long Will It Take?

AT TEN THIRTY that night, after I had practiced the form alone in the garden, Dashiell and I headed back to Bank Street T'ai Chi. Avi opened the door before we reached the landing, his finger to his lips. Without speaking, I dropped my jacket onto one of the couches, changed into Lisa's black cotton shoes, and followed him onto the floor.

Standing behind Avi, I could see the strength of his movements, as if he were moving not through air but water—not springwater, cleansed of all impurities, but ocean water, thick with salt and life. It was as if he were swimming in the air.

After three hours of work Avi stopped, and we walked to the couches in the area between the office and the studio and sat opposite each other.

"How did you and Lisa meet?"

"So late, and still your head is full of questions," he said.

"You said, first the t'ai chi, then the questions."

Avi sat silently.

"You didn't mean after I learn the *whole* form?"

Was he meditating, looking straight ahead like that at nothing, as if he hadn't heard my question?

"Or not even then, right? When I get to the end of the form, you'll tell me we need to do corrections, that I am not good enough yet to ask you questions. Is that it? I am working so hard, staying up all night learning t'ai chi, and you will never help me learn what I need to know."

He lifted his big hand like a stop sign.

"A student once asked his teacher, 'Master, how long will it take me to learn Zen?' 'Ten years,' the master told him. 'But what if I work extra hard, then how long?' 'Twenty years,' the master replied."

"Avi, I—"

"You are so busy thinking about the destination, you cannot keep your mind on the journey."

"Avram, my aunt and uncle have asked me to help them understand the death of their daughter. They are in pain."

"And they will not be in pain when you tell them why she is gone?"

Now I was the one who was silent.

"Avram," I said after a moment, "I appreciate what you're trying to do, but I don't have ten years for this."

"Then we should stop wasting time. Tomorrow come earlier, come at seven."

I stood and picked up my jacket.

"I am only trying to help you make room for Lisa," he said, "so that you will understand her."

"Yeah, yeah," I said. "It's like dog training."

"Like dog—"

"Some people approach a dog so full of themselves, there is no room for the dog. They are full of ideas, full of answers. They think they know everything there is to know. And without looking at what is in front of them, they are sure that when the dog misbehaves, it's out of spite. They are so busy grabbing, punishing, being angry, that they never wonder, Who is this dog, what is he feeling, what does he understand, what confuses him, and why is he confused, what are his special abilities, and how can I use these to teach him what he needs to know? They are so sure they are right, they never examine their insubstantial conclusions. No matter what the dog might be able to tell them, they cannot learn it. There is no place inside them to put the information."

"So tomorrow, when you come, you'll wear your Everything I Know About Zen I Learned from My Dog T-shirt?"

"I didn't say I knew anything about Zen. I was only talking about dogs. I used to be a dog trainer," I said, "until I came here."

"I understand," he said.

"I'll see you tomorrow, then."

He stood, reached for the jacket, and helped me into it. He put his warm hand on my cheek and looked into my eyes.

"I'll be here," he whispered.

Then he walked to the door and held it open for me.

"Lisa was here every day. This was her life."

He stopped and blew his nose.

I didn't breathe for fear he'd stop talking.

"There was nothing more important to her, nothing that took precedence over her studies. We spent many hours together, studying, talking, or silent, working on the form. One never stops trying to perfect one's ability to do the form. We do not think, Ah, now we have learned it. We pay attention to one detail at a time, taking pleasure in each. We do not think about what isn't. We pay attention to what is. Now, go, child. I will see you tomorrow."

He closed the door.

Here I was, obeying him again.

Well, he was the *master,* wasn't he?

I heard the lock turn.

So what did that make me? I wondered as Dashiell and I headed down the stairs.

And more important, what had it made Lisa?

8

I Took the Stairs

WHEN I WOKE up it was afternoon, three thirty to be exact. If I was going to be at Bank Street T'ai Chi by seven, I had to move. I cleaned and medicated Dashiell's ear, gave him his monthly heartworm preventive, and spent an hour in my office paying bills, now that I could, and taking care of paperwork.

Since I had to repark the car anyway, I drove five blocks to Lisa's street and in only forty-five minutes was able to find a legal spot. Waving to the concierge, I passed the elevators and took the stairs to the second floor. Paul Wilcox had made me more than curious about the strong resemblance to my *cousin*, and I wanted to look more carefully at the pictures of Lisa that were among the books in her living room.

I picked up one of the photos and took it over to the window, holding it so that the light would fall on it. Lisa's eyes were as blue as the Caribbean; mine were more the gray-blue of the Atlantic. Her skin was white, like her mother's. Mine was fair, but not pearly or translucent, not as delicate looking as Lisa's.

Lisa's hair was very much like mine, darker, but about the same length and also curly. In the photo she wore a little braid on one side. I put the picture back on the shelf and, taking a small strand of hair on the left side, braided it as Lisa had done; then, holding the end of the braid, I went into the kitchen, where I had seen some lavender string on top of the refrigerator. I secured the end of the braid, then looked for scissors to cut off the piece of string.

I ran upstairs and opened the closet door, zeroing in on a sheer black silk shirt, black velvet leggings, the Chinese-style quilted jacket, and those fabulous pink high-tops. Leaving my own things in the closet, I put on Lisa's clothes and shoes. Everything fit, so I took some soft black pants and a black T-shirt for t'ai chi as well, folding them carefully and putting them in a nylon mesh tote bag I found in Lisa's closet. Halfway down the stairs, I turned back. I needed a bathing suit, didn't I? Before leaving, I also borrowed some jewelry to go with my new clothes, a jasper heart necklace from Tiffany's and a pair of silver earrings that sounded like small bells when they moved. I left my small gold hoops in their place.

I dropped the clothes off at home, and once again Dashiell and I headed toward the heart of the Village, Washington Square Park. Radiating out from the fountain at its center were paths that led north, east, south, and west, to the hanging tree, an old elm once used for executions, to playgrounds, to enclaves of the down-and-out asleep or sitting up and smoking on the benches that were the closest things they had to home, and to the dog run. Dashiell began a hip-hop ballet with a broken-coated Jack Russell terrier, and I took myself to the southwest corner of the run and, listening to the crunching sounds of the dogs playing on the pea gravel, faced north, eyes on the horizon, and became meditation in motion in Lisa Jacob's beautiful, expensive clothes.

Near the dog run, a mounted policeman was putting his horse through its paces. A nurse was pushing an old man in a wheelchair, a plaid blanket over his legs. A nanny pushing a baby carriage walked by, a handsome young man was headed in the direction of the NYU law library, people sat on the grass reading. No one was imitating Bob Dylan or Janis Joplin, and it was a bit early for the drug dealers. Later in the day, if I asked Dashiell to "find the grass," he'd go nuts.

It was quiet, so I stayed for a long time, watching Dashiell play and thinking about Lisa Jacobs. At six I stopped at the Cowgirl Hall of Fame for a burger, then headed over to school.

I took the stairs. Avi had said it would help me do the form. Lisa, he'd said, always took the stairs, never the elevator.

Avram looked startled when he opened the door, but said nothing. I slipped off Lisa's jacket, put on her black cotton shoes, and followed Avi into the studio. Dashiell had already taken his usual spot in the sitting area, his big white paws just touching the wooden floor where we worked.

As is tradition, we did the form without speaking. Then Avram began again, and I followed him. This time, as I continued, he came near me to make corrections, gently moving an arm or a hand or readjusting a foot by placing his next to where mine should have been and leaving it there until I'd lifted mine and placed it next to his.

Most of the form is done with knees bent, as if you

were in a low-ceilinged room. Avi helped me to sink lower, until my legs felt as if they were on fire. He had explained that the burning meant that the blood was seeking new pathways, and so my legs were getting stronger. Unfortunately, so was the pain.

Suddenly I was flushed with heat. All I wanted to do was hang out the window and get some air, but Avi kept on working.

"Did you ever notice how clumsy people can be?" he asked, leaving me with all my weight on my right leg.

"When your step is empty, no weight at all in it," he said, taking the same posture he had left me in sometime back in the Iron Age, "you are steady *before* shifting your weight."

He flexed his knee, lifting his left foot off the ground. Then he placed his foot back down, heel, toe, and shifted his weight forward, as slowly as honey oozing off a spoon.

"Remember that t'ai chi is a martial art, Rachel. You must always be connected to the earth, both figuratively and literally. You do not want your opponent to be able to push you over."

It was long past dark, but neither of us stopped to put on the lights. Lit by the bright light of the moon shining in through the big windows, reflecting in the mirrors, and shining on our faces, we continued to practice, mostly in silence.

"Okay, shake out your legs," Avi finally said.

We stood quietly for a moment, neither of us speaking. Something was bothering me, jabbing away at the edge of my consciousness. I turned and looked at the windows. Then I looked into Avram's face.

"Which one?" I asked.

"The second from the left," he said. He turned and walked back to his office, leaving me alone.

I walked over, unlatched the window, and pushed it out, letting the cold, damp night air hit me in the face.

The street looked very far away, and just looking down made my knees turn to water.

The door had been locked, I thought, but the chain hadn't been latched.

I felt a wave of nausea as I pictured Lisa looking down, just as I was doing, then climbing onto the sill and falling into nothing.

I thought about the second curious thing in Lisa's calendar. All those appointments. All those plans. The days after her death were filled with things to do.

No handprint on her back, Marty had said.

Most jumpers were men, I thought, looking down. Female suicides usually used carbon monoxide or some other form of poison, not something that would disfigure them, like a gunshot wound. Or defenestration. Vanity at play, right up to the very end.

I thought about all Lisa's pretty things, about those roses, dozens of bouquets, hanging upside down from her ceiling.

I thought about her pretty face.

I thought, No *way* did Lisa Jacobs jump out of this window.

There was a reason none of this made sense. Lisa Jacobs hadn't killed herself. Someone had done it for her.

I leaned out and looked down.

Then, quickly, I straightened up and stepped back, bumping into Avram. He leaned past me, pulled the window shut, and I latched it.

In those black cotton shoes, he had been so silent I hadn't heard him approach me.

I began to shiver. I had stood in front of an open window in a dark room in the middle of the night with a stranger behind me, a man strong enough to lift me and toss me out the window as if I were a sack of trash he was tossing into a Dumpster.

His hands were trembling.

So were mine.

When he moved, I felt myself jump.

He reached into the pocket of his soft cotton pants.

"Will you lock up after you change your shoes? I must go now."

"Of course."

He handed me a set of keys.

"Tomorrow, five o'clock?"

I nodded.

"Good," he said. "I'll have a surprise for you."

My heart was pounding so hard I thought I might have a surprise for him too, another of his protégées dead in the middle of the night, this one right in the studio, of a fear-induced heart attack.

But he never noticed anything.

He grabbed his jacket from a hook near the door, and in a moment he was gone.

I was going to leave, too. In fact, I couldn't wait to get out of there. But then I noticed the door to the office. It was ajar.

I walked inside and sat in Avi's chair, putting the keys he'd given me down and placing my hands on the smooth surface of his ruddy teak desk. The computer was to my left, the files to my right. The bookcase behind me covered the entire wall. On the wall to my left, in a simple oak frame, was a photo of Lisa frozen in the middle of doing Cloud Hands. I hesitated for only the briefest moment before turning on the computer.

"Insatiable curiosity," Frank Petrie used to say, "it's what makes you broads so damn good at the job."

I slid the chair closer, preparing to work. So many

secrets, I thought, so little time. But then I looked back at the keys. I already had these. Lisa's mother had given them to me.

No one had taken Lisa's keys to lock up after the murder.

Whoever killed her already had a set.

9

Forever, She Said

THE LAST TIME in her life a woman feels really comfortable about being seen in a bathing suit is when she's six, and God knows, I hadn't seen six in a dog's age. Nonetheless, there I was in the doorway of the ladies' locker room at the Club, wishing I had a dog to hide behind. Unfortunately, I'd left him at home.

At least it wasn't rush hour at the pool. There were only three people in the water. One of them was the coach.

I stood watching him do laps for a long time. He seemed tireless, cutting through the water the way Avi cut through the air when he did the form, as smooth as a thread of silk being teased from a cocoon. When he reached the deep end, he curled around underwater and shot out in the opposite direction, not coming up for air until he was nearly halfway to the other side. A fish. But what kind of fish? I wondered.

I dropped the towel onto a bench, then stood next to it, trying to keep my balance as I wiggled the elastic band that held the key to my locker onto my ankle. Suddenly I saw feet, so close I could have reached out and touched them.

"Ah, the cousin."

I straightened up.

"I didn't expect to see you again."

"Out of my way. I'm trying to get a tan."

He smiled.

"So what are you doing here?"

He was staring.

Perhaps it was Lisa's black bikini bathing suit, which barely covered the stuff my mother said no one but my husband or a doctor should ever see.

Or maybe it was Lisa's jasper heart necklace dangling just below my modest but attractive cleavage. Or was it the cleavage itself? since that's where he seemed to be looking.

"If I want to compete in the next Olympics, it's practice, practice. Anyway, I'm here. So, hey."

"Hey, yourself," he said, finally bothering to look at my face. "So, let's see that stroke you're so famous for."

I turned and walked to the deep end and, one heart hanging around my neck, another in my throat, dove into the now-deserted pool. I began swimming laps, and just when I was really getting into it, I noticed that Paul was back in the water, hanging on to one side at the deep end. I swam over to hang out with him. After all, this was work. I wasn't here for my health.

"Hey."

He reached out and picked up the jasper heart, holding on to it for a moment before dropping it.

"Lisa had one just like this."

"No kidding?"

"If memory serves," he said.

"Well," I said, "sometimes it plays tricks on one. Instead of serving."

"You have similar taste to Lisa. It's interesting."

"It's a family thing," I said.

"Take that suit, for example."

I did, I thought.

"Lisa had a similar one. Not exactly the same. But very similar."

"Yeah? How are they different?"

"Hers had more cleavage," he answered.

Rule number whatever of private investigation is, Never take the job personally.

Yeah, right.

I pushed off the wall to swim away, but something stopped me. It was the coach's hand. He had hooked it into the back of the bottom of my bathing suit, what there was of it.

"You don't leave a person much dignity," I said, flailing around until I could turn and get a grip on the side of the pool again.

"How much do you need?" he asked.

"I thought saving face was a big deal with Orientals."

"I'm nowhere near your face," he said, finally letting go of my bathing suit bottom.

Clinging to the edge of the pool, chlorine wafting up at me and stinging my eyes, I wondered what Lisa had seen in this guy. Sure, he could swim. I'd give him that. But so could a fucking sturgeon.

Maybe it was the t'ai chi. Maybe they had that in common, too. "Did you meet Lisa through t'ai chi?" I asked him.

He shook his head. "What are you up to, Dog Paddle?" he said. "Why are you here?"

"I told you, Paul. I'm trying to help Lisa's parents. May aunt and uncle."

"Okay," he said, "let's talk."

"Here?"

I started to tremble. If my mother were here, she'd probably tell me my lips were turning blue.

"I'd rather we had more clothes on," he said, looking at me as if I were a pastrami sandwich and he were a starving Jew.

"What about—" I said, feeling as if someone else were speaking through my mouth. It was probably the echo from all the tile.

"What about this evening?" he said.

"I'm busy."

"Me, too. I have to take my grandmother shopping. But I could meet you afterward, at ten, say."

Apparently Paul Born in the USA Wilcox was no banana, the Asian equivalent of an Oreo.

"Should I come up or wait for you downstairs?" he asked.

"Downstairs?"

"Bank and West, isn't it? Two buildings in from the corner, south side of the—"

"Oh, *that* downstairs."

"That *is* where you'll be, isn't it?"

I nodded.

"I'm coming prepared to talk. Et tu, Dog Paddle?"

I could feel his breath on my face.

"I'll be prepared to listen," I said.

"That's a start," he said.

He put his hands on the edge of the pool and hoisted himself up and out of the water. I put my hands on the edge, too, but before I could propel myself out of the pool, Paul Wilcox did it for me. He had taken my wrists, and then there I was, standing too close to him, rivulets of chlorinated water running down my thighs and onto the wet tile beneath my bare feet.

"God," he said, his voice suddenly husky, "your hair does the same thing Lisa's did when it got wet."

His was jet black and thick. It stood straight up when it was wet, in spiky little clumps.

"Another family thing?" he asked, his voice soaked with sadness.

I pulled my hands away and brushed the hair off my face.

"Nah, it's a Jew thing. We all have curly hair and big noses." Big Nose was what the Chinese called Caucasians.

He smiled and ran his finger down my nose. "Your nose isn't so big. It's just about perfect," he said.

"Yeah, yeah," I said. Next thing he'd be telling me I was a hard-boiled egg, white on the outside, yellow on the inside, a Caucasian with an Oriental soul. Like my cousin.

I'd forgotten how dark his eyes were.

He turned and headed for the men's locker room.

For a moment in the pool, he'd seemed so angry, I'd been afraid he was going to push me under. But that couldn't have been my real fear. Hell, my sister did that all the time when we were kids. The real threat was becoming sucked in. The real fear was that something about this man was making me lose my objectivity, even my judgment.

"Wait," I shouted at his back.

"You bellowed?" He came back to where I was standing.

"About tonight," I said. Avi had said he'd have a surprise for me. I thought he might be ready to talk. "I can't meet you tonight. How about—"

"How about now? I'm ready for lunch."

"Lunch?" I said, as if I were a parrot.

He simply waited.

"Okay, lunch. That sounds fine."

I had to talk to the man. He was an important source. Lunch was better than the deep end of the pool. For one thing, I'd be dressed. Suddenly, lunch sounded safe, it sounded perfect. What the hell could happen at lunch? I asked myself, feeling smug now, as if it had been my idea all along.

"It'll take me ten minutes to get dressed. Can you wait that long? You seem to be a pretty impulsive person." He picked up a corkscrew strand of my wet hair, shook his head, then let it go and headed for the locker rooms.

"I'll meet you at the front door," I said to his back, watching his adorable little *tochis* as he walked away. "In seven minutes. Don't keep me waiting."

I'm not one for fussing. I was showered, dressed, and in front of the gym in six minutes.

"We can go right across the street," Paul said a moment later, not breaking stride as he joined me on the steps and swept me along onto Varick Street.

The mystique of perfect timing pervades the literature of dog training. Correct a dog precisely at the moment of his indiscretion, and he'll learn to mend his ways. Make your correction a minute later, and he won't. Had we come out of the Club a minute sooner, or a minute later, I never would have seen him.

I was supposed to look across the street, see the ordinary-looking luncheonette that, according to the Zagat survey, had the best fried chicken north of the Mason-Dixon line, and agree to have lunch there. That's all. But trouble never asks permission. Like that proverbial bad penny, it just keeps turning up.

There, across the street, standing right in front of

Edna Jean's, was a middle-aged man I knew, a man who shouldn't have been there. It was Saturday, wasn't it? He should have been home, having lunch with his wife of twenty-four years, admiring his panoramic view, listening to his children bicker. Instead he was on Varick Street, so absorbed in the blond at his side that he never turned and noticed his sister-in-law staring at him from across the street.

Was she one of his models? She was all in black, of course, except for her perfect, long blond hair, which she wore loose, even on such a mild day. Didn't it make her neck too warm? *I* was certainly hot under the collar.

Not the blond. She looked cool holding his arm and smiling up at his face. Totally cool. Maybe you could do that when you had zero percent body fat, flawless skin, teeth that were probably perfectly even and actually white—but that was just a guess, because surely I wouldn't get close enough for the bitch to bite me. She might have rabies.

I thought about my sister and her big dimpled ass, her size-eleven feet, her mouse-brown hair. Until that moment, until seeing her husband hanging on every word of a stunning slip of a blond—or was that actually a *dress* she was wearing?—I'd thought of my big sister as beautiful.

Suddenly I began to panic. My brother-in-law was turning in my direction. So I did the only thing I could.

I grabbed Paul's shoulders and pulled him toward me, as if he were a Chinese screen I could hide behind. I moved my arms from his shoulders to his neck, then into his wet black hair, and keeping him between me and what I was still watching across Varick Street, I whispered, "God, I feel so terrible about Lisa," and buried my face in his neck.

I heard his voice, so close the words reverberated on my skin, heard him say, "Poor Dog Paddle," and when I felt him stepping back, what could I do, I had to keep him there, I lifted my face and found his lips. And then the most surprising thing occurred. Despite the fact that my only motive was to protect myself from being seen until I'd figured out what to do if I were, I found myself being kissed by a complete stranger, his long fingers in my hair, the tip of his tongue tracing my lips, a guttural sound like the one Dashiell makes when I scratch inside his ears coming from only God knew which one of us.

Then over his shoulder I could see Ted's arm up, waving for a cab.

"Hold me," I whispered, pulling him closer, so close you couldn't slip a slip of paper between us.

"Rachel," he said, "Rachel."

A cab stopped. I watched Ted and the blond get into it. Were they lovers? I wondered as the cab moved into traffic and pulled away, heading downtown. Maybe there was another explanation.

Yeah, right, maybe.

That's when I realized that something else wasn't right. The cab was gone, but Paul was hanging on to me, breathing audibly. And something was pressing into my leg, something hard. What the hell was it, an egg roll in his pocket?

No, I thought, not an egg roll, it felt more like a knockwurst.

I stepped back.

"Oh God, Rachel," he said, his dark eyes all gooey with lust. He sure did have a way with words.

"Look," I said, "something just came up. I have to reschedule our lunch."

He turned and looked the other way, his face now more the color of rose hip tea than jasmine.

"I'll call you," I said. "I'm sorry." And like a steak left out to defrost in the same room with an untrained dog, I was gone.

Walking home, thinking about my sister, I remembered another kiss. Well, it was sort of a kiss. That time I'd been a child, and the person I'd sort of kissed had been Lillian.

I was too young to know how ridiculous her original idea was. We were lying on the glider on Aunt Ceil's screened-in back porch, after a day at the beach. We were face-to-face, so close I could see the fingerprints on Lili's glasses.

Let's become blood sisters, she said.

How? I asked.

First you have to put a match under the needle, like when Mommy takes a splinter out, she said. Then you stick your finger, and I stick mine. Then we press them together, mixing the blood, Lillian said, pressing her two pointers together to illustrate. That makes us blood sisters, forever.

I began to cry.

Okay, okay, she said. There's another way. Stick out your tongue.

Wug iz dis thaw, I asked.

She didn't answer. She stuck out her tongue and made the smooth tip of it touch mine.

Forever, she said.

Thawevah, I repeated obediently, afraid to pull in my tongue. God only knew what germs were on it, I thought. Even then.

Could you even let your own sister's tongue touch yours nowadays? Probably not. Not if her husband was maybe running around doing God knows what with God knows whom.

The bitch wore black, a short, slinky thing that went

in and out wherever she did. Her hair was long and straight, shimmering where the light hit it, moving as gracefully as seaweed in the ocean. I hated her on sight.

But what could *I* do about this? Tell my sister? Mightn't she simply kill the messenger?

Not tell her? Then what?

Confront my brother-in-law? And say what? Who was I supposed to be, the sex police?

Was this even what it appeared to be? And if it was, mightn't it blow over without Lili getting hurt?

Without Lili getting hurt, I thought. How could she not get hurt, even if the thing was a one-night-stand? Doesn't infidelity, even the briefest sort, always damage a relationship? Even if Lillian never found out, wouldn't the very fact of it change everything? Forever.

10

Something Was Different

WHEN I GOT home, I made two urgent phone calls. Then I sat in the garden with Dashiell until it was time to see Avi.

As soon as I opened the downstairs door to Bank Street T'ai Chi, Dash knew something was different. His nose dipped down to the floor in front of him and soaked up information unavailable to mere humans. His head pulled up. It appeared he was looking up the stairs, but it wasn't his eyes that were working so hard. His nostrils flared as he tuned in on the scent cone hanging thickly in the air. Whoever had recently passed this way interested Dashiell greatly. He turned as if to ask if my hands had fallen off or my feet were nailed to the ground, and he whined. I unhooked his leash and watched him disappear.

A moment later, they were both standing on the landing, looking down at me. He, the Arnold Schwarzenegger of the dog world, a can-do machine, was all muscle. Except for the black patch over his right eye and the black freckles on his skin that show through his short, smooth coat, Dashiell is white. He has a broad head with great fill in his cheeks, a jaw so strong he can hoist his own weight, a chest as hot and powerful as a blast furnace, and a heart so elastic you'd think his dam was Mother Teresa.

She reminded me of Lisa's mother, refined where Dashiell was crude, decked out where he was no-frills, feminine where he was clearly one of the guys, champagne to Dashiell's beer.

The bitch wore black, a double coat of medium length, thick, lush fur, the splash of white at her front like a bib of pearls. Her feet were white, too, as if she had delicately dipped them in gesso. Her tail was tossed majestically over her back, the white tip resting lightly on her flank. A symbol of good health in the breed's native country, she radiated her own vigor. She stood above me, her head cocked to the side, her brow wrinkled, her intelligent brown eyes alive with light. I loved her on sight.

I looked at Dashiell. He had fallen hard and fast for the Akita, too. His eyes were absent of all intelligence. He had moved, lock, stock, and rawhide, into pheromone city.

As if on a signal from each other, the dogs turned, taking the stairs at a speed I couldn't even aspire to, and disappeared. I climbed to the fifth floor at my usual pitiful, human pace. Because Lisa never took the elevator.

"She's called Ch'an," Avi said. At the sound of her name, the Akita turned and looked at him. She was large for a bitch, probably about eighty-five pounds. "Outside," he said, waving his arm toward the windows, "they call her Charlie. But of course Lisa did not name her Charlie Chan."

"You mean she gave a Japanese dog a Chinese name?" *Ch'an,* I had read recently, was the Chinese term for Zen, or meditation.

Avi's eyebrows went up. "You've been studying. You are so like Lisa."

"It's just that I'm walking in her shoes, trying to understand her life so that I might, one day, understand her death." Avi winced. "I love the t'ai chi, Avi, but I don't know much more about Lisa now than I did the day I met you, certainly nothing that would explain in the slightest what happened."

"In China," he said, "if one wants to study t'ai chi, seriously study it, the way Lisa did, it is necessary to be accepted by a master. You cannot go to a school, pay your money, and be taught t'ai chi, the way you can here. Every family guards its secrets," he said. "They will not teach just anyone."

"I—"

He raised his hand to stop me. Both dogs, thinking his gesture was meant for them, lay down.

"In China," he said, "tradition dictates that the student follow the teacher, and that is how he learns. Here we place great emphasis on education. It is different. But even the way we teach here, giving our students helpful images and patiently correcting postures, we still count the time of study in decades instead of years. Even that may be optimistic. So we try to find peace and beauty along the way. Now, about Lisa"—he pointed to the black shoes, their toes touching the wall—"a few days, Rachel, would be on the optimistic side in this study, too, wouldn't it?

"Twenty years or forty years, there isn't enough time in the world to know someone after they are gone. It's just not possible to get a true portrait of a human being from the detritus of his or her life and the opinions of others.

"Zen teaches you who *you* are, Rachel. Once you know that, you will know everything you need to know."

Then why, I wondered, had Alan Watts said, "Trying to define yourself is like trying to bite your own teeth"? Or was that my grandmother Sonya, the night her false teeth fell into the split pea soup?

"And t'ai chi—" I interrupted him.

"Yeah, yeah, Zen in motion."

So what else could I do? I took off the pink high-tops, put on Lisa's t'ai chi shoes, and silently, standing behind my mentor, I practiced the form. Afterward Avi asked me to do a silent round, and this time, instead of working with me, he watched.

Something was different. Perhaps the study now had forged a link with the past, with the t'ai chi I had studied so long ago and thought I had forgotten. Or perhaps concentrating on what I was doing rather than on watching Avi was what made the difference. Now when I placed my foot in an empty step, it felt as flat as a sheet of paper. I felt at ease, my body remembering everything, energy moving up my spine, over my head, spilling down my chest, connecting me to the earth beneath my feet and the universe above and beyond.

"Better," he said, stroking one side of his beard and then the other with the back of his hand, like a cat cleaning its whiskers.

But the moment I stopped moving, all my confidence fled. I felt only the enormous weight of my ignorance. It was a familiar feeling. The work I do is like driving in heavy fog. Sometimes it clings to the windshield, and you can't see an inch in front of you. At best it rolls a foot or two away, or lifts for a moment and allows a tantalizing glimpse of the road ahead before closing in all over again. Most of the time I feel as if I were driving blind.

I slipped off Lisa's shoes and put on her sneakers. When I looked up, Avi was holding Ch'an's thick, black leather leash.

"Come in the morning Monday. We have a staff meeting. You can meet the others. Maybe *they* will answer some questions for you. And leave your boy at home. Only bring Ch'an with you."

I began to shake my head.

"Can't you do this one thing for me?"

He didn't wait for an answer. The master was used to obedience.

"Lisa—"

"Yeah. I know," I said. "Lisa never took the elevator. She always took the stairs. And I do, too. But *this* I can't do for you."

"But Lisa always brought Ch'an to school with her."

"Lisa always brought *her* dog to school. And I—"

But he wasn't listening. He was looking toward the big windows.

"Even on the night she died," I said.

He nodded.

"I was asleep when the police called me. They said there was an emergency and asked if I could come right away with the keys. They didn't say what it was. They didn't tell me what had happened here. I thought a pipe was leaking. I had no idea.

"There were so many people here, so many. I could see them from down the block. I got confused. I couldn't understand why. A fire, I thought. There must have been a fire.

"Then I saw.

"She was lying on the street, under a yellow tarp. I

could see one of her hands, the palm up"—he turned his hand to show me—"sticking out from under the plastic.

"They asked me to look. They asked if I could identify her. One of the detectives slipped his hand around my upper arm and another one drew the tarp back, uncovering her face, her beautiful face."

Avi shook his head and began to cry. He took a wrinkled handkerchief from his pocket and wiped his eyes.

"We walked up the stairs," he continued. "The door was locked, of course. Lisa wouldn't have left it open when she was here alone late at night, even with Ch'an to protect her. I unlocked the door, and one of the two detectives who came up to the studio took my arm and pulled me aside. The other drew his gun, he shouted 'Police' and waited, but there was no sound, nothing. We stayed in the hall and he went in.

"For a moment I was just blank, just seeing the hand, turned up, like so, as if to catch rain. Then I remembered Ch'an and was polluted by the fear that the detective would be frightened of her and shoot.

" 'Don't be afraid,' I called out to him. 'Don't shoot the dog.'

"The second one opened the door wide, and we both stepped in. The room was dark, the way we worked last night, you and I, the studio lit only by the moon. It was empty.

"The first detective was just walking into the office, and I heard him gasp. I thought to myself, God, no, someone else is lying dead on the floor.

"We went to the doorway to see, myself and the other detective. But it was Ch'an who had startled him. That's all it was. She was lying on her mat, her head up, her front paws crossed, one over the other, looking at us, as if nothing at all had happened." He put a hand on his chest and rubbed it, as if by doing so he could erase his grief.

"What about the note, Avi? Where was the note?"

"It was on the desk, in front of the computer. 'There's a suicide note,' the first detective said. I am not ashamed to tell you, the tears were flowing from my eyes that night, too, Rachel. I don't know why, but the thought of her sitting at my desk and writing . . . Poor Lisa."

"Did you read it? Did they show it to you?"

"Yes, yes, I read it," he said. "First the second detective read it. They each leaned over the desk to read it. No one touched it. They asked me to do the same. To read it, but not to touch it. I did. They asked me if it was Lisa's writing, I told them it was." Avi took a few breaths. When he had calmed himself, he continued. "Even then," he said, "with all three of us in the room, Ch'an never moved. She just stayed on her mat, watching us. I guess she was in shock."

"She was just being an Akita," I said.

"What do you mean?"

If he didn't understand Ch'an after living with her, how could I explain her to him?

I looked at my watch. "I have to get up early," I told him. "I better go." I tapped my leg for Dash, but then hesitated at the door. "Will you keep Ch'an, Avi? I don't think Lisa's parents want her."

The Akita had gotten up when Dashiell did. She stood quietly next to Avi, looking off to the side, as if she were in another world and none of this had anything to do with her.

"She belongs here, Avi, with you."

"Go home, Rachel," he said. "It's late. Let me not keep you any longer."

11

Was There a Message Here?

I COULDN'T REMEMBER if it had been the homeopathic veterinarian or the holistic dentist who had told me about Rabbi Lazar Zuckerman, but he hadn't asked how I'd heard about him, so I hadn't had to lie to a man of God.

I had left a message for him yesterday afternoon. He had left one for me after sundown, when he could use the phone without breaking the laws of God. He said I could come the following morning. But since I hadn't spoken to him, I hadn't had the chance to say I was bringing a pit bull with me.

He was seventy-five if he was a day, but crouching so that he could embrace Dashiell, he looked about eight. His eyes, behind rimless glasses, were a faded hazel, but wise and full of light. I think it's a job requirement. He had a full head of hair, steely gray ringlets, a black yarmulke held onto the back of his head with a single bobby pin, and the obligatory rabbinical beard, long, full, and wonderfully unkempt.

"Rabbi Zuckerman," I said.

He stood and looked intensely into my face.

All the way here I had been expecting short and stout, perhaps because of his deep, rich voice, but the rabbi was as tall slender as a young tree, if not quite as lithe.

"I hope it's okay about the dog?"

He waved his hand in front of me, as if he were saying hello, to stop the false apology. "Come, come, both of you," he said, leading me into a dining room off to the right, "we have important work to do."

We sat at a dark mahogany table on chairs so huge I felt my feet wouldn't touch the ground. Or was it the rabbi who made me feel as if I were a child? There were heavy velvet drapes on the windows, wine colored, swagged back with white curtains beneath, but still the light came into the room, showing the sheen of the much-polished table and the age of the faded, flowered wallpaper and worn oriental rug.

Rabbi Zuckerman placed his hands on the table and waited. After the long walk, Dashiell didn't need to be told to lie down. Sighing heavily, he plotzed right next to the rabbi's chair, showing his innate respect for such obvious authority. I reached into my pocket and drew out the copy of Lisa's suicide note and the samples of her known handwriting the rabbi's message had asked me to bring along, letters I had found in the briefcase her mother had given me what seemed like a hundred years ago, in Sea Gate.

He pushed his glasses up onto his forehead and into that mess of curls and brought Lisa's note up close to his face. I thought he was speaking to me, but realized he was humming—Bach's Sonata no. 1, if memory serves. He studied the three words for a very long time. Then he carefully placed the copy down on the table, smoothed it flat with both hands, and looked at it some more.

Next he picked up one of Lisa's letters. These had been written to her mother and father, and so, like anyone else's letters home, they were fairly egocentric, bland, and reassuringly cheerful. But it wasn't the content that the rabbi was studying. For him, the writing itself was the message. What I'd remembered hearing was that a Rabbi Zuckerman on Eldridge Street had a passion for graphology, that he'd been studying handwriting and the things it revealed about character for thirty or so years.

"Suicide, you said, yes?"

I nodded.

He began to hum again, this time keeping time with his foot tapping away on the threadbare carpet. By now five letters were spread out in front of him. He studied them and nodded.

"Su-i-cide," he said. "Hmmph."

"Rabbi Zuckerman, I was wondering if you—"

"Shah," he said. With one hand he reached up and brought his glasses back down to rest on his nose. He got up, causing Dash to momentarily lift his head, and disappeared into the kitchen. I could hear the water running. So could Dashiell, who got up and followed him. A moment later I could hear the sound of one dog drinking, considerably louder than the sound of one hand clapping.

The rabbi returned with two jelly jar glasses, which he placed on the table. He bent and opened the server at the wall behind the head of the table, taking out a bottle of sherry. As he poured, he hummed. Then, handing me one of the glasses, he said, "So."

"Rabbi Zuckerman," I started again, "I was wondering if you could tell if the same person, if Lisa Jacobs, who wrote the letters, also wrote the suicide note. I realize that the note only has three words, well, two and a signature, but—"

"There's a lot of energy in her writing. Strength of body, strength of mind. A remarkable woman. Remarkable."

He took a sip of sherry.

So did I. When in Rome, so to speak.

"Ambition. Optimism. Self-control."

"But—"

Dashiell had remained in the kitchen. I could hear his tags as he flopped over onto his side on the no-doubt-cooler kitchen floor.

"The hand holds the pen," the rabbi said, "but the brain controls the hand. Thus the writing reveals character."

He picked up one of the letters and pushed his glasses back up onto the crown of his head.

"You have never before used the clues from handwriting in your detective work?"

"No, never."

"But you are hoping for a definitive answer. She did. She didn't. If she didn't, who did?"

"No, not that much."

He took a sip of sherry.

"Rabbi Zuckerman, Lisa's parents—"

"Yes, I know," he said. "I can see from her letters. For the parents, there is no more sun to rise in the morning. The world is now dark for them. So, Rachel, what do you hope to give them?"

"What they asked me for," I said. "Some understanding of why."

He nodded.

I waited.

The rabbi hummed.

"This young woman," he finally said, "the woman who wrote with such a regular hand, everything in balance, the proportions pleasing, she was tenacious, self-willed, powerful, a determined person. The writing, you see, shows a person's hand."

I nodded.

"She was confident, more confident than vain. There are no flourishes, no embellishments, no hauteur. Do you know this word?"

I nodded.

"Young people nowadays," he said, "they have no vocabulary. They read only what is sprayed on walls. Do you own a dictionary, Rachel?"

"Yes, Rabbi."

"That's good," he said. He looked back at the letters. "I don't believe this was an empty person with an insatiable craving for attention. No, no, no, a focused person, a strong person, but a self-centered person too, someone who put herself first. A disciplined person, the writing up and down, up and down. Vertical. A thinking person."

"But Rabbi Zuckerman, did she write all five letters? Did she write the last letter?"

"Did she write the last letter? You think she did not?" he asked.

"What I think is that she did not kill herself, Rabbi. I think someone else did that. I can't buy suicide. It makes no sense. There was no history of depression—"

"Look here, Rachel, in these letters, the lines are straight or sometimes they rise ever so slightly, up, up, up, like so," he said, pointing, "and so and so, showing optimism, not depression. Depression makes the lines go down, sometimes off the page, as if the person were too weary of spirit to notice their writing had walked off the paper. Not your Lisa."

"That's what I mean. Her home is serene and lovely. She loved her work. Her parents doted on her. It doesn't seem she could have, would have killed herself. It—"

"So, forgery. Is that what you think?"

"I—I don't know any other way to explain the note."

"When someone forges another's writing, Rachel, they tend to pay attention to the obvious, in this case, the *L* in Lisa, the loops, the flourishes. But Lisa did not embellish. Her writing is small, neat, and simple. The forger tends to forget the smaller items, the little letters in between, and these areas can give him away. But we have so little to go on here. Three words."

"So you can't tell?"

"Can I tell? Can I tell?"

I watched quietly as he studied one of the letters again, his nose nearly touching the page. He was so focused, nearly obsessive in the attention he paid to each letter. Yet he was clearly sensitive, too, not the kind of man who would ignore the needs of his guests, even when one of them was a dog. He was old, but he was strong, the way a tree is, able to sway in the wind and not break. You could see that when he moved. But he was also soft. You could see that in his eyes, his yin and yang in perfect balance.

For a moment I pictured myself living here, making gefilte fish every Friday morning, going to the *mikveh* once a month. Was there a message here?

"The last letter was written more quickly than the other four," he said. "Forgery is almost always written slowly, deliberately." He stood and began to pace. "Even if the forger practiced Lisa's writing, one does not dash off a note in someone else's handwriting. When copying, one takes his time." He leaned over the table now. "Not only does the *L* look like Lisa's writing, Rachel, but the *I* in *I'm sorry* looks as if she wrote it. And the small *i,* see how straight, how precise, now look in her other letters, see, the same, the same, and here, the same."

The rabbi fished in his jacket pocket, came up with a magnifying loupe in a green leather case, and took his chair again, sighing as he sat. He held it over the suicide note, moving it slowly over each letter in each word.

"Here's something interesting," he said, holding the paper right up to his face again. "Look at the periods in her older letters."

I took the loupe and slid it over the letters. Magnified, Lisa's periods were tiny dashes that turned up at the end. I picked up the xerox of the suicide note. Again, a tiny dash that with the naked eye looked like a dot. A dash that had an upward movement, that told you the direction her pen was lifted off the paper. The same, the same, the same.

"And her *s,*" he said, "in 'sorry' and in 'Lisa.' "

"The same, the same," I said.

He nodded.

"I don't get it. She couldn't have killed herself. I feel it so strongly."

"No one is saying she did, Rachel. We are just saying that it seems she wrote, 'I'm sorry. Lisa.' "

"Oh, God," I said.

The rabbi nodded and began to hum.

"She wrote the note. But not necessarily for the purpose everyone assumed."

"She wrote the note," he repeated. "But unfortunately, the only person who could have told us the purpose is dead."

"Maybe not," I said. I picked up the jelly glass and downed the sherry. "Maybe one other person knows, the person who wanted us to *think* it was a suicide note. The person who killed Lisa."

The rabbi turned sideways on his chair so that he could look toward the window. He sat like that for a while, nodding to himself, his face and hair illuminated by the afternoon sun.

"Perhaps so," he said. "Perhaps so."

After a while, he picked up one of the older letters.

"See how the letter is framed, Rachel, the broad margins left and right, top and bottom, as if it were a painting. She had, your Lisa, a passion for beauty, did she not?"

I pictured the roses hanging upside down over Lisa's dining room table.

"Yes, I believe she did, Rabbi."

He sighed. *"Azoy gait es,"* he said.

"So it goes," I agreed.

I folded the letters and put them back in my pocket, wrote a small check to the building fund, called Dashiell, and suddenly remembered the black Taurus sitting down the block from my house. A true New Yorker, I was so used to walking I hadn't remembered I had a car this month, and now, having walked all the way to the East Village, I would have to walk all the way home.

I stopped for fresh hot bialys, giving the bag to Dashiell to carry for me, and then stopped at Guss's for a fresh, crisp pickle, the kind that gets fished out of a wooden barrel. This no one had to carry for me. This I munched noisily as we headed back to the West Village.

We walked along Houston Street, past the Mercer Street dog run, which you have to be a member to use, past the thirty-six-foot-high bust of Sylvette by Picasso, set on the grounds of University Village, and past Aggie's restaurant on the corner of Houston and MacDougal, which made me realize the pickle was only a first plate.

Across MacDougal from Aggie's was a large, fenced ball field. I went to a far corner, took the bag of bialys from Dashiell, and unhooked his leash. I sat on the ground, legs folded in front of me, eating a bialy and thinking about Lisa's dog, there with her the night she'd been killed.

The Japanese consider all their breeds to be more courageous than any Western breed. It is courage in the face of adversity that the Japanese most admire, a trait, by their own admission, of national character that they also assign to their dogs, the Akita, the Sanshu, the Shika, and even the cute but bratty Shiba.

If the note that I'd carefully put back into Lisa's jacket pocket had not been a suicide note, if Lisa had not climbed up on the windowsill and tossed herself straight into eternity, what, I wondered, would the Japanese say about the fact that someone had murdered her while her Akita stood by doing nothing?

The American standard for the Akita—*American* meaning the standard approved by the American Kennel Club, the main U.S. registry of purebred dogs—says the ideal Akita should be "alert and responsive, dignified and courageous."

Whatever the truth was, whatever had happened that night, Ch'an was living proof of the beauty of the breed. If truth be told, Ch'an, with her deep-set, triangular eyes, her powerful, wedge-shaped head, her thick, dark coat, was breathtaking.

And isn't beauty what most of us go for anyway?

Wasn't it what was motivating my brother-in-law's apparent indiscretion?

Wasn't beauty what killed King Kong? Just try telling any one of the single apes you know that you want to fix him up with a woman with a great personality. *See* how far you get.

At least the Akita standard says *something* about temperament. Many of the AKC standards have nothing at all written about character, as if a dog were an assembly of parts covered with fur.

Had Lisa been fooled by the words of the Akita standard, all that overblown, flowery stuff the national clubs write about each breed—loyal, dignified, courageous? Or, since she embraced things Eastern, had she merely wanted an oriental dog?

I opened the bag and pulled out a second bialy, giving half of it to Dashiell.

The same, the same, Rabbi Zuckerman had said.

But who's to say what its purpose was?

I'm sorry. Lisa.

It could have been about anything.

I thought about stopping at the Sixth Precinct on my way home, but what would I say—that I'd made the astonishing discovery that Lisa Jacobs had actually written the suicide note they already knew she wrote? Or that, despite that fact, I had a strong *feeling* that she'd been murdered?

You mean an *intuition*? Marty might ask.

Or would he say, "Handwriting analysis? Pretty flaky, Rachel, even for you. What's next, a Ouija board?"

Just thinking about it, I could almost hear them snickering.

No way. If their motto was Cover your ass, well, so was mine. I didn't need to be thought a fool by my local branch of New York's finest.

What, after all, did I have so far? Cops say the criminal always leaves something of himself at the scene, and that he always takes something away from the scene when he leaves. Could the note, written for another reason, be what was left? That could mean the killer had planned Lisa's death. So what might he have taken away? A hair? A thread? The scent of her perfume? But so what? Whatever he took, whatever he left, a fingerprint, some dandruff, even his damn wallet, couldn't he have been leaving things and taking things away from the scene for years? After all, he had the keys. Didn't he?

Or she?

It was way too soon to talk to the cops. All I had was Lisa's note. And the nagging idea that its purpose had been universally misconstrued.

12

Are You Seeing Anyone?

IN THE EVENING I walked Dash to where the car was parked and drove to Rockland County to visit my sister. Maybe there I'd discover something telling, like if my sister's husband had suddenly started wearing turtlenecks to cover up the hickeys on his lousy, philandering neck.

I made a mental note. Check bald spot for signs of hair transplants in progress. Check bathroom for Grecian Formula for Men. Get Lillian talking.

The gate was open, and I parked just outside the two-car garage. What a different life from mine my sister had—two children, an expensive suburban house, a fully stocked and equipped kitchen, a washer and a dryer, even a freezer. And now, or so it appeared, a cheating husband.

I walked down the long, skinny deck. The door was ajar. I called Lili's name and walked in. She was in the kitchen making soup, her sleeves rolled up, the chopping board deep in carrots, celery, parsley, and parsnips, a cut-up chicken in a bowl to her right.

"Oh, I didn't hear you," she said, her face without makeup, her hair uncombed and sticking out around her face as if she'd stuck her finger in a socket. She was wearing one of Ted's old shirts and what we used to call fat pants, baggy, wide-legged jeans. Maybe those were Zachery's. She had a dishcloth tucked into her waist with assorted stains in various colors on it, and she wore fuzzy slippers, black-and-white ones, in the shape of pandas. If not for the size of her feet, eleven, I would have thought the slippers were Daisy's.

I thought about Lisa's mother, perfect in her gray silk dress and simple pumps. My sister used to dress like that, fussing with her hair, wearing makeup and pretty clothes even when she was staying home. Then I thought about the blond and wondered what difference dressing up would make anyway.

Lili held her arms out to the side as I hugged her, so as not to get raw veggies on Lisa's gorgeous clothes. Since she always complained about the way I looked, I thought she'd notice the improvement. But she didn't. She just turned back to the cutting board and resumed her chopping.

"Zachery is bowling," she said, as if I'd asked. "Daisy is sleeping over at Stephanie's. Teddy had to go in to the city and take care of something at work this afternoon. Inventory? Was that what he said? Whatever. So it's just the two of us." She looked up now and flashed me a Kaminsky grin.

"Are you hungry? There's cold chicken in the fridge. Make some tea for us, too."

I filled the kettle and lit the stove, watching as the blue flames momentarily fogged the pot.

"I thought Ted would be home for dinner." Lillian

shrugged. "He's such a workaholic, that man. You know, I thought he'd get better as he got older, but he's worse." She stopped cutting and looked at me. "Sometimes I worry that something's wrong," she said. She turned back to the cutting board and carefully began taking the skin off a clove of garlic.

"What do you mean?" I asked, feeling as if I hadn't taken a breath since Nixon made his Checkers speech.

"Like if the business is in trouble and Ted won't say. He's so good, Rachel. He's never wanted me to worry about our finances." She began to peel another clove.

I took two mugs off the shelf, put a tea bag in each, and began to make the sandwiches.

"Sometimes I think I should get a job."

"No kidding."

"The kids are always off with their friends, they don't even eat supper at home half the time. And Ted's been working late a lot, like last week the accountant was supposed to come at two thirty and he didn't show up until ten to five. Can you be*lieve* that?"

I didn't offer an opinion.

"It's always something. Maybe it would help if I earned some money, too. There'll be college to pay for soon."

"What would you do?"

"Well, that's precisely the trouble. It's a great idea, but what am I trained for? Who's going to hire someone my age with no real work history?"

"You could always become a detective," I told her, and then ducked out of the way as the dish towel snapped through the air.

"This is stupid. I have such a lucky life," she said, signaling that she'd had about enough. We took the sandwiches over to the table. "Are you seeing anyone?"

She was obsessed with me getting married. Well, I

had, hadn't I? And where had that gotten me? Where, I thought, did anything get anybody—love, marriage, having a child? Where had it gotten the Jacobses? And where had it gotten Lillian?—all her ambitions to be a lawyer instantly put aside when Ted had gotten a terminal case of ring fever and insisted, even before she finished law school, that they get married and she stay at home and play house.

"There must be some job you could get," I said, deciding against telling her that my social life consisted of recently having kissed a total stranger in order to avoid being seen by her husband, who was at the time Velcroed to someone young enough to date her son. "Lots of women go back to work when their kids are older."

"You get so detached from everything," she said, "staying at home. Why am I complaining so much? I live in the most beautiful house in the world, on top of a mountain, with this wonderful"—Lili stopped and sipped her tea—"view."

"Still, a job might be interesting. Look, even if things are fine with Ted's business, working is not only about money."

"I know, but there is so much to do around here."

She pushed her half-eaten sandwich away. I picked it up and gave it to Dashiell. "Let's go for a walk," I said.

Lili changed to mud-stained sneakers and put on Ted's old leather jacket. I put on Lisa's quilted one. Dashiell rushed on ahead. We proceeded more slowly, following the circle from Lili's flashlight so that we wouldn't trip over roots or fallen branches. We went up the path that led into the state park that surrounded Lili's house, walking arm in arm where the trail was wide enough.

"Have you talked to Ted about it, about going to work?"

"I don't think he'd like it, Rach. You know how Teddy is. He wants his dinner on the table the minute he gets home. He wouldn't like the inconvenience of it."

"So you haven't discussed it with him?"

"He has his own problems, Rachel. I don't know if I told you, but a few months ago he seemed so tired all the time that I got really worried. Maybe you should join a gym, I told him. They say it really helps, you know, exercise. It's even supposed to reduce stress, and you know Ted's work, well, the garment district, it's ulcer country."

"So what did he say?"

"He thought it was a great idea. He found this gym right near work. He's already lost that big gut. He looks good for fifty."

Fifty. Maybe that explained it.

"With Teddy working so hard and making all these changes, how can I—"

"You need to talk. You guys are best friends," I said, as if I still believed it. "That's how you stay close, by communicating. That's what you told me, when Jack and I—"

"You're right. It's all my fault. I haven't been talking to him." My sister turned and headed back toward the house. I whistled to Dash and followed along behind her.

"I didn't say it was your *fault*, Lili. I was just repeating what you always told me, that good relationships are based on good communication," I said to her back.

Once inside, Lili picked up her lukewarm tea and began to drink it. Then she began talking about something she'd seen on television. I waited for her to use the downstairs bathroom so that I'd have an excuse to use the one off her bedroom. I quickly checked the hamper, finding it empty. That's when I got really depressed. I expected to find out that designer briefs had replaced my brother-in-law's baggy boxers. Instead I discovered that my sister had nothing better to do than the laundry.

13

Frank Would Be So Proud

I WOKE UP early enough to make a much-needed raid on Lisa's apartment. Her workout clothes were getting a bit ripe, and unlike my sister Lillian, I had more pressing things to do than the wash.

I took Dashiell to the strip of land along the river, now gussied up with benches and called a park, and let him run for a while. Then we headed for Lisa's. When I unlocked the door, Dash made a beeline for the water bowl. I dumped Lisa's mail on the small table near the door and headed upstairs. I had brought along my leather backpack to use as a shopping bag.

I began my shopping in Lisa's bureau, taking a few more black tops and some leggings. Next I decided I needed a change of jewelry. I dropped the musical earrings back into the top drawer of the jewelry box and fished around to see what else I liked. I decided on little silver hearts, simple, with a dot in the center of each.

In the second drawer, in keeping with the theme, there was another heart piece, tucked into a robin's-egg-blue Tiffany bag, as the jasper necklace had been, a heavy silver link bracelet with a heart dangling from it. It was engraved, but not with Lisa's name or initials. It said, Be My Love. Pretty corny, but I wouldn't have thrown it away had someone I loved given it to me. I held it in my hand for a while, warming the silver and feeling its weight. In the end, I put it back in the little blue bag and left it.

I changed to one of Lisa's black sweaters and a clean pair of faded jeans. It was sort of like playing dress-up, only it was morbid. Still, I was just following Avi's advice, wasn't I? I was walking in Lisa's shoes. And her earrings, necklace, and clothes. I was reading her books and letters. I had just barely escaped from having to sleep with her dog. And in a short while I'd be back at Bank Street T'ai Chi, where it was possible I'd be meeting the person who had last seen her alive.

I put the rest of the clothes into the backpack and headed for the stairs. I planned to put most everything back, of course. I'm often a liar, but only rarely a thief. On the way out I snagged the book of Zen quotes I hadn't finished reading, tucking it under one arm. It was time to go, but first I had a guilt pang at the front door. The pile of mail was growing. One of these days, I knew, I'd have to look through it. But not this day. If I didn't hurry, I'd be late for the staff meeting.

I could see light coming into the hall as together Dash and I climbed to the fifth floor. The door had been propped open. I could hear their voices as I approached.

"—a matter of time," I heard Avi say impatiently.

"But you're not denying—"

"I am not denying. But length of time does not determine—"

"I have been here for seven and a half years. I have done—"

"Janet, there is something important you have *not* done. Now, could we discuss this, you and I, at a later time? I have something important to talk to all of you about today."

I was a few steps from the landing when I put my hand into Dash's collar to stop him. Someone had left an expensive camera, a Nikon, on the shelf where the shoes were stored, an odd thing to do in New York City. I wondered which of them was so trusting.

"But it's the same old story, Avram. Exactly the same. And I need—"

"*You* need. There is barely room for oxygen in this place with all this overblown ego. I, I, me, me!" There was a silence and then Avi spoke again, slowly and calmly. "The study we have all embarked upon is a lifelong investment in loss, letting go of ego, letting go of tension, letting go of fear—"

"Avi, you—"

"I have only taken on an apprentice. You act as if—"

"That's what you said last time."

"But *who*?" It was a man's voice this time. A young-sounding man.

They were all young. Howard Lish, a massage therapist who worked out of his home on Bank Street, only a block and a half east of the school, I had learned by surfing around in Avi's computer files, was, at thirty-eight, the oldest on staff. Stewart Fleck, a social worker who apparently had no compunction about signing out to the field and then coming here to study or teach, was thirty-four, just two years older than Lisa. Hey, it'll be nice to meet a couple of young men for a change, I thought, even if at this point in time they were both murder suspects.

Like *I'm* perfect.

"You mean you've ignored my request again, Avram?"

That was Janet again, Janet Castle, thirty-three, a bodybuilder who earned her living as a personal trainer and, like the others, did t'ai chi on the side.

"Enough. I want you all to accept her. To help her learn."

They all lived in the neighborhood, all close to the school.

"Where did she come from? Where were you hu-hu-hiding her? Lisa's only been d-dead two—" A man's voice.

"*Enough.* This pushing, this ambition, this jealousy, where does it get you? Not where you say you want to go. You come here so full of yourselves, all of you, how can I teach you anything? Look at the sorry lot of you."

I could picture their heads hanging, like three reprimanded golden retrievers. If they had tails, just the tips would be hopefully beating against their chairs as they waited for some sign of forgiveness.

"I was hoping," Avi continued in a softer voice, "that when she comes, you would welcome her, teach her, embrace her."

"Em*brace* her?" Janet said.

I let go of Dash's collar, and together we sauntered into the staff meeting.

"Ah, it's Rachel and Dash. Come in, come in," Avi said, beaming at me as the other three all turned in unison and stared daggers in my direction. "I'd like you to meet the others."

"Hey," I said, offering one of my most dazzling smiles. "Great to be here."

There was an empty chair next to Avi, so I took it, dropping the full backpack and the Zen book next to it, then slipping Lisa's jacket off and letting it drape, inside out, over the back of the chair. I crossed my legs, adjusted the sleeves of Lisa's soft black cashmere and cotton sweater, and began to play with her jasper necklace.

Avi extended a big red hand. "Rachel Alexander, Howard Lish—"

"Hey," I said.

"Stewart Fleck—"

"Hey, Stew."

"And Janet Castle."

"Hey, Janet."

I might have gotten a more animated response from Mount Rushmore.

The phone rang, and Avi excused himself. It was the first time I'd seen him interrupt anything he was doing to take a call, and I could only think he wanted the others to have a chance at me. You could just see they were dying of curiosity. He'd probably sit in his office listening as they circled and closed in for the kill.

"Now I see what my problem is," Stewie said, staring after Dashiell as he followed Avi into the office. "I don't have a dog."

Janet smirked and ran her fingers nervously through her short hair.

"So, Rachel," Howie said, his big face flushed, his hands trembling, "wh-what did you do before coming here?"

That's New York for you. Skip the foreplay and get right down to it. I stared for a moment, making him even more nervous than he managed to be on his own. He was wearing a plaid shirt and jeans that both looked as if they had come from Goodwill, and I'd bet a day's pay he had at least one hole in his socks.

"I was a brain surgeon," I finally said.

I heard a chair scraping in the office. Avi had probably just fallen off it.

"Oh, great," Janet said in her Texas twang, "another one. Oddly enough, we were all brain surgeons before finding t'ai chi." She began to laugh. "Looks like the old man got a live one this time," she said, "got to give him credit." Her hair was boyishly short and blond, nearly white, with a small splash of green at the crown, a case of better living through chemistry.

"We all have d-day jobs, so to speak," Howie said, his forehead wrinkled as he waited for me to volunteer something. Good fucking luck on that one. I was only sorry I wasn't chewing gum. It was definitely the missing touch.

Fuss, fuss. Lisa had been heavily subsidized by daddy, five or ten thousand dollars at a time, for birthdays, Hannukah, Simchas Torah, whatever, in order to have the privilege of being Avi's apprentice. So what was this all about? Being teacher's pet?

"You live in the neighborhood?" Stewie asked.

Where were his manners? Next he'd be asking me what my rent was.

"I'm staying at my cousin's place," I told him, "for now."

"Your cousin?" Janet asked.

"My cousin Lisa."

Stir things up, Frank used to say; it makes the shift float to the surface.

"You're Lisa's cou-cousin?"

"Didn't Avram tell you?" I asked.

"I'm a massage therapist," Howie said, his bulldog jowls trembling as he spoke. "It's good to know, in case you ever get a crick in your neck or anything. So wha-what were you up to, before?"

Maybe he *was* a bulldog. He sure didn't know when to let go.

I looked into my lap and smiled. "Look," I said after a while, "Avi says now is all there is. Now I'm here."

No one spoke. Not one of them appeared to have taken a breath since Eve reached for the apple, sending the human race on its downhill slide.

Frank would be so proud.

"How long have you known Avi?" Stewie finally asked, as interested as if he were a cocker spaniel and I were holding a liver snap.

"It's hard to say."

"Just what we need around here," Janet drawled, "another bitch."

Stewie shot her a look.

Avi returned and with a motion of his arm called us for rounds. Howie, Stewart, and Janet went out into the hall to change shoes. I picked up Lisa's shoes from right behind my chair and slipped them on. We were off to an auspicious beginning, I thought as I took a place in the back so that I could watch them from behind as well as in the mirror.

Howard Lish, a sad-looking fat man, was off to the left. He was about five-eight, flabby, and had apparently found the very potbelly my brother-in-law had just lost.

Stewart Fleck was as small and chary as a rodent out on a raid in some street cat's territory. He was barely my height, on the gaunt side, and pale, as if he stayed indoors too much. I could see his dark, beady little eyes watching me in the mirror. Fuck *him*, I thought and watched him right back.

The only other person I knew with muscles like Janet Castle was my pit bull. She was wearing a shocking pink cutoff singlet that showed off her rocklike abs.

You could see her perfect quads under the floral latex tights, and her glutes looked as if they were made of concrete. Holy steroids, Batman, what a construction site *she* was.

I looked around at the sorry group. Not one of them was quite what I'd expect to find if I opened the latest edition of Who's Who in Zen in America. Where did Avi find all these nerds?

But who was I to talk? I still cared far too much about what my family thought about me, even though most of them were dead. The strongest substance I'd abused lately was sherry out of a jelly jar with a seventy-five-year-old rabbi. And it had been a dog's age since I'd shared my bed with someone who wasn't wearing a flea collar.

14

Janet Gave Me a Wink

AFTER ROUNDS STEWIE and Howie left immediately, and Avi went into the office and closed the door. Janet gave me a wink, as if we were old buddies and we'd just pulled off another good one. While I was changing my shoes, she came up to me.

"Listen," she said, "I'm sorry I came down so hard on you. It's not your fault, what happened. It's just the way things are." She shrugged. "I mean, Avram's great, I love him to pieces, but he does things his way. Shit, it's his school, am I right?"

I nodded.

"So why don't we go have lunch, my treat, to, you know, make it up to you for me being such a bitch?"

"Why not?"

"Great," she said, slapping me on the back and nearly knocking me through the wall.

I put Lisa's shoes back where they belonged and, with Dash trailing along after me, met up with Janet in the hall changing to her thick-soled, multicolored cross-trainers. Was she figuring we'd run to the restaurant?

"You like Chinese?" she asked. She'd covered her short hair with a baseball cap, worn backward.

"Who doesn't?" Actually, I'd had a yen for it for days now.

"Great. We'll go over to Charlie Mom's. Did you ever try their vegetable dumplings? They're *fab*ulous."

The waiter's erased blackboard of a face never changed as he regarded Dashiell's credentials and his yellow Registered Service Dog tag. I was pretty sure he had no idea what they meant, or what the law said, but he let him in anyway. We were led to a table in the back. Dash slid to the floor right behind my chair and fell immediately asleep. As usual, no one else in the restaurant seemed to notice he was there.

Janet ordered soup and dumplings for both of us. By the time we'd unfolded our napkins, the soup was in front of us.

"It's so cheap here. I come every chance I get."

"So why the fuss over Avi teaching me t'ai chi, Janet? He must teach lots of people. It's what he does, isn't it?"

"But there's only one apprentice," she said, picking up the baseball cap and placing it back on her head.

The waiter brought the dumplings even though we hadn't touched the soup yet.

"What's the big deal?"

"It means he thinks you have special ability. And so he gives you lots of time. What else do you think we're talking about? Sure, the man teaches t'ai chi, we get to work with him in *class*. It's not the same. His special student gets to spend time alone with him, I mean, hours at a time. That he doesn't do with everyone. And that's what this is all about, time with Avram. The man goes, Get that, will you? when the phone rings, and he changes your life. It's not what he does. It's what he is. And just being around him, I don't know. It does things to you, Rachel. The man's amazing."

"He sure is," I said, dipping one of the crispy noodles in duck sauce, then just hanging on to it. "Janet—"

She looked up from her soup.

"What do you make of the note?"

"The note?"

"You know. The one Lisa left?"

"Oh, *that* note. Here's how I see it," she said, taking a handful of noodles and tossing them into her soup bowl. She leaned forward. "We had talked, me and Lisa, what, a month ago. I mean, I was pissed."

"About Lisa being Avi's apprentice instead of you? But you were both at the school for *years,* weren't you? Why did you wait so long to tell her?"

"It wasn't *that,*" she said. "I mean, in the beginning, when she came, well, I knew it wasn't *her* fault that Avi spent the time with her, not me. It was his decision, so how could I blame Lisa for taking a wonderful opportunity?"

"Of course. You couldn't," I said.

But of course, you could.

"So, what was it?"

"A few months ago, something changed. Lisa changed."

"In what way, Janet?"

"She got real la-di-da, like she was more important than the rest of us. So finally one day I got her alone, and I went, What got into you, and she goes, What are you *talking* about, Janet, and excuse me, but can't you see I'm busy here? and I went, This won't take long, it's just when are you going to stop being such a bitch, woman?"

"What did she say?"

"Nothing at first, you know. She just looked, well, shocked. I mean, we had been close, me and her," Janet said, holding up two fingers that appeared to be glued together at the sides. "So then she goes, Janet, I had no *idea*. There's a lot of stuff going on in my life right now, a lot to deal with. She looked like she was going to lose it, you know. I actually felt bad for her for a minute. But then she goes, I guess that's why I've been short with you people. You people! Give me a damn break. I mean, isn't that pathetic, not to know the effect you're having on the people around you. And to call us *you people,* as if we had just fallen out of her nose or something."

"What else did she say?"

"*Nada.* She just shook her head and walked away. And then, well, it happened. I mean"—she made an arc with her chopsticks and whistled—"out the window."

"I don't get it, Janet," I said, leaning over the table to get closer. "You're not saying she killed herself because of what you said to her, because you were upset—"

"Hell, no."

She drank some tea and picked up a dumpling with her chopsticks.

"So what *are* you saying?"

"I figured the note just took care of our unfinished business."

"Such as?"

"She'd explained herself, you know, a lot of stress, blah, blah, blah, like *that*'s an excuse. But she didn't really apologize, you know what I'm saying? Now she has. That's all."

"And you forgive her? Now."

"Absolutely." She popped the dumpling in her mouth and chewed thoughtfully. "She was perfect, you know," Janet said. "She'd never leave anything undone. It's like a dis-*ease,* being like that." She picked up her bowl and drank some of her soup.

"Why did she do it, Janet? She was so young, and she was doing what she wanted to do, wasn't she? I just don't get it. Did you ever find out what she was talking about, the stuff she said she was dealing with?"

"Not really. I figure there'd been big trouble with her boyfriend, because he'd stopped coming by to pick her up. But that had been a while before. Maybe there was some new guy busting her chops. Who knows? Or maybe she just got tired of having to be perfect. *That* can be a real drag."

"What do you mean?"

Janet shrugged, picked up another dumpling, and dipped it into the little dish of soy sauce before putting it into her mouth. I spooned up some soup.

"See," she said, pointing at me with her sticks. "That's how Lisa ate. She'd never pick up her bowl. Afraid she might drip a little soup on her chin." She wiped her mouth with the back of her hand. "Like it would be the end of the fucking world if she did."

"Janet, what did Avi mean when he told you there was something important you hadn't done?"

"We were that loud?" she said. "You heard us fighting before you even walked in?" Janet put both hands over her mouth.

"I did."

"No wonder you were such a bitch!"

"I couldn't help hearing you all, Janet," I said, leaning over the table and punching her playfully on her concrete arm. "The door was open, and I was walking—"

"Because Lisa never took the elevator," she said.

Then she crossed her eyes and stuck her tongue out to the side.

"So, the thing Avi said—"

I picked up a dumpling and dipped it in the soy sauce. The strong flavor made my eyes tear.

"The bodybuilding." She lifted her right arm and flexed the most astonishing biceps I had ever seen. "Avi says t'ai chi makes learning everything else easier. And everything else you do, physical stuff, like sports or exercise, makes it more difficult to learn t'ai chi."

"Is that true?" I asked, thinking of all the hyperbole I had read in one of Lisa's books, particularly the sweeping statements about health and longevity.

The waiter arrived with the check. I reached for my wallet, but Janet shook her head.

"Yes," she said, looking down. "He gets really pissed when I come to class so sore from weight lifting that I can hardly move without groaning. T'ai chi, he goes, is about letting go, relaxing the muscles, strength from softness, all that shit. He goes, Ach, you know how he does that? So what do you do, he goes, you make rocks out of your muscles. You're not happy until you're in pain.

"What happens when the most pliable element meets the hardest? he goes one time. But he doesn't wait for an answer. He'd be one unhappy dude if you ever answered one of his questions. He has to ask and answer. Am I right?"

I nodded.

"The rock yields, he goes. It is worn away by the water. Nothing, absolutely nothing can withstand the force of water." Janet leaned forward and lowered her voice. "He got so mad at me once, he can be a cranky son of a bitch, you know, so he goes, How long are you going to go on trying to be superwoman? like one word

from him and I'm going to burn my cape and throw
away my shirt with the red S on it."

"What did you tell him?"

"Nothing. I didn't say squat. So he goes, Janet,
haven't you noticed that it gets more and more difficult
to find a phone booth nowadays? And when you finally
do, someone's already gone and pissed in it." Janet covered her mouth when she laughed. "The man's a fucking riot."

"Have you ever thought of giving it up?"

"Shit, no. You done any? It makes you feel so *good*."

"Pumping iron? Not really."

Janet raised one eyebrow. "Never?"

I pushed up the sleeve of Lisa's sweater and flexed my
biceps. She wasn't impressed.

"You're coming to the gym, woman, for a *real*
workout. I want you to *feel* what I'm talking about.
Hey, it's on me. No charge. Okay?"

She took out her appointment book and a pen, and
we made a date for my bodybuilding lesson, for Thursday at five. She carefully wrote my name in her book,
holding the pen with her left hand. This would have
been a huge issue, perhaps even exoneration from my
suspicions, had I not already seen Rabbi Zuckerman
and heard his opinion that Lisa had written the note
herself, the note that Lisa's parents, Paul, and now Janet thought had been an apology to them.

As Janet wrote, her tongue out to the side and moving with each word, I took a good look at her arms. She
could have carried Lisa up the stairs and pitched her
out the window without stopping to catch her breath.

"You coming to sword class tonight?" she asked.

I pictured myself as a *New Yorker* cartoon. The cap-
tion would read, "Oops."

"I'm sort of a klutz. I'd probably cut off my own foot."

"No problem, as long as you don't cut off *my* foot." She winked at me. "Everyone says that. Beginners use wooden swords. Your foot'll be safe."

"I have some stuff to do tonight," I told her. "Maybe next week. Hey, thanks for lunch. And for not holding a grudge."

"No problem," she said.

"Janet, you aren't going to get mad at *me* now, are you, because Avi—"

"Nah. I was pissed at Lisa for all of a sudden acting so nasty to all of us. Shit, Howie was in *tears* one day. Truth is, I wouldn't be the favorite even if you never showed up. Avi likes pretty girls. He says I look like a boy." She picked up the cap and ran her hand through her short hair. "I don't get my period anymore," she whispered. "Not enough body fat. Are you eating this?" she asked, picking up her chopsticks and pointing them at my last dumpling.

"No, go ahead."

"You sure, woman?"

I nodded.

She didn't have any breasts to speak of. She had well-developed pecs instead. Even her skin had coarsened, and her jaw was as square as a boxer's, the human kind.

She ate the dumpling, dipped the rest of the fried noddles in duck sauce and ate those, and then drank the rest of her soup.

"What happened between Lisa and Howie to make him cry, Janet?"

"I don't know. Neither of them would tell me. Say, that's your cousin's necklace, isn't it?" she asked after wiping her mouth and dropping the napkin onto her plate.

I felt for the jasper heart. It looked as if it had been molded from melted crayons and the artist had left a thumbprint dead center before it hardened.

"Like I said, I'm staying at her place for now."

"And using her stuff?"

I shrugged. "What's the big deal? It's not like *she* needs it anymore."

"Ain't *that* the truth."

She got up, and Dashiell and I followed her out. On Sixth Avenue she handed me a card with my appointment on it and a pass to the gym at the Archives building, on Christopher Street.

"I trained Lisa, you know," Janet said, nodding.

"Lisa? Even though Avi—"

"Look, Rachel, if you haven't found out yet, you will. The man's got a Napoleon complex. Everything has to be done his way, no exceptions whatsoever. You have to draw the line *some*where, at least if you're going to keep your sanity you do."

"So he knew that Lisa—"

"Nah. It was our little secret." She winked. "Lisa said it helped her with sword class. Those mothers are *heavy*. You need strength here," she said, slapping her left shoulder with her right hand. "You'll see." Then she feinted a punch toward *my* shoulder and took off.

That evening I took Dashiell for a long walk along the waterfront. Playing with a flirty husky bitch, he seemed to forget the rest of the world existed. Later, after reparking the car, I read unfathomable Zen stories to him as he lay snoring at my side.

15

This Is Going to Hurt

I COULD HEAR the rain tapping lightly on the roof when I woke up. I told Dashiell to find the cordless phone and, when he had, dialed Lili.

"I was just thinking about you," she said, the way she almost always does.

"Me, too," I said. "That's what I was calling to say."

"Ted's working late tomorrow, some buyers in from out of town, I think. Why don't you come out? We can go to that nice Japanese place in Nyack."

"Can't," I told her, in a rush now that I'd gotten what I needed from the phone call. "I have to work."

"Bummer," she said.

"Maybe next week." I hung up without waiting for an answer.

Wednesday. Excellent. I had the car. Now I needed a driver. I dialed again.

"Paul?"

"Rachel? Is that you?"

"I'm sorry about the other day, running off like that.

It's just that I remembered something I'd forgotten. An appointment I'd scheduled."

"I thought it must have been something important, for you to run off like that."

"I was wondering if I could make it up to you, buy you dinner?"

"Rachel, you don't have to—"

"How about tomorrow night?"

"Tomorrow?"

"Just say *yes*, okay?"

"Let me check."

I heard him put the phone down, but I couldn't hear him walking away. Maybe he was barefoot. Or his appointment calendar was right near the phone. Or he was pretending to check his calendar in order to save face.

"Yes," he said. "Consider yourself lucky. Tomorrow's okay."

"Great. I'll pick you up at the Club. Is five okay?"

"Rachel—"

"It was all my fault. Okay?"

Once again, I hung up without giving the person on the other end of the line a chance to say another word.

It was eleven fifteen. Stewie was teaching a noon class, so Dash and I headed over to Bank Street T'ai Chi.

Avi had just finished practicing the form. "Do you have a moment?" I asked him. "I need to ask you something, about the note Lisa left." Show him proper respect, I thought, and he'll be putty in my hands.

"Are you familiar with the story of the young man who wanted to study Zen?"

"Oh, *please*."

" 'Have you had your breakfast?' the master asked him. The young man nodded, just the way *you* always do. He had. "Then wash your bowl," the master told him."

"So, what does that mean?"

But didn't I know what it meant? After all, Avi had announced that I was his new apprentice, a role I'd had experience with. I had learned dog training as an apprentice to another trainer. That meant I would get lots of private lessons, a chance to assist in class, that I'd answer the phone, do the bills and mailings, lick the stamps, sweep up, dust, pinch dead leaves off the plants, run out and buy him cigarettes, and wash the coffee cups after class because he thought ceramic cups were more friendly to the environment than Styrofoam, a man clearly ahead of his time.

"Did you want me to sweep up out here?" I asked. "Or vacuum your office?"

Avi sighed.

"That won't be necessary. We have someone to do that, Rachel," he said, as if I were a few logs shy of a full cord.

"Then will you answer my question?"

He merely waved his arm impatiently and headed for his office.

"Or not?" I said after he'd already closed the door.

"Being a de-tec-tive sounds like *fun*," my nephew Zachery had said the night I'd made my official announcement to the family.

Yeah, right.

Thank God our mother is dead, Lili had added, because if she weren't, *this* would have killed her.

I sat down on the studio floor, against a side wall, to wait. The students began to arrive at ten of twelve for the lunch-hour class, changing shoes in the hall and then sitting in the area between the office and the studio until they were called to begin. Stewie arrived late, changed his shoes, and after nodding to his students, turned to face the mirror and began to do the form. I joined the class, taking a place in the back.

Stewie's eyes, which should have been half closed and half open, darted nervously from side to side, watching his students in the mirror. He was watching me, too, but when his eyes met mine, his moved away quickly.

He spoke softly as we moved slowly through the form. The empty leg is yin, he said, but when you shift your weight into it, it becomes yang, yin and yang, dark and light, soft and strong, these are constantly changing.

I thought about the way a bitch plays with her puppies, moving gracefully from her role of natural authority to a submissive posture so that the puppies can play at being alpha, then taking charge again when the game is over, never leaving them with a false impression of the way things are.

I was hoping I'd end up at lunch with Stewie after class, the way I had with Janet. Clearly I wasn't the only one of us who was curious, but before I had the chance to change my shoes, he was gone. I never did get to ask him any questions or find out how he felt about my cousin Lisa. Not wanting to waste the rest of the day, I got another idea.

I waited until I was downstairs to use the phone, calling information first, for Howard Lish's number, then asking to see him, for an emergency. My calf, I told him, was throbbing and cramped.

Come right over, he said, not stuttering at all. I'll take care of it.

I smiled as I hung up and, Dashiell at my side, headed east, just past the HB Acting Studio, to the building where Howie Lish lived and worked.

"The crick is in my leg," I said when Howie, wearing

a white jacket as if he were a dentist rather than a masseur, opened the door. "Instead of my neck."

"You're pushing yourself too hard," he said, turning and walking toward an open door just down the hall and on the right. "You're trying to learn t'ai chi too fast, working too many hours."

I heard the sound of a television set from somewhere else in the apartment. Howie closed the door to his office.

"Hop up on the table," he said. "Let me have a look at it." I signaled Dash to lie down in a corner of the room. Then I panicked. Had I told him which leg it was? I hoped not, because I couldn't remember. Luckily, my normal rocklike tension saved me. Howie began prodding the muscles in my right leg, and before I knew it, I was screaming. Then he squeezed the calf on my left leg, pressing his fat fingers in so deep they could have touched each other. Again, I embarrassed myself.

"Hey," I said. "Easy."

"It's only a matter of time until the other one goes into spasm," he said, as serious as an undertaker. "You're very tense."

I guess he'd be eligible for Mensa now that he'd figured that out.

"I only have time to work on your legs today. I have a client coming in twenty minutes. But you'll need to do more than just this if you want to stay out of trouble."

He handed me a cotton smock, telling me to strip from the waist down. Right, like guys weren't telling me that since I grew tits. Leaving my underpants on is sort of a rule I have when I'm around strange men. And if ever there was a strange man, it was Howie Lish. Wearing the smock, I got back up on the table. Now what? Was I supposed to call him? Or just lie around in my skivvies hoping he'd eventually return?

Howie came back into the room carrying a thick blue towel, which he laid over one leg, and a bottle of lavender-scented oil. Standing at my side, he put a strong, gentle hand on my back.

"Howie, I can't tell you how—"

"Shh," he said. "This is going to hurt."

I heard him rubbing his hands together. When they landed on my bare leg they were warm, wet, and slippery. He began to massage my leg in long strokes, first up the back of the leg, then on the sides, and after it had gotten warm, the blood circulating nicely, thank you, he began to dig into the calf, and I heard someone cry out in pain and realized afterward that since it hadn't been deep enough to have been him, it must have been me. Again.

Saying nothing, his hot, slimy hands never stopping, going back and forth between the painful kneading and poking and the delicious long strokes that ended right at the edge of my tiger-striped underwear, Howie worked on my legs for over half an hour. At the end he took my feet, one at a time, in his big, strong hands and did exquisite things to them. I was sure it couldn't be legal to feel this good.

"Better?" he asked.

"Wonderful," I told him. "Thank you."

"I'll go out so you can get dressed."

I pulled on Lisa's leggings, then turned. Howie was standing in the doorway. Had he just come back? Or had the little weasel been there all along? I picked up Lisa's turtleneck and put that on too, breaking eye contact with Howie for the moment the shirt slipped over my head.

"When you get home, take a long, warm bath," he said, as if nothing untoward had happened. "Not hot," he added. "Hot baths make you more tense." His face looked hot. At any rate, his nose and cheeks were as red as if he had been in a sauna. "You're pushing yourself very hard, physically and mentally. Your body gave you an important message today, to lighten up on yourself. You ought to pay attention to that. And I'd like to see you again on Friday."

I bet you would, I thought.

"I can fit you in at three thirty."

"Perfect," I said. I could always call and cancel later.

I wondered what Lisa had said to make him cry. I didn't think it would take much.

"You're probably eating badly, too," he said.

"What am I supposed to be, a vegetarian or something?"

Howie smiled. "No, but raw, organic vegetable juice can really help give you the stamina you need for t'ai chi. You don't need to be a vegetarian, but you certainly should watch your fat intake—"

Look who's talking.

"But I'm not—"

"It's not for your weight. Your weight is good. Fat's been linked to—"

"*Stop*. I'm feeling too good to hear the list of diseases you get from each food group. I read the papers. The trouble is, they change their minds every week or so. You know, one week it's oat bran, the savior of the human race, then it's selenium, or green tea or beta-carotene. You know what I'm saying, Howie?"

"I do," he said, shifting his weight and looking uncomfortable. "Sometimes you sound just l-like her," he said, looking down at his Fred Flintstone feet.

"You mean Lisa?"

Howie's face got all splotchy, and his neck flushed red. He nodded.

"It's hard to get a handle on her," I said. "We were

cousins, but I hardly knew her. And now I hear so much about her, being at the school and everything. But it's inconsistent. Sometimes she sounds so special, so smart, so graceful, the way her parents saw her. Other times—" Something in Howie's eyes made me pause. "You'd want to toss her out the window."

Howie blinked once.

The doorbell rang.

Dashiell stood, ready if needed.

"Do you miss her, Howie?" I asked as he headed out of his office to answer the door. "Were you and Lisa close?"

He turned to face me. "Of c-course I m-miss her," he said, his voice as flat as Kansas. "She was my teacher—and a client."

"That's all?" I asked him.

"I-isn't th-th-that enough?"

He ought to do something about *his* tension, I thought. The man looked as if he were ready to implode.

"How much do I owe you for fixing Mr. Leg?"

The bell rang a second time.

"I'll catch you next time," he said, a kind of pain showing on his face that couldn't be fixed as easily as a bogus spasm could.

16

You Think Too Much

WHEN I LEFT Howie's, I headed for Lisa's. I'd decided I'd sort through her mail and check her answering machine messages and then reward myself with a bacon burger and some fries. I was feeling really tired, probably a fat deficiency.

The concierge handed me even more junk mail than was waiting for me upstairs, the stuff too big to fit in her mailbox, catalogs and magazines folded and held together by a fat rubber band. Just the volume of stuff started depressing me. If I liked paperwork, I would have become a CPA. By the time I'd gotten upstairs, I'd convinced myself, just as I did at home, that I could pitch out Victoria's Secret and L. L. Bean one day later.

The answering machine was flashing, but instead of rolling it back and listening to the messages, I picked up the cordless phone that sat next to it, walked over to the black couch under the windows, and dialed my aunt Ceil.

"Hello?" she said, her voice strong and gravelly.

"Ceil? It's Rachel. I was wondering if I could come and see you tomorrow afternoon. I have a favor to ask."

"Of course, tootsie. Come early. Stay late. I'll make us a little lunch. When can I expect you?"

"Is two okay?"

"Two is perfect, darling. See you then."

Was Ceil the only one in my family I had an easy time with because she had been married to my father's brother, so she wasn't a blood relative? Maybe, like dogs, people just got along better with others that were not from their own gene pool.

I meant to get up and listen to Lisa's messages, I really did, because the tenth law of investigation work is, You never know. I thought again about dumping the junk mail and doing whatever was appropriate with the rest of it. But I felt almost drugged. Perhaps it was the massage. With some of my tension gone, there was nothing left to hold me up.

I'd heard Dashiell going up the wooden steps. I'd heard the bed creak as he'd gotten onto it. I thought of joining him, but the black couch was so soft and inviting, and I was already there. So I leaned sideways, pulled up my legs, and fell immediately asleep, Lisa's cordless phone still in my hand.

When I woke up, it was dark in the apartment, and for a moment I had trouble remembering where I was. Dashiell was lying next to the couch now, and when I sat up, he looked up at me, reminding me that a dog has needs, too. I looked at my watch. It was after seven. I pulled myself together, and we headed for the waterfront so that Dashiell could stretch his legs and use his muscles before dinner.

We crossed over at Christopher Street and headed

north, Dashiell running far ahead, ecstatic to be free to move, running back to check on me every few minutes.

There was a Great Dane wearing an American flag bandanna waiting up ahead, and in no time they were jumping in circles, eyes dancing, feeling each other's strengths and weaknesses as they practiced a dog version of Push Hands.

When I felt someone right behind me, I turned.

"Stewie. Hey."

It was my lucky day. I was now looking into the small, dark eyes of Stewie Fleck. He was wearing a heavy black turtleneck and black jeans, a beatnik in the age of grunge. When I turned, he smiled, and I could see the strain in it.

"I was going to practice the form out on the pier," he said, looking at his feet now, "but it's too crowded tonight. Avi says to be careful practicing outdoors, because someone might see you and challenge you."

That seemed a remote possibility to me where we were. The Greenwich Village waterfront was a gay pickup area, especially after dark. People came here to make love, not war.

"I was just going out for a bite to eat. You feel like some food, or a beer?" I asked him, never one to let a serendipitous opportunity slip through my fingers.

"Well, if—" he said, looking like one of those Fresh Air Fund kids seeing trees for the first time.

"Sure you do," I told him. "I know a great place. Dylan Thomas used to drink there. Of course, where didn't he used to drink?"

Stewie smiled his nervous smile. I took that as a yes and led the way. Ten minutes later we were seated at a booth at Chumley's, drinking beer, Dashiell lying under the table on my feet.

"So I was working as a carpenter, making cabinets,

fixing things," Stewie said, continuing the story of his life he had begun as we'd crossed West Street, "living in Ohio of all places, and I'm not exactly happy, but I have no idea what I want to do with the rest of my life. I'm all of twenty then." He flashed me his tense little smile again. Like a lot of shy people, once he felt it was okay to talk, there was no stopping him, which was just fine with me.

"So one night," he continued, "I go to sleep and I have this dream that I'm walking in the woods and I meet an ancient man, right, and we begin to talk, we just sit on the ground and talk, and he says he's going to tell me the secret of life, right? Just like in all those shaggy dog jokes, you know, life is a bowl of cherries, those jokes? But when I wake up, I know he told me the secret, but I can't remember what it was. Jesus, I thought. Maybe I can go back to sleep and ask him again. But then I thought, No, you can't do that, if someone tells you the secret of life, you can't go back to them and tell them you forgot it, right?"

I laughed and tried to look fascinated. "So what happened then?" I asked.

"Get this, Rachel. I'm sitting there and I'm really depressed, and then I think, No big deal, I'll have to find it out for myself."

"Wonderful," I said, thinking this guy would be talking to a lamppost if he hadn't run into me, the way this stuff was pouring out of him. His last conversation was probably when he ran into Adam and Eve as they were leaving the garden.

"And that was the beginning," he said. I sipped my beer, and our food arrived. "That's how I found t'ai chi." He sat back, nodding, really pleased with himself. "You take a lot on faith here," he said. "It's too dark to see what you're eating."

He had ordered the vegetarian chili. I had gotten a bacon burger, the bacon and the beef so rare it must have been only moments since they had their own dinner. It didn't occur to me until the first delicious bite that the sight of a fresh kill might offend Stewie. On the other hand, on my list of things to worry about, offending vegetarians doesn't even show up.

"How long after the dream did you come to New York?" I asked, hoping to catch up to the present before arthritis set in.

"There was this girl I met, said she was moving to California, so I went out there, too. But I had to wait about six weeks after she left, to finish up the jobs I had started. And when I got to where she said she'd be, she wasn't there." He took a spoonful of his chili. "I tried to find her, and when I couldn't, well, I was out of money by then, so I stayed anyway, and that's when I began to study t'ai chi. It was really popular out there. The yellow pages were full of schools."

"How did you end up in New York?"

"I met this guy who was out on the coast on vacation, and he was taking classes where I studied t'ai chi. People do that all the time, if they're serious. They don't take vacation from going to class. And after rounds one evening, I overheard him talking to another student, about the school he studied at in New York, and he started to talk to him about Avi. Two months later I was in New York. And two weeks after that I was working for the welfare department and studying t'ai chi on Bank Street, living in Greenwich Village."

"What about the carpentry?" I asked, noticing how rough and stained his hands were. "Do you still do that?"

"Why? Do you need some work done?"

"I might," I said.

"I still make things—boxes, bookshelves. I made the shelves in Avi's office, and the supply closet. I did Lisa's shelves for her, floor-to-ceiling, in her living room. When I have time, and someone I like asks, I build for them. I like to work with my hands."

"Nothing for Howie, or Janet?"

"Howie's always tight on money. He has, you know, a lot of responsibilities."

"Like what?" I asked. "He's married, he's got kids?"

"I told him once, whatever you need, I like to do the work. You just pay for the materials, labor's free. But he couldn't do that," he said. "No way."

"Too proud?" I asked.

Stewie shrugged.

"Nothing for Janet?" I asked, realigning my bacon burger as I did. "She's got a cash flow problem too?"

"Janet? What would she need bookshelves for? She practically lives in the gym."

"Really?"

"You don't get to look like Janet lifting weights three times a week. That's dedication. She competes, you know. She was Miss Tex Pecs before she came to New York." Stewie began to laugh. "I'm not sure of the *exact* title," he said. Then he sort of lost it, tilting his head back and sounding as if he were sneezing backward.

I looked up from my fries. Fleck was loosening up. Maybe it was the beer. I signaled the waiter to bring another round.

"She talks tough, Rachel, but she's a good egg, Janet. It's just that she's like a kid. She likes to do what she's not supposed to, get herself into trouble."

"Yeah, she seems like great fun," I said, picking up my pickle. "She ever get you into trouble?"

"Me? No. Not really. I got other stuff to do in my free time."

"What about Lisa and Janet? Were they friends?" I reached under the table so that Dashiell could clean my greasy fingers for me. "Did they hang out? Put glue on the master's chair? Become juvies together?"

"I wouldn't necessarily say *that*. Lisa was a serious student. She didn't have much time to socialize. Like me. Anyway, Avi says it's not appropriate for teachers to form personal relationships with their students. He says it interferes with the teaching process if you become emotionally involved."

"Even friendships?"

Stewie nodded.

"Avi says we should rely on ourselves, not on each other."

"So Janet and Lisa didn't spend any time together outside of class?"

"Lisa was at the school until all hours. Always working. Or staying up half the night studying. This is my *life*, she used to say, there's no room for anything else. Or any*one* else. And Lisa, she wouldn't go against Avi the way Janet does, doing something he wouldn't approve of. Not Lisa."

"She must have been very disciplined," I said.

"What about you?" Stewie asked. "What were you doing before—" He stopped in the middle. "Never mind," he said. "I just remembered. Now you're here. Eating dinner with me at Chumley's."

"This is true," I said, finishing my second beer. "Stew," I said, waiting for him to look up from his dinner. "I'm seeing my aunt and uncle tomorrow."

"Lisa's parents?"

I nodded. "I feel so confused about what happened. I was wondering, I mean, you worked with her, Stew, were you shocked by what she did? Did she seem troubled to you? Do you know of any problems she was having? I don't know how to talk to her parents. I don't know what to say to them."

Stewie looked down at his plate. "When I told you the dream I had, well, I don't think Lisa ever found herself wondering what to do with her life. She was so focused, this was the life she seemed to want, and it was the life she was living."

"But what about her personal life? Was that going well, too?"

"She could have had anything she wanted," he said, his eyes shining in the dark of the former speakeasy. "I don't get it. The truth is, nobody gets it, Rachel. It's a mystery."

"So she didn't seem unhappy near the end? There was nothing—"

Stewie shook his head. "I would have to have to talk to her parents, because what could you say to someone who lost the one person they loved most? There's no way they'll ever get over it."

I skipped dessert. Stewie had some obscene chocolate thing that seemed to grow larger as he ate it. He said he lived on Bedford, but he'd walk me home. Dashiell walked a few steps ahead, the leash loose, automatically turning right on Hudson Street, toward home. Without thinking, I turned right, too, until I felt Stewie's hand on my arm.

"Where are you going?" he asked.

Lisa's place was to the left. I looked toward Dashiell, who had stopped when I did. Now they were both looking at me as if I were crazy.

"I wanted to pick up a muffin," I said, "for the morning."

Stewie nodded and walked me to Sacred Chow, which of course was closed. Then we turned around and headed for the Printing House, where I got to see

Stewie's crunched-up, embarrassed little smile once more as we said good night.

I walked in through the front door, greeted Eddie, and walked out the side door. A few minutes later, driving around looking for a legal spot for the Taurus, I was thinking about Stewie Fleck.

There was a Zen version of his dream. Avi had told it to me one day during a private lesson.

"In the middle of the form, having gathered your energy, you return to the mountain. There you seek the teacher, but the answers you seek," he'd said, late one evening, "are already within you."

"What about the answers I need about Lisa?" I'd asked him.

"You think too much," he'd said. Then he'd turned north, toward the window Lisa had been pushed out of, and begun the form again.

17

What Do You Suggest?

CECIL WAS DRRESSED to the nines, all in black, her white hair slicked back in a twist at the nape of her neck, the only color her bright red lipstick.

"Come, darling," she said, swooping me into her arms and then leading me to her sunny kitchen. "Let's eat."

Dashiell sneezed at her perfume, then padded along behind us, wagging his tail.

Over the table were pictures of my cousin Richie as a little kid. He must be somewhere in his late forties by now. "What do you hear from Richie?" I asked, more to be polite than out of any real interest. In truth, I was thinking only of the reason why I had come.

"That kid," she said, "what a hoot he is."

"How's his writing going?" I asked, digging into my salad niçoise.

"Writing? Writing? Is that what your mother told you?"

I nodded. "She said he moved to Key West to become

a writer, like Hemingway. She even emphasized the writer part, meaning why don't *you* do something that would give your mother *noches*?"

Ceil roared. "She always worried about what other people would think. She had a cover story for everyone, even my son. You know, before you got married, she always told people you'd been engaged, but your fiancé had died in a tragic accident, so of course they wouldn't ask you anything." She laughed again. I felt my face flush. "Oh, darling, I didn't mean to upset you. Except for funerals, we never see each other. I hardly know you now."

"I—"

"I know. I know. You're a busy professional. So, today we'll get acquainted again." She smiled and took a sip of her coffee. "Richie's not a writer, Rachel. He's a drag queen."

My eyebrows must have gone up.

"A female impersonator. Come on, cookie, you know what that is. He dresses up in women's clothes, he sings a little, he makes a nice living."

"My mother knew this?"

"Of course."

"And Richie, what, he just told you one day?"

"He never had to tell me, Rachel. I used to catch him trying on my bras when he was a kid, putting on nail polish, falling all over himself in my high heels. He even bought me a wig once, for Mother's Day, so that he could wear it when I wasn't home. He's too much, my Richie."

"So where did my mother get this story?"

She pricked a tomato with her fork and held it aloft. "When Richie was at Yale, he *did* talk about becoming a writer. He also talked about becoming an architect, a veterinarian, an engineer. It was all talk. I did think he might take up acting. They had a wonderful drama program at Yale, and I thought that would be right up Richie's alley. But he didn't take to it then. Of course, he does all sorts of skits now."

"So my mother fixated on the writing?"

"Why not? He did write a poem once. When he was ten. Your mother didn't make up the story from air. She put together a little this, a little that, some imagination, and her enormous pride. Your poor mother. That was her obsession, that everything should look just so." She popped the tomato into her mouth and chewed.

"Did Richie go to Key West right after Yale?"

"No, he lived in New York for a while, in Chelsea. He worked in a restaurant, he was a singing waiter, darling. And every winter he went to Key West. One winter, he bought a little place. And that was that."

"Does he know you know?"

"Sweetheart, he calls me for advice. Mom, he says, my skin is breaking out from the base. What do you suggest? Would aloe help? And he gives advice. Tells me what to wear. Tries to get me to color my hair. Mom, he said, last time I was down, for my eightieth birthday, Mom, he said, if you dyed your hair, you'd look ten years younger." She roared.

She didn't ask about the Jacobs case, and I didn't bring it up. After lunch, she showed me pictures of my cousin Richie on stage, as Liza Minelli, Judy Garland, and Marlene Dietrich.

"He has fabulous legs," I said.

"Takes after me." Ceil pulled up her skirt and stuck one long gam out from under the table for me to admire.

After lunch she went rummaging around in a closet and came up with a lace and velvet shawl wrapped in tissue paper. "This was your mother's," she said. "She gave it to me once when she came to visit. I'd like you to have it now."

"Ceil, I can't take it from you. It's too beautiful."

"Of course you can. It should be with you." She handed me the shawl. "You know, darling, your mother was just a human being. One day, it would be nice for you if you let go of some of your disappointment."

"I—"

She lifted one long-fingered, bony hand to silence me. "Do you remember the summer you stayed with me for a month, when you were eleven?" I nodded. "And do you remember Margaret?"

"Of course," I said. "How could I forget? That was my first job."

"I'd met her late one afternoon, the week before you came. I was admiring the ocean, talking out loud to myself. You know how I am. She asked if, as long as I was looking anyway, I'd watch her swim. At first I thought, What chutzpah, what a loony request. And then I saw the white cane folded up and lying on the corner of her towel, so I said yes, I'd watch. Stand on the shore, she said, and shout to me if I'm headed in the wrong direction. So I watched her swim. And when she came out—"

"You said, I have a very responsible young woman coming to stay with me next week, for the whole month of August, my niece Rachel, and she'd be delighted to meet you here every afternoon at five and watch you swim."

"We all need that," Ceil said, "someone to shout and tell us if we're headed out to sea. But when you can see," she said, picking up her coffee cup, "well, most of us don't have someone responsible standing on the shore to make sure we stay headed in the right direction. Now, come, I know why you're here."

I was truly amazed. I hadn't said a word about Lillian and Ted, not even on the phone.

"So let's take that adorable creature of yours to the beach." She turned to Dashiell, his big mouth agape in adoration as she spoke. "Aunt Ceil knows why you came to visit. For the same reason your mommy used to come when she was little. She loved the beach, just the way you do," she said to him. "Marsha told me you showed up *wet* for your meeting with them," she said to me. "That's the girl I remember, I thought when she said it. Come," she said, talking to Dashiell again, "we'll take our walk."

"You have to give him what he needs," Ceil said later, as we watched Dashiell running along the sand. "You're responsible for him."

Of course, I didn't for a minute think she was talking about Dashiell.

"He always loved dress-up," she said, walking next to me but with her thoughts far away. "He liked to pretend he was something he wasn't. Some*one* he wasn't. He enjoyed that. He still does. I never told him to try to be anything different. People are who they are. I never tried to tell him what to do or not do, how to live his life. It's harmless, what he does. It gives him pleasure. He's my son, and I love him. That's all there is to it. That's what I told your mother, too. She thought I ought to *do* something. Do what? I asked her. Beatrice, I said, all I can *do* is alienate my son. No one wants to be told what to do. People have to handle their own lives, their own way."

I had come to talk about Lillian.

"Do you believe in fate, Rachel?"

"I don't know," I told her.

What do you suggest? I'd meant to ask. But what with one thing and another, I never did get around to it.

18
Follow That Cab

I WAS NEARLY dry by the time I arrived at the Club. Paul wasn't out front, but as I got out of the car to go get him, he appeared in the doorway. I winced. He was wearing a black T-shirt, a black jacket, and black slacks. As soon as the car began to move again, it would be aswirl with white fur. Dashiell, who was sitting behind the driver's seat, was shedding.

Without saying a word, I walked around to the passenger side, and Paul got in on the driver's side. Some things are easy to arrange with men. You never have to ask them to hold the remote either.

He got in, fastened his seat belt, then checked to make sure I'd fastened mine. "I thought we'd be alone," he said, looking toward the backseat, "so we could talk."

"You can talk in front of him. He's tight-lipped."

"Where to?" he asked.

"Forty-fourth, between Fifth and Sixth."

He gave me a funny look and began to drive. I looked

out the side window to avoid obsessing about his strong, beautiful hands.

When we got to Forty-fourth, I told him where to pull over.

"We can't park here," he said. "Not unless you want to get towed."

"We're not parking," I told him. "We're waiting."

"For another couple?" he asked, looking disappointed.

"Sort of."

He nodded, watching me as I slid down a little in my seat, my eyes glued to the door of 17 West Forty-fourth. Perhaps it was the expression on my face that kept Paul Wilcox waiting in silence. As we sat there, I had murder on my mind.

He wasn't even there yet, but already I could almost feel my hands around his throat, choking the life out of him.

I could push my gun into his chest, tell him why, make him beg, then pull the trigger anyway.

Or I could poison him, slowly, painfully, with something impossible to detect.

Fuck it, I thought. As soon as he steps out the door, I'll have the driver gun the engine and run him down. My sister looks stunning in black. Come to think of it, who doesn't?

When he finally appeared, *she* was hanging on to his arm, smiling up at his face. He *had* lost weight. Even scrunched down in the seat, looking past Paul, I could see he was thinner. And wasn't that a new sport coat the bastard had on?

He leaned over and kissed the blond on the mouth, then his arm went up, and a cab pulled over to the curb for them.

"Follow that cab," I told my driver. But he did nothing. Unless you call staring something. "Follow that cab," I repeated. "And don't spare the horses."

"Ah, so," he said, nodding. He pulled out and caught up to the cab, which was waiting at the corner for the light to change.

"Good *job*," I told him.

Dashiell's tail beat against the backseat.

"I'm quite experienced at covert pursuits," he said.

"Is that right?"

"Exactly. My grandmother is dying to know where her neighbor, Mrs. Chiang, buys fish. She always finds the freshest fish for the least money, but she refuses to tell my grandmother where."

"How frustrating," I said as the light changed. We followed the cab onto Fifth Avenue and began weaving in and out of traffic to stay behind it as it turned east, then south, heading downtown. "So you and your grandmother follow Mrs. Chiang's cab?"

I thought we were going to lose Ted and the blond when their cab went through a changing light, but Paul zipped right after it, risking a ticket.

"Not exactly," he said.

"Meaning?"

"We follow her rickshaw."

"Ah, so," I said as we careened toward the Manhattan Bridge. And me without my passport, I thought, but the cab kept heading downtown, turning a few blocks later into Chinatown. After an impossible final few minutes trailing behind the cab through the crowded, twisty, narrow, one-way streets, it stopped at 63 Mott Street, outside of Hong Fat. I ducked way down as the cab door opened.

"You can get up. They're inside now," my driver said.

He was a fast study.

"Thanks," I said, as casually as if, instead of going through a red light and driving like a maniac, he'd just held a door for me or lit my cigarette.

"Do you have anything to tell me?" he said, turning sideways to face me, an inscrutable expression on his face.

"Yeah," I said. "Pull in as much as you can and cut the engine."

"That's it?" He waited patiently, his eyebrows raised.

"We're eating Chinese," I told him.

"Let me guess. At Hong Fat?"

"Don't be ridiculous," I said, unzipping my teddy bear backpack and pulling out my cell phone. "We'd be towed in a nanosecond if we parked here." I called information for the number of Hong Fat and, before dialing it, smiled at Paul and in my sweetest voice asked him what he'd like for dinner. He laughed so hard tears came to his eyes.

"Surprise me," he said when he'd regained his composure.

"No problem."

I dialed Hong Fat.

"I'd like an order to go, please. No, delivery. Well, it's not exactly an address. I'm parked across the street in a black Ford Taurus. *T* as in *to go*, *A* as in *appetizer*. Taurus. A car. Car. *C* as in *chow mein*. Yes. An order of steamed dumplings with oyster sauce. Do you want soup?" I asked Paul. He shook his head. "We'll skip the soup tonight. One order of kung po chicken and one crab with ginger and scallions. White rice or brown?" I asked Paul, but he just waved his hand at me. "White rice," I said into the phone. "And chopsticks, please. Thank you."

"Chopsticks okay?" I asked him.

He merely stared at me.

"How about a drink before dinner?"

I didn't wait for a response. I reached back to the floor behind his seat and pulled out a plastic shopping bag. I handed him a bottle of merlot and a corkscrew, and I held the two plastic glasses.

As if he ate dinner in a car every night of his life, he anchored the bottle between his legs, peeled off the foil that surrounded the cork, and began to twist the corkscrew carefully into the center of the cork, which a moment later came out with a satisfying pop.

He filled the glasses and took one for himself.

"To you, Dog Paddle," he said, touching his plastic glass to mine.

We sat back and sipped our wine. I thought about music, but Dashiell was asleep and I didn't want to drown out the sounds of his snoring. I had thought about candlelight, too, but there really wasn't anyplace safe to put candles. I'd checked it out.

When the confused-looking little man in the white jacket came out of Hong Fat and looked around, Paul rolled down his window and motioned him over to the Taurus. I leaned over with the money, but Paul brushed my hand away, taking some folded bills from his pants pocket and paying for the food himself. The waiter said something I couldn't understand, and then Paul nodded and laughed. He pulled the bag in through the open window and turned back to me. "So, how do you want to do this?" he asked.

"One course at a time, starting with the appetizer," I said, opening the bag and pulling out the dumplings and the little clear plastic container of dipping sauce.

"Would you like to tell me what this is all about?"

My mouth was full of dumpling. I shook my head no. "I thought we were going to talk about Lisa," I said around the dumpling. "You promised."

He took a bite of dumpling. "You want to talk about your *cousin*?"

"I do."

"This is delicious. How did you find this place?"

"It was recommended, so to speak, by someone I thought I knew."

He refilled our wineglasses.

"Seriously, Paul, I—"

"She wanted to marry," he said, leaning back and gazing out the windshield. "She said it was time to formalize our commitment to each other. I told her I wasn't ready." He turned toward the food, hoisting the final dumpling with his chopsticks. Then, chopsticks poised, as if he were about to conduct an orchestra, he looked at me. "Okay?" he asked. There was a flash of white between us. I could hear Dashiell swallowing the dumpling behind me.

"You said *okay*. It's his release word."

"The chicken next?" he asked, as if nothing untoward had happened.

"But you loved her, didn't you?" I asked, thinking about the jasper heart necklace and the heart bracelet, thinking about all those roses.

Paul turned away from me and looked out the side window. Sitting on the sidewalk, to the right of Hong Fat, there was an unshaven, disheveled-looking man leaning against the wall, a cigarette dangling from his crusty lips. He wore a purple sweater that was too big for him and was frayed at the bottom, stained, wide-legged brown pants, shoes without laces. In one hand he held a live crab.

He put the crab down on the sidewalk.

"Come here, Donny," he said in his gravelly voice. The crab didn't budge.

"Goddamn you to hell, Donny," he shouted at the

crab. "I said *come*. When the fuck're you gonna learn to mind me?"

He took the cigarette from his mouth and, holding it between two stained fingers, touched it to the rear end of the crab. I grabbed Paul's arm and squeezed it.

"That's a good boy, Donny," he said as the crab moved forward. "See," he said, leaning down into the crab's face, "it ain't so hard to be a good boy."

He picked up Donny by one claw and quickly dumped him into a paper bag that he had anchored under his legs, struggled to his feet, and holding the bag out in front of him, staggered down the block.

I didn't feel hungry anymore, and apparently neither did Paul, because neither of us picked up the bag to take out any more of the food.

"What did she say?" I asked. "My cousin Lisa?"

"That she had wanted to bring me into her family, to have my children, for us to grow old together."

"And when you told her you weren't ready, she didn't want to see you anymore?"

"No," he said, looking straight ahead again, as if he were driving instead of parked. "I didn't want to see her after that."

"Why not?"

"It had all been spoiled," he said. He looked back toward the street, but the little man with the crab was gone.

"But you still loved her," I insisted.

"Yes," he said. "She was . . ." He looked down, into his lap, the chopsticks still in his right hand. "I had hoped . . ."

He took off his glasses, placing them on the dashboard, and put his fingertips over his eyes. I don't know what got into me then. Maybe it was all the walking in Lisa's shoes. Once again, I reached over and slid my arms around his neck. But this time, it was different. When he moved his hands away and looked at me with those hurt, dark eyes, I leaned closer and kissed him. My lips gently brushed one cheek, then the other. When I kissed his eyes, I tasted the salt of a tear. Then I felt his chopsticks against my back as he embraced me, his other hand on my neck, his long fingers reaching into my hair. I felt a familiar heat starting and spreading quickly, as if someone had dropped a match in straw. Live in the now, Avi had said. So I did. I sank into it and let it happen.

That's when something caught my eye. Over Paul's shoulder, I could see them as they came out of Hong Fat and stood just across from where we were parked, kissing. They talked quietly for a moment, then Teddy's arm went up, for a taxi.

I pulled away from Paul and ducked.

He put his glasses on and turned.

"Why do I get the nagging feeling you're using me?"

"Because I am."

"I thought as much. Follow that cab?" he said.

"Wait until they *get* one," I told him.

You had to give him this. The man was a good sport.

Men like this don't grow on trees, my mother would have said.

But only if he were Jewish and a professional man.

A cab stopped. We took off after it. Ten minutes later, I knew where the blond lived. Had I been alone, I could have rushed in and told the concierge she'd dropped her pen on the street and gotten her name. Or I could have waited in the car for my brother-in-law to emerge.

And then what?

"Rachel?"

He touched my cheek with the back of one hand.

I had gone to Sea Gate to ask about my sister's situation, to find out if Ceil thought I should say something, or do something, to see if between us we could think up a way to prevent the shattering of my sister's marriage, of her life. Interfering, after all, was my family's stock-in-trade.

Leave them alone, Ceil would have said.

But, I would have said, in my usual articulate fashion.

Exactly, darling, she probably would have told me. Butt out. It's not your life. It's not your problem. Let it go.

What on earth had I been thinking?

"Let's go home," I said.

"And where is that?" Paul asked, his voice as soft as the fur between Dashiell's round brown eyes.

"I've been staying at my cousin's," I said.

"I thought so."

"You did?"

"You don't have anything on that didn't belong to Lisa. All finished here?"

I nodded.

Paul drove to Lisa's and found a spot that was good for the next day. On our way across the street to Jimmy Walker Park, we pitched the Chinese food into a corner trash basket. Let some poor homeless person who didn't know Donny eat the crab. I certainly couldn't.

Leaning against the fence, watching as Dash left notes for the other neighborhood dogs, *I was here, and here, and here,* I wished I were still a dog trainer and that the man whose shoulder was touching mine were really a date and not part of a criminal investigation.

I'm sorry. Lisa.

When I'd told him about the note, he'd thought it had been written to him.

But why would Lisa have been the one apologizing?

Of course, if it had been the other way around, if he had done the asking and Lisa had been the one to refuse, then her note might have been an apology to Paul for turning him down.

Why had she?

She hadn't brought him home. Had she been worried about Daddy's disapproval? She was still dependent on him, still taking lots of his money so that she could live the way she wanted to.

The Village, the Village, David had sad, so he'd bought her a condo. But at what price?

None of the ubiquitous concierges was at the desk, so I used my key to get into the lobby. I picked up Lisa's mail. There were still bills coming in, postcards and letters from real estate brokers asking her to call them should she want to sell, coupons for a free car wash or half-priced lunch, and the usual pile of mail-order catalogs. Upstairs, I unlocked Lisa's door and dumped the new pile of mail on the little blue table to the right of the door, right next to the old pile, which looked tall enough to topple over.

Paul took off his shoes and put them against the wall, under the coat hooks on the wall to the left, then went to give Dashiell some dog biscuits and make us tea. I hung my jacket and backpack on one of the hooks.

I could hear Dashiell crunching loudly, the hiss of the boiling water as it was poured into the teapot, water being poured into the sink. The first potful was to warm the pot. The second potful brewed the tea.

"Honey?"

"What?"

He poked his head into the living room, smiling.

"Honey in your tea?"

"Oh. Sure," I told him.

I heard the spoon against one cup, then the other.

We sat on the black couch in the dark living room, neither of us touching the tea he had made us.

"Do you have a life of your own, Dog Paddle?"

"Not lately," I said.

I heard Dashiell on the steps, then I heard the bed sigh as he climbed on, circled, and lay down to sleep.

"You look tired," he said. "I should go."

I turned and looked at him, his eyes shining in the light that came in from the window. One thing about New York City, it never really gets dark.

"I had fun tonight," I told him.

"Me, too. You're"—he stopped and laughed—"you're not like anyone I know."

"Not even . . . my cousin?"

"Especially not your cousin."

"Well, we were—"

"*Distant* cousins," he said, finishing my sentence.

He leaned in and kissed me, gently, on my lips.

Okay, he was completely adorable, but no way was I going to bed with this man. I hardly knew him.

"How are we different, me and Lisa?"

"You have a sense of humor," he said, removing the lavender string from the little braid and undoing the braid with his long fingers. "Warped, but clearly evident."

If I were *truly* walking in Lisa's shoes, shouldn't I reconsider?

The trouble with sex was where it might lead.

First I'd go to bed with him, next thing I knew, I'd be letting him touch the parts of my body that never got suntanned, then I might start necking with him in the car until all hours, I'd let him hold my hand in the movies, and who knows, one fine day after that, I might give him my phone number.

What kind of a girl did he think I was?

"Come on," he said, pulling me up from the couch. He held my hand and walked me to the stairs. He led the way up and gently guided me to a spot near Dash. When he leaned down, my steely resolve took a powder. Even sitting, my knees felt weak. I closed my eyes. That funny brush fire had started up again and was spreading fast.

He picked up the pillow and fluffed it and then stood straight again.

"*Shuijiao hao,* Dog Paddle," he whispered. "Don't let the bed-bugs bite. Stay put, *xiao yue.* I'll see myself out."

"What did you say?" I asked him.

"How would I know?"

He grinned, letting me see those cute dimples again.

"I better go," he said.

"See," I said in the dark, "it ain't so hard to be a good boy."

"That's what you think," he answered.

You had to love this man. Or was the delicious rush I was feeling just the *feng shui* of Lisa's apartment?

"Before you go . . ."

"You need?"

"Tea. That nice cup of tea you made me."

"It'll be cold by now. I'll make you a fresh cup."

I waited until I heard the water running before opening the nightstand drawer and feeling around in the dark for what I knew was there. When I heard him coming up the stairs, I quietly closed the drawer.

He put the tea on the nightstand.

I was waiting for him to kiss me again, but instead he just touched my cheek, turned, and headed down the wooden steps.

I ached to call him back.

I slid quickly off the bed and went to the top of the stairs, just in time to see Paul lean over the little blue table, pick up an envelope from the pile of Lisa's mail, and slip it into his jacket pocket. Then he put on his shoes, tied the laces, and reached for the door.

I heard the knob squeak. It needed oiling.

I watched the door open, then close.

Damn. Why hadn't I opened Lisa's mail? I had to see what he had taken.

At any cost.

I tore down the stairs, praying he'd still be in the hall. Not knowing what I'd do or say, only knowing I had to get that envelope, I pulled the door open. There he was, just standing there, facing me, his hands at his sides.

"I couldn't go," he muttered.

"I know," I said, my hands around his neck, pulling him back inside.

As I backed into the living room, he was kissing me, my eyes, my mouth, my neck. He took one of my hands from behind his head and pressed the palm to his lips. I could feel his heat on me, and my own, setting me on fire.

"We can't," I moaned into his neck.

There had to be another way to get that letter back, I thought. Hell, I could just ask for it.

"Of course we can," he said, "I'm a coach. I'll see us through."

And then we were on that soft black couch.

Was it my grandmother Sonya, right before Hannukah, who had said, To receive everything, one must open one's hand and give? Or was it Taisen Deshimaru?

Either way, I opened one hand and held it up for Paul to see what was in it while I slipped the other hand into his pocket. He took the foil-wrapped condom I had taken from Lisa's nightstand and put it carefully on the floor next to the couch, where he could easily find it when he needed it. Then he took off his glasses, folded them, and placed them there, too. While he did that, I stuffed the envelope that had been in his pocket between two of the couch cushions. Then, the lamppost light shining in on us like moonlight, he began to take off my clothes.

Later we moved upstairs. Dashiell grunted as I slipped into bed next to him. Paul said he had to go, but apparently he didn't mean immediately. Once again I opened my arms to him, even though it was patently clear that this time there were no pockets to frisk in his outfit.

No one could ever accuse me of not giving my all to the job.

It was past eleven when he finally got up to leave. I strained to hear his bare feet on the stairs. As he got dressed, Lisa's place began to seem so lonely I could hardly stand it.

I slipped out of bed and went to the head of the stairs, figuring I'd snag one more good-night kiss. But the door was already closing.

I thought of tearing after him again, leaving myself not a shred of dignity in the bargain, but something else happened, something that made me freeze in place.

I heard a key slipping into the lock. Holding tight to the railing, I was barely breathing when the tumbler turned over.

I suddenly felt chilled. I went downstairs and pulled the velvet shawl from my backpack, slipping it around me as I walked into the dark living room.

I walked over to the couch and slid the envelope out from between the cushions.

Lisa and Paul had been lovers, I told myself, trying to stop my heart from pounding.

Of course he'd have her apartment keys.

That didn't mean he had her work keys.

Did it?

19

She Rolled Her Eyes
When She Read It

SITTING ON LISA'S couch, I tore open the envelope I had retrieved from Paul's pocket and by the light of the lamppost coming in through the windows discovered what it was that Paul Wilcox had not wanted me to see. As soon as I had, I went through the rest of the mail, finding yet another real surprise.

I pushed the play button on Lisa's answering machine, listening to the lonely sound of the dial tone as I got dressed. Then I woke Dashiell, locked up, and took the stairs down to the lobby.

"Ms. Alexander?" the concierge said as soon as he saw me. "Wait up. I have something for you."

"For me?"

"Yeah. I'm sorry I didn't catch you on your way in. I must have been on my break. I see he's back," he said, handing me a bouquet of roses. "These came this afternoon. I guess he wanted you to have them, you know, before."

"What are you talking about?" I asked, looking for a card and not finding one.

"The old boyfriend. I mean, Mr. Wilcox. I guess he wanted you to get those before he came over," he said. Then he began shining up his brass name tag with the heel of his hand to distract me from the fact that, according to his job description, he was out of line in commenting on my personal life. Since I didn't raise my eyebrows or inhale sharply, he looked back up after a moment.

"You mean *Mr. Wilcox* sent these, Eddie? There's no card."

"Wouldn't be the first time," he said. He leaned over the high desk. "After he and Ms. Jacobs split," he said, "he got pretty weird. Used to stand across the street, the other side of the ball field, so he'd like be out of the way, looking up at her window." He shook his head. "He must of had it real bad for her, to do that. No chick's worth *that*, far as I'm concerned, but, hey, not everyone thinks the same, am I right?"

"What are you talking about?" I asked him.

He leaned over the counter. "Well, I guess they had some kind of fight, you know, a breakup, like over the holidays. But he kept coming around for a while, asking if Ms. Jacobs was home. But when I went to ring her, he always said, Never mind, and he'd just leave. I was really embarrassed for the guy, coming around like that but not even calling up. It was pretty humiliating."

"And he'd go wait across the street, like until she walked the dog?"

"No, it was way later, like after midnight. Ms. Jacobs, she never walked Charlie that late unless she worked late and Charlie's last walk was the walk home. This was when my shift was over. Twelve thirty, one o'clock."

"When you were leaving for the night?"

"Yeah, right. I'd see him, not right here, you know, not so obvious, but way on the other side of the ball field, where the bums hang out?"

"You mean the boccie court?"

"Around there, right. I'd see him, you know, lurking in the shadows, like leaning on a tree, a baseball cap pulled low over his forehead, like I wouldn't recognize him, right? It was real dramatic, like something out of a movie, you know what I mean, the ex-boyfriend watching the building, standing there all alone, just staring like that. Gave me the creeps."

"But he never came late, used a key to get in?"

"No, ma'am."

"How do you know?"

"We're covered here twenty-four hours. If the night man is late, I wait. We never leave the door uncovered. I would have seen him."

Of course, he had missed me coming in with Paul.

"He just stayed there and watched? How long?"

"From, you know, after they broke up to until she died. Sad thing, about her dying, your cousin. Such a pretty girl. Always considerate, too. Not like some of them," he said, tilting his head toward the elevator doors to indicate those residents who were less considerate than my cousin Lisa.

"I meant, how long did he stand there? Ten minutes? An hour?"

"Oh, that I couldn't tell you, Ms. Alexander. I don't know how long he was there because I stay behind the desk, you know. So I only noticed him when I was leaving. But figure it was winter, right, so how long could he a stood it out there in the cold?" He shrugged his shoulders. "Musta been really stuck on her, your cousin, to take the breakup so hard."

"You mean to stand out there in the cold watching her windows?"

"Yeah, and all the stuff he sent."

"Stuff?"

"The flowers, for example. A half dozen roses, sometimes a dozen, two, three times a week. All like this, with no card," he said, pointing to my roses. "The delivery guy would have his slip with Ms. Jacobs's name and the address, but there was never one of those little envelopes pinned to the cellophane. Like Ms. Jacobs was fooled. You know what I mean?"

I nodded.

"There were presents, too. I mean, money was no object. Little packages used to come, UPS, just her name and address on them, never a return address. She worked late sometimes, Ms. Jacobs, so I'd hold them here for her. Once she opened one in front of me. It was, you know, from Tiffany's, in that little blue box they have, with a white ribbon tied in a perfect bow on top, kind of thing you women go crazy for, am I right? But Ms. Jacobs, she didn't go crazy for it. She was *pissed*. 'Can I leave this with you, Eddie?' she said, and she left the box and the ribbon for me to put in the trash, but, you know," he leaned over again and whispered, "I didn't. I took it home. I'm saving it for my girlfriend's birthday. I'll get her something, put it in the Tiffany box, you know what I mean?" He winked.

I forced a smile. "So what was in it? What'd he send her?"

"A silver bracelet, with a heart on it, and some writing. I didn't get to see what it said, but she, your cousin, she rolled her eyes when she read it, put it back in the little blue bag, and stuffed it in her pocket. There was some other stuff too, but that was the only one she opened here. That was the last one," he said. "That one came right before she did it, a day or two before."

"And then afterward, Mr. Wilcox wasn't around? You never saw him again?"

"Not until tonight, forty, forty-five minutes ago, when he left."

"Thanks, Eddie."

Lisa's daddy had done well by her. The Printing House was like living in the fucking Plaza. They had maid service, if you wanted it, and you could drop off your laundry and dry cleaning at the desk and have it back, clean and ready, by the time you got home from work. If you needed gossip, protection, opinions about your private life, that was available, too. I wondered if you could put your shoes out in the hall at night and find them back and polished in the morning.

"Can you hold the flowers another minute for me, Eddie. I forgot something upstairs."

"Sure I can. Anything you say, Ms. Alexander. Anything to help."

Back at Lisa's apartment, I took the steps two at a time, opened the second drawer of Lisa's jewelry box, and took the silver bracelet out of the robin's-egg-blue bag. I opened the clasp and put it on, feeling the silver warm up where it was touching my skin.

I turned the heart over and read the inscription.

There wasn't scratch on it, no patina from use. Lisa hadn't worn the bracelet. But I would. Like it or not, I had taken over where she'd left off.

Down in the lobby, I picked up the roses. Outside, where Eddie could no longer see me, I lifted them to my face and inhaled their perfume.

Never, I remember Frank saying, holding my shoulders and looking into my eyes as he spoke, never go to bed with a suspect until you find out who the murderer is.

I had nodded dutifully.

And it's someone else, he'd added.

Right, Frank, I'd said. And what number law is that?

Sex is no laughing matter, he'd said, shaking his head. In this job, it can kill you.

Who did I think I was, walking down Hudson Street with a dozen roses in the crook of my arm, fucking Miss America?

When I got to the corner, I pitched the bouquet into the trash basket. Then Dashiell and I headed home.

20

I Don't Know Anything for Sure

I OVERSLEPT ON Thursday morning. There was barely time to call Lisa's mother and check out my landlord's house before getting to school for a noon instructor's session with Avi.

Once a week or so, Dashiell and I went through the Siegals' town house to make sure that no homeless person had noticed it was empty and decided that sleeping indoors under crisp percale sheets would be preferable to sleeping in a cardboard box on a grate on the sidewalk. I even checked the smoke alarm, which was admittedly ridiculous since, should it go off, no one would be there to hear it. But Norma had a thing about smoke alarms, and in New York City you don't argue over an easy job that gets you a terrific place to live at an affordable rent.

Everything was covered with dust and grime. When I got back to the cottage, I called the cleaning service and arranged for them to come the first of May, which is when the Siegals usually showed up to spend a month or two in the city before heading out to the beach. And in an extravagant gesture, I told them I'd like my house cleaned as well this time.

Wearing my own clothes, and nothing of Lisa's, I headed for Bank Street. Once inside, I ran up the stairs, following behind Dash. Rounds had started, and I walked in on a startling scene. There were Janet, Stew, and Howie, each with a string of bubble gum running from the tip of the nose to the *t'an t'ien*, a spot a couple of inches beneath their belly buttons.

"Nose-navel alignment," Avi said without turning. I watched him watching me in the mirror. "Gum's on the coffee table. Chew it first." Just like my mother, I thought, always assuming I had the mental prowess of an idiot.

"The gum will remind you to keep your nose where it belongs," he added, rather personally, I thought. My nose was everywhere, usually in someone else's business, and that was precisely where I wanted it.

After class the other teachers all went to change their shoes and get back to work. "Gotta run," Janet said, looking at her watch. She caught my eye and winked, mouthing, "See you at five." When they had all gone, Avi motioned me to follow him into his office.

"How is your project coming along, Rachel?" he whispered, even though we were all alone.

"I don't know anything for sure," I said.

"Excellent," he said, then he sat and turned his full attention to his computer.

It was one thirty. If I was going to get to Sea Gate on time, I had to hustle. After passing muster with the guard at the gate, I headed not for the Jacobses' house but to the beach. Marsha was already there, standing by the gate, a scarf covering her hair, a bag of groceries in her arms. I parked the car and went to join her.

"I told David I had to do some shopping," she said, hiking up the bag of food and looking terrified. "What did you want to tell me?"

I took the bag of groceries and set it down on the ground. "Walk with me," I said, looking down at her stockings and heels after I did so. She slipped off her shoes, leaving them next to the bag of groceries. I took off my running shoes and sweat socks and gave them to her to put on, feeling the coolness of the sand as I did.

She took my arm, and we walked down the beach, then headed to our right, where the spit of land that is this private community abuts Gravesend Bay.

"I wanted to see you without David because I thought that if you were alone—"

"David would be very upset with me if he knew about this. Very angry."

"Why is that, Marsha?"

I felt the envelopes I had brought with me in my pocket, all that was left of Lisa's mail after I'd pitched the catalogs and junk mail and filed the bills for her parents to deal with later.

"Certain things, he says, belong in the family, only in the family." She lifted her free hand and wiped her cheeks. "But I know you can't really help us if you don't know the truth. Your aunt Ceil said we should trust you completely. But we haven't done that. We've kept secrets from you."

I took the envelopes from my pocket, the one I'd slid out from between the couch cushions after Paul had left and the one I'd found in the pile of mail I'd gone through later.

"What is that?" she asked.

I showed her the contents of both envelopes.

"I knew that one day I would have to talk to you

myself. I am only ashamed that I waited for you to call."

For a moment, there was only the sound of the seagulls, their beaks wide open as they cawed loudly to each other.

"When you asked about Lisa's note to us—"

"The suicide note?" I asked.

Marsha nodded. We walked past the jetty, where there was a small pool of water caught between the rocks and the sloping shore. Dashiell began fishing for crabs, and I called him to follow us as we slowly headed toward the bay, the light so bright it was difficult to see.

"We had seen her several times in the months before, and there had been many phone calls, more than usual. She was usually so busy, she'd only come on the holidays, and only call once a week. Sometimes less. Her father would try to call her in between, but he would only get the answering machine. She worked such long hours at the school, she couldn't return her calls the same day. Sometimes not for several days. David would get impatient and call her at school, too, but there they do not answer the phone when they are teaching or practicing t'ai chi, and Lisa told us they were always doing one or the other."

"But then something changed?"

"Yes. She started calling more often, then she came to see us, because she had something on her mind."

I stopped walking, loosened my arm from Marsha's, and turned to face her.

"China," she said. "Again, China." She began to weep, covering her face with both hands.

I put the airline ticket, one-way, to Beijing and the signed contract to sell the condo back into my pocket, then took off my jacket and spread it on the sand for Marsha to sit on so that she wouldn't ruin her good

152/ CAROL LEA BENJAMIN

coat. And for a while, my arm around her, she cried against my shoulder. When she sat back up, eyes swollen and pink, her lips were shaking, her hands, too.

"Tell me what happened, Marsha."

"Lisa came to visit us, at the holidays, for Hannukah, in December, and she told us she was going to go to China."

I reached for her hands.

"Not to visit," Marsha said, her voice cracking. "To live."

When I'd first seen the envelope from a travel agent, I had assumed it was like the ones I get, junk mail, a brochure touting a guided tour to Africa or a discount trip to Rome with Mr. Italy. I'd assumed, even though the fifth law of investigative work is, Don't jump to conclusions. I'd also assumed all those letters from real estate brokers were like the ones my landlords always got, letters that started, "Dear Owner, If you've been thinking of selling your apartment, if you've ever wondered what it would be worth in today's seller's market . . ." But one of them had been a countersigned contract to sell the condo Lisa's father had bought for her so that she could walk to work.

"This didn't make her father very happy, did it?"

"He was wild. Just like the first time. Saying the same things. Only now Lisa was a woman, not a child. She didn't *need* his permission, his approval. Perhaps that's what she *wanted*, for her father to approve of her decision, to give her emotional support. But that is not what happened."

Her head was down, the scarf covering part of her face; her arms clutched each other, and she rocked as she spoke.

"She, too, flew into a rage. 'Daddy,' she said to him, 'I'm a grownup now. This time you can't force me to do what *you* want me to.' 'It's for your own good,' he said, just like before, when she was a student, a young girl, 'for your protection.' She jumped up from where she was sitting, Rachel. 'This time I'm going,' she said, cold, like the inside of a refrigerator. And she was gone. Out of the house. I thought we wouldn't hear from her or see her for a long time. Or ever. I thought she might just go, and never write us. But she called, she pleaded, she explained, she wanted so much for David to let her go with his blessing. She was not so grownup that she didn't still need this from her father."

"What did *you* say to Lisa?"

"I gave her my approval. Of course, I thought my heart would break, that if she went to China, that would be the worst tragedy that could occur to me, to have Lisa so far away. What did I know then about tragedy?"

She looked away for a moment, toward the shore where gulls were landing and taking off and Dashiell was constructing a long, curvy trench, shoveling the sand with his big front paws and backing up as he dug. When she turned back to me, her cheeks were flushed, her eyelashes wet with tears.

" 'David,' I told him, 'you have to let her go. She's not a child.' When we were alone, he wouldn't talk to me, not about this, but I said to him, 'David, if you let her go, you will still have her. And if you don't, if you make her defy you in this, you will lose her.' "

"What did he say when you told him that?"

"He said, 'How could she do this to me?' You see where it is, was, between them?"

I nodded.

"It didn't get resolved?" I asked, thinking of the sad way things can be in families.

Marsha shook her head.

"And that's why you thought the letter was written to you, or to David?"

"Yes. I feel my daughter was torn in half, wanting so much to study in China, to live there. And wanting so much to please her father. To have his love. I believe we did this to her, Rachel, this terrible thing. That the apology she wrote was for hurting her father so much. I don't think Lisa could do that. She was never able to defy her father. So, I think, perhaps she changed her mind, but that made her so unhappy—"

"And you hired me—"

"We were hoping," she said very slowly, "that you would find out—"

"Something else," I said. "Another reason for this tragedy."

"Another reason," she repeated. "So that we could begin to make peace with this one day." She looked back toward the ocean where Dash was now racing back and forth where the waves hit the sand.

More than anything, I wanted to help. But what could I say—that the note may have been written to her and David, but that I didn't believe it was a suicide note? That I felt this, I didn't feel that, or I thought this happened, or this didn't happen. Not knowing how to comfort her, I sat there biting my lip until I tasted blood.

"It took courage for you to be able to say what you did. A lot of courage," I finally said. "This should help me find out what we need to know."

"Do you really think so?"

I nodded.

I followed her back to the gate where her groceries and shoes sat.

" 'Why did she want to go over there to live with those goddamn Communists?' he asked me a few days ago. 'To ride a bicycle to work. Here she could have had a car. I would have bought her a car. She knew that. I would have given her anything she wanted.' "

When she handed me back my shoes, I put my arms around her.

"I'll call you as soon as I can," I said.

She nodded, picked up the groceries, and headed toward home.

When I turned around, Dashiell was pleading with his eyes. I waited until Marsha was crossing the street, then, leaving my shoes and socks near the gate, I headed slowly down the beach, toward the surf. We headed back to the point, where the bay flows into the ocean and where you can see the Verrazano Bridge looming over the narrows, connecting Brooklyn to the once isolated Staten Island.

I stopped and picked up a short, fat driftwood log, which I swung back behind me and let fly into the ocean. Dashiell dove into the chilly water, all his attention on the task at hand.

I sat where the sand was hard but not wet, rubbing my hand on the cold sand and feeling it adhere to my skin. It's not only at a crime scene that we leave something and take something away. I had come here with Lillian and Ceil after my mother had died, to scatter her ashes in the ocean.

"She always wanted to travel," Ceil said as the ashes arced gracefully across the surface of the water. "But with two young children and no money, you can't go far. Then with your father dying so young, poor man, only fifty-two, where would she go by herself? And then," Ceil sighed, "the cancer. So she traveled to the hospital and back. And now here."

I picked up a broken shell and began to write in the sand.

I'm sorry. Lisa.

"The same, the same," Rabbi Zuckerman had said.

I wished he hadn't. I wished I had been able to tell the mother that her daughter hadn't written the note. One way or another, I was always wishing for things to be different, the way I had wished last night, first in the park, next in Lisa's bed, that the beautiful young man at my side were not connected to a criminal case.

But he was. He was right in the middle of it.

Last night, sitting on Lisa's couch, my fingers trembling, my mother's soft velvet shawl wrapped around me, I had opened the envelope I'd slipped out of Paul's pocket. There, with the ticket, I'd found the list of immunizations required for bringing a dog into China. Lisa hadn't abandoned Ch'an. She had planned to take her along.

I thought about Beatrice again, the way her ashes hadn't floated out to sea, as we foolishly thought they would, but had come right back to shore with the next wave. We could see them lying still and sodden on the wet sand in front of our feet. I hadn't known there were so many shades of gray. Lillian, ever the hostess, had brought a bottle of wine to the beach, and plastic cups.

"To Mom," she said, lifting her cup and draining it.

"To Beatrice," Ceil and I said as one, and we drank our wine and thought our private thoughts.

I hadn't made peace with my mother before she'd died. Now it was too late. I'd left her remains here, but I hadn't left the bitterness I'd felt, nor the sadness. Those I had carried away with me. Those I still held on to.

For a while I just sat there, looking out over the ocean, toward the horizon. Then, scratching at the hard sand with my broken piece of shell, I began to dig a little hole, watching it fill with water from beneath.

When Lili and I would dig in the sand, back when we were kids, Beatrice would poke my father to get his attention. Look, Abe, she'd tell him, they're digging to China.

I called Dash, dried his ears carefully on the end of my shirt, and following the lacy footprints of the gulls along the shore, we headed back to the car.

21

I Thought I Spotted a Sadistic Gleam in Her Eye

ON MY WAY to the gym to see Janet, I stopped at Lisa's. When I had gone through her drawers and her closet, I had noticed a Lycra bodysuit, like Janet's, and a pair of cross-trainers. Leaving Dashiell there because the gym with all those machines moving and heavy weights swinging around was too dangerous a place for a dog, I changed quickly and headed out.

Janet, wearing men's boxer shorts and a cutoff T-shirt with the logo of the gym on it, was on the phone, making faces as she listened.

"Go warm up on the treadmill," she said, as if I were a hamster. Minutes later she came to fetch me.

"Most women have more strength in their legs than their arms and chest," she said. She had a clipboard with her and a form with my name on top of it. "Let's start with your legs and work up."

"What?" I said. The music was deafening.

She took me over to a machine that you lie down on and took the pin from where it was, moving it down for more weight. I would have thought the other direction more appropriate. Getting on the machine, I was squinched into a little knot, my knees practically inside my mouth. When I pushed against the plate my feet rested on, I was propelled backward and my legs, which felt as if the bones might shatter, partially straightened out. Janet positioned my feet and told me to begin. I thought I spotted a sadistic gleam in her eye, but I couldn't be sure. It might have been a trick the fluorescent lights played with reality.

"This hurts," I said, after a dozen or so leg flexes.

"It's supposed to," she said. "If it doesn't hurt, you're not going to get stronger."

Just about when I thought someone had set fire to the whole damn gym, Janet looked up from her notes to offer some encouragement.

"Okay, Rachel, you're doing good, now let's see three more. Five, four, okay, good form, woman, keep it up, four, three, two, let's do it, don't give up now, three, two, one, excellent."

The woman, besides being an admitted and practicing sadist, couldn't count her way out of kindergarten. My legs felt as if someone had torn them out of my body and sewn them back in without anesthesia.

Janet stopped counting, but when I stopped, she flicked her hand at me, a motion that I assumed meant I was to continue.

"So how are you doing with Avi?" she asked absentmindedly, but instead of waiting for an answer, she resumed. "It's like I said, isn't it? Just being around him. Okay, rest," she said, but by the time I'd taken one breath, she was flicking her hand for me to push again.

"You can tell him anything," Janet said, sighing. "He's like the parent you always wanted and never had, very wise, and really interested in you. No one listens like that man. Okay," she said, "three, two, one. *Good.*"

To my surprise, when Janet expressed her approval, I wanted to double the weight and do twenty more reps. Fortunately, she was off to the next machine before I got the chance. I got up and trailed after her, as imprinted as Conrad Lorenz's geese.

All around us, half-naked, muscle-bound men were grimacing in pain, grunting even louder than the ear-splitting music, lifting weights as big as compact cars, and looking at themselves in the mirror any chance they could. There were females at the gym too, thin, pretty young girls reading magazines full of new hairstyles as they rode their stationary bicycles, others with earphones running on the treadmills, and some passing through on their way downstairs to step aerobics class. There were heavy women, too, two of them, both working on the thigh machines.

"Come on," Janet said, "we're going to work on your butt."

I followed her across the gym to yet another torture machine and listened carefully while she told me how far back to push the lever and how long to squeeze my glutes before releasing the lever so that it could come forward again.

And here I thought this would be mindless.

"He's such a stitch," she drawled. It took me a second to realize she was talking about Avi again. "Like he always says, 'You talk too much,' the minute you finish." Janet shook her head and laughed. "You talk too much," she repeated, and laughed again. "But only after he'd listened to every word you had to say, and only as a way of telling you it was time to do the form, to get your energy moving again."

She began to count, "Only three more, woman, let's

do it," reminding me of the dentist my family used when I was a kid, always saying "Almost done" as he was about to set the all-time world record for drilling without a pause.

"You're going to be wearing that butt of yours behind your knees if you don't work it," Janet said on one of her many breaks in the middle of counting.

"What did you say?" I asked, the blood pounding in my head, my breath sounding like the ocean during a storm.

"Your butt, woman. It's going to sink if you don't work it. Five, four, three, good work, Rachel, hold it, hold it, okay, bring it forward, three, two, one. Other leg."

"My butt's going to sing?" I asked her.

"Yeah, but please don't let it do that until I'm out of the way," she said. "Just keep working."

We did shoulders, arms, back, chest, calves, quads, abs, and a few dozen parts I didn't know I had. When Janet's six o'clock showed up, I wanted to offer him a car. I thought we were finished. But I was wrong. While he warmed up in anticipation of *his* torture session, I got to stretch. It would have felt terrific to stretch out the muscles I had just worked so hard to tighten up, except for Janet, who pushed each limb a few inches farther than where I took it on my own.

"Doesn't that feel *good,*" she drawled. "Don't forget to keep stretching later today and tomorrow. Don't you feel just fabulous?" She began to laugh in a way that made me think she knew *exactly* how I felt.

I left Janet in her world of grunts and groans and headed back to Lisa's. I had taken off the silver bracelet in order to work in the gym. I reached into my pocket and put it back on, feeling the cold weight of the metal first in my hand and then on my wrist.

Be My Love.

It had arrived *after* Paul and Lisa had broken up. After he had proposed. After she'd told him she was going to China and turned him down. Rejected him.

Had this been his way of asking again?

I had hoped, he'd started to say in the car.

I had hoped.

What? That Lisa would change her mind and stay? That she'd marry him after all?

He had reversed the truth, telling me that it was Lisa who had wanted to marry when it was he. And he had tried to take away the proof that his story had been a lie. To save face.

Big deal. Everyone had a story, the facts skewed to fit his own needs. They were probably *all* lying to me. Even Avi.

Everyone lies, my shrink used to say. People need to puff themselves up, she'd said, to make others believe they're more special than they themselves *feel* they are. Maybe there's something they want they wouldn't get with the truth, she'd said. Or maybe they're really lying to themselves. It's something they need to believe, and you're almost beside the point.

Lisa had been scheduled to leave the day after tomorrow.

Who else knew that?

A little while ago, I had wondered what the questions were. Now I had too many that needed answering. As I stood in Lisa's shower, the hot water pounding my sore muscles, they were swimming around in my head like fish. I needed to get dressed, take my dog for a long walk, and think things through.

22

Be Prepared

EARLY THE NEXT morning I took Dashiell straight to Bank Street, climbed the stairs, unlocked the door, and taking off my shoes, walked onto the polished studio floor and just sat. There wasn't a sound in the place, not even the ticking of a clock. I sat still, my thoughts still spinning like the specks of dust swirling in the sunlight.

I don't know how long I was there by myself before Dashiell heard him on the steps. He stood and wagged his tail.

"What are you doing?" he asked, pushing up the elastic that held his ponytail.

"Nothing," I told him.

"Good," he said.

He went into his office to change his shoes, then came back to where I was sitting.

"How long have you been doing nothing?"

"Long," I told him.

"Excellent," he said. "May I join you?"

"Suit yourself," I told him.

He sat next to me. Now we were both doing nothing. Well, truth be told, I wasn't exactly doing nothing. I was watching those dust motes twirling in the air, wondering what made them move so fast.

Avi wasn't doing nothing either. He was scratching Dashiell's thick neck. Dashiell began to moan.

"There's a saying that trying to understand Zen is like looking for the spectacles that are sitting on your nose," he said after a while.

"I don't wear spectacles," I told him.

"Give it time," he said with a wicked grin. "You will." He pushed up the band around his ponytail again. "Come," he said, "let's get to work."

We practiced the form twice without speaking. The third time, Avi stopped working to correct me. Suddenly he grabbed one wrist and pulled me off my feet, into him. "T'ai chi is a martial art," he said. He spoke softly, but he was still holding on to my wrist. "When someone wants something, you give in to them."

I thought he would yank me into him again, to illustrate the lesson, but he didn't.

"Watch," he said, releasing my wrist as suddenly as he'd snatched it and taking the position I had been in. "Take my wrist and pull me toward you."

I closed my fingers around his wrist and pulled him in to me. Where I had gone crashing into his chest with my other hand, Avi's other hand bent against my shoulder. I felt his wrist, then his arm, then his shoulder as his arm melted against me.

"Again," he said, taking the position I had been in when he'd pulled me off balance. "Slowly," he said, "see how I give in, I fold my hand, my wrist, my arm, like so. I give you what you want, but what have you accomplished?" When he grinned, I could smell the woody odor of bancha tea. "The same holds true if you fall, if you trip, if you are pushed to the ground. Fold. You won't get hurt."

"When you talk about folding with dogs, it means giving up," I said. "When you work a nasty dog, a miscreant, you need to get the dog to fold, to give up, to demonstrate that he knows you are top dog. Otherwise, he is. And he'll use his teeth to prove it."

"That sounds like a dangerous battle."

"This is true. Some dogs won't give up. They'd sooner die than fold."

"Some people, too. But in t'ai chi, the goal is to win without ever fighting. T'ai chi is an art of peace."

"So is dog training," I said, "properly done. But sometimes an owner only calls for help after the war has already started."

"In that case, it's best to be prepared. As in t'ai chi. Come, I'll show you."

He stood facing me, his arms in front of his chest. He merely looked at my arms, and I raised them up, as his were, understanding what he wanted in the way I know to fill Dashiell's water bowl when he indicates with his eyes that it's empty.

Avi placed the backs of his hands next to the backs of my hands, not touching, but close enough so that I could feel the heat of his skin, and slowly we began to shift, small movements that changed the balance of our relationship, back and forth, like the glider on Ceil's back porch, yin and yang, as graceful as a dance, but, as Avi had just reminded me, not a dance, a martial art. His hands began to push lightly against my wrists, against my arms, my shoulders. Moving slowly, we felt each other's strengths and weaknesses, we felt each other's total beings, without speech, using only touch, the way a human and a dog telegraph the facts of life to each other up and down the leash.

If you looked casually at what we were doing, it resembled the way Lili and I used to fight when we were kids, hands everywhere, pushing, shoving, circling round and round, each trying to get the upper hand. But if you looked carefully, the same, the same, only ritualized, like the dominance displays among dogs or wolves, each posture full of significance and information, each touch revealing the strength or lack of strength, both mental and physical, of the opponents.

For a single moment I thought about Paul, about the way his lips brushed my skin, barely touching it. In that instant Avi pushed, catching me so completely off guard that he sent me flying backward across the studio.

"Keep your mind *here*," he said, waiting for me to approach and begin again. "Concentrate on getting out of the way." He motioned for me to push him and he turned his body slightly to the side, deflecting my push and letting my own force take me off balance, using my own force against me.

The next time I felt my attention drifting, I was able to bring it right back. I'd once let myself drift for a split second when working with a scoundrel of a dog. I had the scar to remind me that, in dog training, the time is always now.

But then, despite trying to remain as riveted to the task at hand as Dashiell always was to a stick I was about to toss for him, I thought about Lisa, at the window. Once again, Avi threw me off balance. When moments later I tried to do the same with him, I failed to budge him. He was as rooted as a great oak, as difficult to capture as the wind.

My legs were burning, and I was out of breath. Avi

motioned for us to sit, leaning against the wall of the studio. We sat quietly for a moment, just resting.

"Avram, were you aware of Lisa's plans?" I asked, trying to catch him off balance with words where I had failed to do so with my *chi*.

He didn't respond.

I pushed again.

"Did you know she was planning to leave? She did tell you everything, didn't she?"

"You have made room for Lisa," he said, not looking at me, not looking at anything. Maybe he was seeing Lisa. "You have been working very hard," he said.

"Yes, I have."

"I knew she was planning to go to China. I knew for a long time, Rachel, since the first day she came to study with me. Only then, then it was just a story, a dream."

"When did it become more than a dream, Avi?"

"Day by day," he said. "Slowly. Then all at once."

"Did the others know, too? The other teachers?"

"No. Lisa had planned to tell them herself, privately, at the last possible moment. She thought that if I announced it, there'd be a feeding frenzy, that they would all be scrambling to take her place, to become, she said, the favorite. She loved them, Rachel. She was, oh, the dearest person—" He reached to wipe his cheeks. "She couldn't bear to see them all lose their dignity."

"And would they have?"

"Ach," he said. "You've seen them. You've heard them. A gifted student, that might happen once in a teacher's life." He stopped and looked at me. "Maybe twice, if you are really lucky. You do your best with what is sent to you," he said as the door opened and Stewie Fleck walked in. He was wearing a shiny orange baseball jacket with plaid polyester pants, and his shoelaces were open and dragging on the carpet. When he dropped the jacket over the back of the couch, his wallet fell out of the pocket.

How did this man get through life?

And how would Avi, now that he'd lost Lisa?

I looked at my watch. It was five minutes to the lunch-hour class. I was supposed to stay, but I knew I'd be unable to concentrate. There was too much on my mind.

It's best to be prepared, Avi had said.

Frank always said that, too. Be prepared for surprises, he would warn me, and I don't mean good ones. He had that annoying habit of pointing when he was, by his own admission, making a brilliant point.

Yeah, yeah, I'd tell him, prepared, like a Boy Scout.

But he was right. It was a dog-eat-dog world out there.

Whoever had killed Lisa had caught her off guard. So when push came to shove, if Lisa hadn't been able to defend herself, what chance would I have?

With t'ai chi, Avi had told me, you can defeat your opponent by starting after him but arriving before him.

Yeah, right, I thought on my way down the stairs. Tell it to Lisa.

23

Did I See What I Just Saw?

DASHIELL AND I walked over to Hunan Pan on Hudson and Perry. I parked him under a table near the window, and when the waiter arrived with a menu and tea, I conferred with him about an urgent point concerning my case.

Then, just to be polite, I ordered a bowl of hot and sour soup, steamed pork dumplings, and some chicken and broccoli. Out of respect for Donny, I didn't order crab.

After I'd eaten, instead of lingering over tea, I pocketed the fortune cookie and headed over to Washington Square Park. Dashiell was looking stressed, and I thought an hour of hip-hop with some other friendly dogs would chill him out nicely.

Dashiell had no trouble living in the moment. As soon as I opened the double gates to the run, he was in ecstasy, rushing into the group of playing dogs, bumping them with his big, strong butt, racing back and forth, engaging in good-natured humping, the whole canine enchilada. Watching him play was usually a be-atific experience for me, sort of a dog lover's medita-tion. But not this time. I was too busy obsessing about Paul.

Why had he told me he didn't speak Chinese? And what other lies had he told me? What was he up to, anyway? And most important, when would I see him again?

It was probably a good idea that I had a massage scheduled for three thirty. I was as tight as the curl of a pug's tail.

At ten after three Dashiell and I headed for Bank Street. When I got to Howie's, I rang the bell and waited to be buzzed in. But nothing happened. I checked my watch. I was right on time. I waited an-other minute, then gave it one more try before leaving, leaning on the bell a little longer than usual.

I heard the intercom crackle, but I couldn't make out the words.

"Rachel," I said into the speaker. "I'm here for my massage."

He didn't respond, but the buzzer sounded, and when I leaned on the door, it opened. Dashiell and I walked straight back down the dimly lit hall to Howie's apartment, and when we got to his door, we rang again. This time we didn't have long to wait.

She filled the doorway. At first, I thought it was Howie, suddenly much older, and in drag.

Her face looked like melting ice cream, formless and sagging, as if there were no bones or muscles beneath the vanilla-colored skin. Or maybe that was powder, making her look as white-faced as a mime. Her eyes were a bleached-out blue, splotches of red from broken capillaries crisscrossed her cheeks, and smack in the middle of the whole mess she had a purple ginger root of a nose. Her face was like a hide-a-bed that had been left open, stuff showing that should have been hidden away, preferably under the sink.

She was short and heavy, leaden looking, as if she were glued to the ground beneath her Minnie Mouse-sized Nikes. Her sparse orange hair puffed out all around her head, making her look like an angry bird. But when she spoke, she was no bird. She barked like a big, cranky dog.

"Wha'd you want?" she asked, a cloud of Scotch and tobacco coming at me.

"I have an appointment with Howie, for a massage," I told her, trying not to make the mistake of inhaling again.

"Not here," she barked, about to close the door.

She was holding a cigarette and now took matches out of the pocket of her sweater and lit it. Dashiell sneezed.

"He's getting one, too?" she asked. "Don't look tense to me."

"No, he's cool. I'm the one who needs help. Howie says—"

"Howie says, Howie says, that kid don't know his ass from the hole in his head. So what're you standing in the hall, c'mon in."

Watching her tree-trunk legs shuffle slowly forward, I followed her down the hall, past the room where Howie worked, toward where I'd heard the sound of the television set last visit. The TV was on now, too. Some lady with iridescent fingernails like the wings of things that live in pipes and drains was moving her hand from side to side so that the ruby ring she was selling for sixty-nine ninety-five would catch the light.

"Sit down," she said, the cigarette dangling from her lips bobbing up and down when she spoke. "If he said he'd be here, he'll be here. He went out to get me my medicine."

There was an empty glass on the coffee table in front of her, the last ice cube down to a shaving now, sitting in cloudy amber liquid.

"What a good son he must be," I said, looking around the dismal room. The little bit of light coming through the windows hit the threadbare green wall-to-wall and the worn, dirty couch that faced the television set. There was one of those aluminum walkers off near the wall and newspapers and magazines stacked everywhere. The room looked and smelled as stale as the old lady's ashtray, overflowing with butts, a crunched-up empty cigarette package lying on top of the whole mess.

"What a good son he must be," she said, snorting as she did. "A lot you know. Dora Lish," she said. "*How*ie's mother."

"Rachel Alexander," I said.

She ignored me, and I sat watching the ashes from her cigarette land on her lap. "Howie's mother," she repeated. "The kid still comes crying to me when someone hurts his feelings, just the way he always has. He's thin-skinned." She looked at me with one eye as the smoke from the cigarette dangling from her lips went up toward the cracked ceiling past the other. "Thin-skinned."

"You mean he's sensitive?" I asked.

"Sens-tive my ass," Howie's mother said. "He's a damn crybaby, is what he is. Always was. Always will be. Whines ever' time I need something, s'if he had to trudge ten miles in the snow 'stead of around the corner." She puffed on the cigarette without removing it from her mouth and stared at me. "You're not from the school, are you?"

"You mean the t'ai chi school? Yes, I am. I'm study-ing there, too."

"*You* the one made him cry?" she asked, looking confused for the moment.

"No," I said, a little too quickly. "I just started there. I'm new. But I heard—"

"That bitch!" Dora said. She took the cigarette and pointed toward me with it. "Wasn't you, you sure it wasn't you? Say, what's your name anyway?"

"Rachel," I told her. "Rachel Alexander."

"No, that's not her name. Not Rachel Alexander. She had a completely different name."

"How did she make Howie cry," I asked, "that bitch?"

"Don't take much."

"So what happened, she hurt his feelings?"

"Feelings? She was going to *fire* him. That's nothing to do with feelings. It's to do with money." She rubbed her thumb and forefinger together. "Like we're rolling in it," she said, indicating the room we were in with a sweep of one hand. "Like we don't need every damn penny he can make."

"Did she say why? I mean, did Howie say what the reason was?"

I took a peek at my watch. Howie was already twenty-two minutes late for my appointment.

Dora Lish suddenly got up and started beating on the couch cushion. I guess she'd lost the ash of her ciga-rette. The cloud of dust came at me like nuclear fallout, and suddenly I was having a sneezing fit.

Satisfied she'd found the culprit and had beat it into submission, Dora sat and relit her cigarette. It was then I heard the familiar pop and looked up to see Dashiell, a huge paw anchoring the Kleenex box on the cluttered coffee table between Dora Lish and myself, a tissue dangling from his big, wide mouth. He walked over and dropped it into my lap. I blew my nose and patted his big head.

"Wait a minute here." Dora started to get up and then sat back down. She pointed at Dashiell with her cigarette. "Did I see what I just saw?"

I nodded.

"Naw. You're pulling my leg, trying to fool an old lady. Bet he wouldn't do it again," she said, suddenly as excited as a child.

I opened my mouth, but before I had the chance to say a word, Dora Lish, who apparently didn't live next door to the HB Acting Studio for nothing, lifted one big nicotine-stained hand toward her face and faked a rhinoceros of a sneeze.

Ever alert, Dashiell turned back to the coffee table and crushed one side of the tissue box with his foot so that it wouldn't fly up, then pulled out half a tissue, which he dropped into Dora's lap. He backed up and waited.

Dora began to cackle.

Dashiell went back for the other half of the tissue. But this time he didn't bring it to Dora. This time he dropped it right on the coffee table, and pop, pop, pop, three more tissues were out of the box.

"Enough," I told him. "Good boy."

Left without praise, like most of us, he finds a way to thank himself, in this case with the heady pleasure of snapping tissues out of the box until it's empty. After that, he'd discover how tissue boxes are constructed. And if his best efforts on behalf of the human race were further ignored, he'd make tissue-colored confetti, blue in this case. Hey, you never know when there's going to be a parade.

Howie was now forty-five minutes late. Dora had seen me check my watch this time.

"He musta got held up at the grocer's," she said, dropping the end of her cigarette into the whiskey glass. "I'll tell him you were here. What'd you say your name was?"

"Rachel."

"Oh, yeah. I remember. Rachel. Got a cigarette on you, hon?"

I shook my head.

"Mrs. Lish—"

"Dora. Everyone calls me Dora."

Everyone? The place didn't exactly look as if she entertained much, but you never know.

"Dora," I said, but she had turned her attention toward the television set. There was a faux pearl necklace being shown, and Dora watched the hand holding it move across the screen.

"You never told me, Dora, why was Howie going to get fired?"

"I'll tell him you were by," she said without turning to look at me. She fished a butt out of the ashtray and lit it. "I'll tell him about the Kleenex, too," she said, the smoke from her cigarette rising in a thin stream, then widening as it headed for the ceiling.

"Just pull th' door closed on your way out, will ya, hon?"

So I did. I closed the living room door, waited a minute, Dashiell and I frozen in place, my hand still on the knob, and when there was no sound other than the drone of the TV, I looked around the narrow, dark hallway and headed not toward Howie's office and the front door, but the other way.

Dora's ashtray of a bedroom was on the left side of the narrow hallway, a small, dark, cluttered hole of a space, its one window facing an air shaft. She had her own bathroom, though. I poked through her medicine cabinet, filled with enough antibiotics, Tylenol with codeine, Valium, Ex-Lax, and Tums for her tummy to start her own pharmacy. I even found her favorite medicine, hidden behind the six-pack of toilet paper under the sink for those times when Howie was too slow getting back from the store. Before leaving Dora's suite, I stopped at her bureau to look at the photo hanging over it, a round-faced boy, already overweight at seven or eight, standing next to a little girl, her dress so starched the skirt stood out, a ribbon in her curly hair, her face as round as Howie's. A sister? So where was she when Mama needed so much care?

Next door to Dora's room was a second bathroom, and across the hall from that was Howie's bedroom, the door so warped it didn't even close all the way. I pushed it open slowly and turned on the light.

Howie slept on what looked like a cot, or a youth bed. It was as neatly made as if Howie were in the army, the single pillow fluffed, the striped blanket pulled tight and tucked in with hospital corners. Howie's slippers were lined up next to the bed on a little mat. I walked in, waited for Dashiell, and closed the door behind us as well as I was able.

There was an old upright bureau on one wall and a small desk on the other. I sat at the desk, turned on the lamp, and opened the top drawer, looking at the neatly lined up pens and pencils, the checkbook, the little packet of rubber bands, the small dish of paper clips, and the box with stamps in it, all carefully torn from their sheets and stacked in neat compartments, everything just so.

The drawers to the left held Howie's business files, every payment and expense neatly recorded. And envelopes of receipts, all marked and ready for tax time. Behind the receipts were letters. I pulled the file and looked through the lot of them, all from patients and doctors relating to the conditions Howie was supposed to treat. And behind that a folder with photographs in it, only three of them, Howie kneeling with a bunch of other boys, perhaps a team shot but without the identifying paraphernalia, Howie's grim little high school graduation picture, and one really good photo, a black-and-white enlargement of Howie doing t'ai chi. It reminded me of the photo of Lisa in Avi's office, the way the subject was off center, the way the light hit the hands, caught in a graceful pose as the subject moved slowly through the form. Howie looked through the Tiger's Eyes, loose circles made by his powerful hands, which in the photo looked as chiseled as the David's.

I checked my watch. It would be nearly halfway into the next appointment, if there were one. Still no Howie. But for how long, I couldn't say.

I became aware of my breathing then, shallow and quick, my head clear, my ears alert to any sound from elsewhere in the apartment. I shut off the desk light and was ready to go when I got one last idea. I knelt and looked under Howie's neat bed, then slid out the magazines I'd had the feeling would be there, carefully sliding them back when I had seen enough silicone and whips to last me a lifetime.

I stopped in Howie's office on my way out. His appointment book was lying open on the cabinet near the head of the massage table. I checked my watch. It was four twenty-eight. Someone was due in just two minutes, on the half hour. Just then, the bell rang. I signaled Dashiell, and we made it out the door before the second ring, a longer one, had summoned Dora.

There was a tense-looking young man waiting to be

buzzed in. Walking past him, I thought about her, about Howie's mother. She had looked as if she'd fall asleep, mesmerized by the TV. I wondered what would happen to the cigarette, but whatever would, it had happened countless times before, and Dora the lush was still here to tell any stranger who'd listen what a fucked-up loser the son who cared for her in her old age was.

24

There Ought to Be a Law

LEAVING HOWIE'S, I felt that crick in my neck he had warned me about the first time we'd met. I had thought about going over to the Club to see Paul. I could say I'd lost Lisa's work keys, ask if I could borrow his set, see what he said, watch his eyes while he said it.

Then I thought about the envelope. What had he thought when he'd reached into his pocket and found it missing, when he'd realized I knew that it had been he who'd been so anxious to get married, not Lisa? All she had wanted was to go to China, no matter what it cost her. So I thought maybe I shouldn't go and see him. I thought perhaps he needed some time.

But then I found myself thinking about the way his skin smelled, about the long, smooth muscles of his back, about the warmth and softness of his hands, about the way he'd said my name, over and over again, like a mantra. Then I *knew* I better not go see him, because the sixth law of investigation work is, Don't get caught with your pants down, and I didn't want to break it again. I cared much too much for this man, considering all I didn't yet know, and I didn't want to break my heart either.

I could hear the phone ringing when I was still in the garden, but by the time I got the door unlocked, it had stopped. It was probably just someone asking me if I wanted to switch back to AT&T. They call at all hours. There ought to be a law.

I went upstairs to run a bath, and while the tub was filling with water too hot to dunk anything in other than a lobster on its way to becoming bisque, I checked my answering machine and found that an unusual number of calls had come in since I'd left home that morning. Eleven. But when I rewound the tape, I discovered they were all hang-ups. As if someone were trying to find out whether or not I was home.

I was tempted to dig my revolver out from the shoe box on the top shelf of my closet where it had been for over a year, but I told myself that that was too paranoid, even for me.

I turned off the phone and turned down the volume on the answering machine. Soaking in the steamy hot water, without the agitating noise of the telephone, I quickly fell fast asleep and stayed that way for over an hour, until the water had cooled off enough to wake me.

It was nearly eight o'clock when I got out of the tub, turned the phone back on, and, still feeling exhausted, plodded downstairs to feed Dashiell. When the phone rang again, I grabbed it on the first ring. This time the person on the other end didn't hang up.

"Rachel?"

"Marty?"

I looked out the small kitchen window into the garden, a tangle of dark shadows at this hour. "What's up?" I asked.

"I need to see you, kid. Can you come over for a minute?"

"Now?"

"It won't take long." Sounding like a cop.

"Sure," I said, looking at the kitchen clock. Eight twenty now. What was Marty even doing there at this hour? He worked days. "Is anything wrong? You okay? Are the dogs okay?"

"I'll wait for you at the front desk," was all he said. And then I heard the click. He had hung up.

Had he made all those other calls? Had he been waiting, for some reason, for me to get home and pick up?

I pulled on one of Lisa's black sweaters and some leggings, stepped into a pair of clogs, combed back my wet hair, and poured some dry dog food for Dashiell. In less than five minutes I was out the door.

Marty was standing near the front desk, and when he saw me, he took my arm and led me to a desk in back where there was no one else within earshot.

"There's been a murder, Rachel. In the neighborhood. Close by." I felt my heart start to race. Who was I, for the Sixth Precinct to suddenly be filling me in on their most up-to-date bad news? "The victim was found on Bank Street, in that outdoor area at Westbeth." He paused, as if the location of the body would be so pregnant with significance I'd burst out with the name of the killer.

"And?" I said.

He was watching my face. I watched his, not blinking, waiting for the other shoe to drop.

"Across from the school," he added, "where your clients' daughter used to work."

"Yes. But what's—"

"He had your name on a card in his shirt pocket, Rachel."

"You mean my card? Maybe it was someone who needed help, you know, a work contact."

"It wasn't *your* card, Rachel. It was actually *his* card. He'd written your name on the back of it. And there was something else written there, too."

"Something else? What else?"

"Something in Chinese."

Suddenly I got a strange rush to my head, as if I were breathing pure oxygen, and the air tasted metallic, the way it does when you take antibiotics.

"Xiao yue?" I asked.

But he didn't reply. Instead he took my arm and backed me into a molded plastic chair next to the empty desk. He pulled the desk chair around so that he could sit in front of me, so close our knees were touching.

"Paul Wilcox is dead, Marty?"

He nodded.

I looked back toward the desk, at the uniforms milling around, at the line of civilians, there at any hour of the day or night to report the kind of minor irritations that build up in a city like New York, things that drive people to the brink of insanity, or over it. I reminded myself where I was and what was at stake here.

"How? What happened?" I asked him, as if we were talking about some stranger and not a man I'd gone to bed with, my voice sounding as if it were coming from far away, or from the other side of a closed door.

Marty took my hands.

"A couple of the detectives want to talk to you. I came back in so that I could do this." He squeezed my hands. "So like I said, he was carrying a card with your name on it, Rachel. Looks like you were pretty important to him."

I felt my face flush, but the rest of me was as cold as a corpse. I had come out without a coat, and my hair was still wet, I thought as I felt myself shiver, my fingers like icicles in Marty's hands.

"Rachel?" he said. He stood, slipped off his jacket, and put it around my shoulders.

"How, Marty? Help me out here, will you?"

"ME says broken neck, unofficially, of course, pending autopsy. They're working on him now."

"When did it happen?"

"Mid to late afternoon. Best guess? Weather conditions weren't unusual, so by the deceased's temperature, he figures four to five, give or take."

I winced, thinking of the medical examiner slipping the thermometer next to Paul's eyeball. Keep your mind *here,* I told myself.

"Who's on?" I asked him. "Who do you want me to talk to?"

"Talk to me," he said.

"He was Lisa Jacobs's sweetheart," I told him, "until a few months before her death, her suicide. I met with him in connection with the case, to try to find out what I needed to know about Lisa, for her parents."

Marty nodded.

"So that I could help them to understand what had happened, I mean, why what had happened had happened, so that I could give that information to her parents."

"And?"

"He wasn't very forthcoming when I first went to see him. He just seemed angry. Turned some of that on me."

"So you tried another approach? Something less threatening, more friendly."

"Swimming," I said, feeling my throat closing.

"Swimming?"

"He was a swim coach. I went over to the gym where he worked, the Club on Varick Street, and went swimming."

"And?"

"And then he was more forthcoming. He opened up," I said, swallowing hard, "about their relationship. I guess that's why—"

"He had your name in his pocket, over his heart?"

I nodded. "How did it happen, Marty?"

"Looks like a mugging. The sort where you not only take the individual's credit cards and cash, you also inflict as much damage as possible, given the constraints of time and place. Sometimes the mugger gets scared off in time, and the victim lives. No such luck this time."

"Was there anything else on him, Marty, besides the card?"

"Handkerchief, key ring, driver's license, small change, nothing much."

"Show me."

"His belongings? What for?"

"Please, Marty. This has to do with my case. It's really important."

"I don't—"

"You don't think I—"

"Rachel—"

"So show me."

A moment later I was looking through a plastic bag at Paul Wilcox's handkerchief, driver's license, two quarters, a dime and two pennies, and a key ring with eight keys on it, three of them Lisa's, three of them for Bank Street T'ai Chi, one for downstairs, two for upstairs, though nobody ever locked the bottom lock.

"That's it?" I asked.

"Just what you see," he said.

"Rachel, you know anything about this man's life, any enemies he might have had?"

"No," I said. "No friends either. We only spoke about Lisa, about his feelings for Lisa."

"If you think of anything—"

"Right," I said. "Can I go now?"

"Rachel—"

"What? You don't want me to leave town?"

"I want you out of this."

I nodded.

"Unless you *think* of something he said, anything he said that might—"

"Yeah, yeah," I said. "I'll call you first thing. I'll beep you. Whatever."

"Or Matthew. He and Dave are in charge of this. They might want to talk to you, but I'll talk to them for now."

"Thanks, Marty."

"Sure thing, kid."

I started to go, but Marty took my arm and stopped me.

"Hey, I meant to tell you, Rach. You were right on the money about Elwood's thyroid." He made a fist and pointed to the floor with his thumb. "Way down. He and Gluck are taking the same pills now. We keep telling Gluck he better watch it, he'll be out of a job, we're going to put Elwood on the phone. The doc says it'll take a few months for his weight to go down, but his energy is way up. You gotta see him. He's like a new dog," he said. "I'll call you as soon as he gets back."

The bomb dogs worked one week, then had two weeks off, what a lot of their fellow officers considered an enviable work schedule.

"You okay?"

I nodded.

"Good. That's good. You take care now. And call me if you think of anything."

It was nearly ten when I got back home, and I couldn't remember having just walked across from the precinct. There were two more messages. Both hang-ups. Of course the calls hadn't been from Marty. He would have left a message.

I sat in the living room for a while, thinking about Paul. There wouldn't have been a wallet. When he'd paid for the Chinese food, his cash had been loose in his pocket. He wouldn't go out without money. No one would. So the mugger had taken whatever cash he'd had on him.

I made a pot of tea, heating the pot with boiling water the way he had. But when it was ready and I'd carried my cup back to the couch, I just let it sit there, untouched.

He'd had the keys to the studio. Had he used them that night? No, of course not. He wouldn't have been so surprised to learn about the note if he had.

The phone rang, and I picked it up, but oddly, whoever was on the other end had nothing to say. That's when it occurred to me that I couldn't remember if I'd locked the garden gate. I grabbed my keys, put Lisa's jacket back on, and walked outside, Dashiell following. We headed toward the dark tunnel that led to the gate. I was going to try it, to make sure it was locked. I was going to shake it, to see if it held, then finally go to sleep. But what I saw stuck in a curlicue of the wrought-iron gate stopped me dead in my tracks.

There, wrapped in floral paper with a layer of waxy green tissue paper underneath, were yellow rosebuds, twelve of them, each perfect. Their perfume filled the night air.

After making sure the gate was locked, I looked at the bouquet very carefully, even turning it upside down and shaking it. But no matter how hard I looked, I couldn't find a card.

25

We Don't Need the Money,
He'd Said

THE PHONE RANG again. I could hear it as I carried the flowers back toward the cottage and laid them on the steps.

Someone had been sending roses for a while now. Someone had waited across the street from Lisa's, watching her windows. And someone knew that I didn't live at Lisa's house, that I lived here. That when the time came, this is where I was to be found.

But it hadn't been Paul. Then who was it? And what was he after now? Or who?

Leaving the roses on the steps, Dashiell in the garden, and the door open, I went upstairs, took the little stool from my office, and carried it into the bedroom closet. Then I climbed up on it and pulled down the Joan & David shoe box, a relic of my eight-month marriage to Dr. Fashion, a box much too heavy to have shoes in it, and put it on the bed.

Under some circumstances, my shrink Ida used to say, paranoia is not such an inappropriate response.

I went down to the basement where I had the formal dining room table I never used and all the cartons of stuff I'd never opened from when I split with Jack and moved here, saltcellars and linen napkins, a dozen sterling silver iced-tea spoons, stemware, Rosenthal china, wedding presents from people who apparently thought Jack had married Martha Stewart. I squeezed my way past a mountain of boxes to the sideboard against the far wall, which held only bullets for my gun and the boxes of gadgets Bruce Petrie used to give me, so full of formal dinner parties was my life. With a box of thirty-eights in hand, I began to pick my way back to the stairs. But then I stopped.

Why was this stuff still here, still part of my life? More to the point, how had I fooled myself into thinking I could be happy spending my days hanging up the clothes someone else tossed over the dresser the night before and finding new things to do with cilantro?

I had moved into Jack's Victorian house in Croton, overlooking the Hudson River, a sort of mirror image of Lili and Ted's modern house on the other side of the river. Lili, cradling her morning coffee, could watch the sun rise over Westchester, pink turning to gold, all brightness and hope. I could watch the sun set over Rockland County, brilliant orange and flaming red, the colors of dying leaves in fall.

Having closed my dog school in the city, I'd figured, no problem, I'd train in Westchester, closer to home. But when I told Jack my plans, he became as still as marble and just as cold.

We don't need the money, he'd said, as if that were all that work was about. Then, after a long frost, he spoke again. He wanted me home when he got home, not running around at all hours of the night getting myself bitten. He wanted to sit down to a nice, home-cooked meal with me and discuss his day. That's what marriage was, wasn't it, for chrissake, he'd said. He hadn't married me, he added, to come home to an empty house.

Where, I remember wondering, was the man who'd found my occupation quirky and endearing? Get a load of this, he'd told his cretin brother Alan, she trains *dogs* for a living. And while I'd answered all his brother's inane questions, he'd looked proud. But as soon as we were married, he'd changed.

The price of my poor judgment had been a divorce. Lisa's may have cost her her life.

I put the box of bullets on the bottom step and began to open those other boxes, cartons containing carefully wrapped champagne flutes, a soup tureen, a fish poacher, grape shears, lobster forks. At three in the morning, having set aside only a hand-thrown planter I could use for herbs in the winter and a small, flowered bud vase, I resealed the cartons and stacked them neatly under the windows. Then I shut off the light, dropped the box of ammo in the kitchen, and went back out into the moonlit garden.

Alongside the house were the logs I had gathered last fall in the woods surrounding my sister's house. The smaller pile, the split logs, was nearly gone. I tossed the jacket over that pile, lifted the heavy tarp from the larger woodpile, and unwrapped the sledgehammer and wedge that lay on top of the wood.

Dashiell lay peacefully on the rich, loamy earth near the oak tree that stretched skyward from the center of the garden. It was taller than the cottage. The moonlight, filtered through its branches, made his white fur look pearly, almost iridescent.

A mugging. Yeah, right.

Mid to late afternoon, I thought, lifting a log from

the woodpile. Where had Howie been? It didn't take an hour and a half to pick up a bottle of cheap Scotch for your mother, did it?

I stood the log on the tree stump near the wood pile and tapped in the wedge. Where had Stewie Fleck been between four and five? In the field, meaning anywhere he damn well wanted to be, the little creep?

What about Janet? Had she been at the gym, where Stewie said she practically lived, torturing innocents?

Come to think of it, where had Avi been? The news was full of reminders lately that no one is immune to human frailty, not judges, Nobel laureates, or even holy men.

If Paul had been killed across from the school, didn't that mean he'd been on the way to the studio, to find me?

If so, why hadn't he called to see if I were there?

But what would be the point? Surely he knew that no one ever picked up the phone. If someone doesn't have the patience to wait for us to call them back, Avi had said once when I was going to answer the phone in the middle of working, they're not going to have the patience to learn t'ai chi. Not answering the phone was a weeding-out process for him, the first in a long string of character tests.

Why Paul? I thought. But the answer to that question hit really close to home. Too close, if you ask me.

I looked back at Dashiell, still lying under the tree. Between his paws, right under his nose, he had serendipitously discovered a scent worthy of his complete attention. I could see his nostrils moving.

I turned my attention to the wood pile and began to split logs in earnest now, tapping the wedge into the next log, swinging the sledgehammer back and then high over one shoulder, bringing it down hard, hearing the satisfying clang of metal on metal and seeing the log cleave in two, opening like a flower that had suddenly decided to bloom, the outside darkened by the weather, the inside raw and vulnerable looking as a wound. I worked until I developed a rhythm, until I was drenched with sweat, until I no longer knew where the sledgehammer ended and I began, nor did I care, until there were no more logs to split. Then I sat quietly on the steps, my dog on one side of me leaning in, those perfect roses on the other, until the stars began to disappear, the color of the sky lightened, the first bird began to sing. And when it did, I sat some more.

26

Be Not Afraid

WHEN THE GARDEN was filled with the sweet, clean light of morning, I spread the yellow roses under the bushes across from the cottage to mulch. Then, sticking my sore hands into my pockets, I felt the fortune cookie I'd never opened. I broke it in half and held the pieces for Dashiell to eat while I read the message. It was a proverb. *Be not afraid of going slowly, be afraid only of standing still.*

I went inside and gave Dashiell food and water, ran a bath, and while the tub was filling, put my gun and bullets on the top shelf of the closet. Later, dressed in Lisa's comfortable black workout clothes, I called Goodwill to arrange for them to pick up the physical evidence of my brief marriage in exchange for a generous tax deduction. When I hung up, I saw that Dashiell was fast asleep on the couch. He was so tired, he hadn't finished his food. I gave him a kiss and headed for Bank Street T'ai Chi alone.

I took the stairs, walking slowly. I had, after all, been

up all night. The door was locked, but when I unlocked it, I found Avi there with Ch'an. He was at his desk paying bills.

"Ach," he said, "I hate this. Lisa used to do this for me. Now the bills pile up, and I have to sit glued to a chair for hours to take care of them."

"I'll do that for you," I told him, one hand on his shoulder. "You shouldn't have to do this. Go. Go for a walk. I'll leave everything ready for your signature when I finish."

I picked up Ch'an's leash and held it out to Avi. He opened his mouth as if to speak, but changed his mind. He merely waved it away with one big hand.

"You keep her," he said, his eyebrows pinched together, his brow tense.

"Okay," I told him. "No problem."

"And give her a little walk before you leave, Rachel," he said without looking at me. "I won't be back for her until this evening."

I waited to hear the door close and the tumbler turn over. Then I pushed the stack of unpaid bills aside. While the computer was booting up, I rolled back the tape on the answering machine and began to listen. Avi rarely picked up the phone, even when he was at his desk.

There were five messages on the machine, all inquiries about beginning classes, requests for brochures. I rolled the tape back and played it again, addressing the five brochures, then began surfing Avi's files, looking at the dates and times the computer automatically adds to each directory. Avi had been working on-screen yesterday, starting at one thirty. Unfortunately, I could see only when he logged on, not when he'd finished working.

There were no classes on Friday afternoon or evening, no way of knowing if Avi had been here or not. I slit open the envelopes in the pile of bills, checked each against last month's billing, and wrote the checks I'd promised I'd write, leaving the stack for his signature when I'd finished, even stamping the envelopes for him. Then, before closing down the computer and shutting off the light, I checked one more thing, Avi's personnel files. I copied down the addresses I didn't already have, making sure to check my own as well. I was listed as living at Lisa's apartment, with Lisa's phone number. I wasn't in the phone book. Still, somebody knew where I really lived.

I patted my lap for Ch'an, and she came and laid her big head across my thighs, sighing as she did. I put one finger inside one of her ears, and she began to moan, the way Dashiell always does. That's when I noticed the tag on her collar. I picked it up and looked at it. It wasn't her license. It was her ID tag, complete with Lisa's name, address, and phone number.

Like Lisa, I would never risk losing my dog. Dashiell too had an ID tag on his collar, a brass plate attached to the leather collar with two rivets, for complete security. His had only my name and number on it, no address, because my life's mission was to raise paranoia to a high art. So my secret admirer had had to be extra clever to have both my phone number *and* address.

No problem. Whoever stood across from Lisa's apartment, looking up at her windows, could have followed me home. But it hadn't been Paul, had it? It had been someone else, someone who had nothing more important to do than to wait, hoping for a glimpse of the person he so longed to see. Not Lisa. Lisa was gone. Now it was *me* he had waited to see, me looking out over the dark street or up at the white face of the moon. It was me, one night when the weather was mild and his patience long, who appeared not in the window, but on the front steps, leaving with my dog.

Was I just giving him a walk? That would be easy enough to find out. At that hour, even in New York, there aren't many people around. You could follow someone from Hudson and LeRoy to Tenth Street, staying far enough away to remain undetected yet still not risking the chance of losing them. Even when your unsuspecting prey turned the corner onto Tenth, there'd be no problem. Dashiell, like any intact male, was infinitely more conscientious about leaving his scent near home than far away. The closer he got to where we lived, the more urgent and time-consuming was his need to mark, and, lucky mutt, he had an owner who had an understanding of and a soft spot for hormone-driven canine necessities.

I left the office, slipped off my shoes, and walked onto the studio floor in Lisa's white cotton socks. Facing north, I did the form, keeping my concentration in the raging furnace beneath my navel. Something was chewing away at the edge of my consciousness, but I didn't know what it was. When I finished, I walked over to the windows, opening the one someone had pushed Lisa out of, and once again looked straight down at the street, so far away.

The first time I'd imagined Lisa doing this, I'd supposed she'd stood here alone and miserable. I'd pictured her climbing up on the sill, then pitching herself forward, into eternity.

Now I was sure she'd had help.

But not from her ex-lover.

Before I closed the window I looked at the courtyard across the street, where Paul's body had been found. Formerly the research facility of Bell Labs, Westbeth was now housing for artists. There was a security guard inside with closed-circuit TV watching the elevators, the hallways, the entrances and exits, the courtyard.

Was the killer someone Paul knew, someone who could have rested an arm over his shoulders in friendship? Two men walking or standing that way wouldn't alert a security guard, not in this neck of the woods.

Or were they shielded from the camera's eye by one of the trees planted in rows across from the entrance? Perhaps the guard was checking another monitor at the time of the murder. No one can watch everything at once. How long would it take to snap someone's neck, slip the money out of his pocket, then disappear? Not long. A life, a complex being, a family, and a future, destroyed in an instant.

I went back into Avi's office and picked up the phone. "Can you meet me at the studio in half an hour? It's important. Good. Lunch is on me."

I put on my shoes, grabbed my jacket, picked up Ch'an's leash again, and headed for the door. Ch'an got up slowly, stretched, and followed me, looking elsewhere, as if it were merely a pleasant coincidence that we were both going out at the same time.

On the way to pick up lunch, I thought about my companion, walking along untroubled at my side. If trouble came, would her demeanor change? Had it changed during the last moments of Lisa's life, or had the dog remained asleep in the other room, oblivious to what was going on in the studio?

Wouldn't there have been loud voices, accusations, recriminations, something to rouse the sleeping dog and make her curious enough to pad out into the studio to see what all the fuss was about, something to make her understand her owner was in jeopardy?

After all, Akitas are reputed not only to be loyal and courageous but to have astonishing powers of reasoning as well. In fact, those very characteristics, one owner had told the *Times,* had enabled his Akita to save his life. The dog had wisely neglected to alert him to a crime in progress the night thieves stole his Lincoln from his driveway. "He didn't want to see me come running out of the house in my underwear and into a dangerous situation," the proud owner said. "And, besides, I didn't really like that car anyway."

Sometimes what seems like a clever ploy on the part of a dog is merely a case of an owner who loves his dog, as many of us do, beyond all reason, and the ability of the human half of the partnership to tell a good story, saving face not for oneself but for one's dog.

Talk about stories, how about the O. J. Simpson case? Here again an Akita was present during the commission of a crime, the double murder that captured the attention of the entire nation. In Simpson's first trial, the dog was part of the case. Since she had been found afterward, wandering the streets wailing, the prosecution attempted to use her cries to establish the time of the killings.

Akita lovers could not understand why Satchmo, formerly Kato, hadn't protected Nicole Brown and her friend Ron Goldman. But if they secretly doubted her courage, no one could doubt the dog's loyalty. There had been blood on her legs and paws when she'd been found, and on her undercoat as well, as if she had in her grief lain down beside her beloved mistress's body.

Days after the crime, the dog's behavior became an issue again. When Simpson returned to Rockingham after the much-televised slow-speed chase, the bitch had cowered as Simpson stepped out of the Bronco. Some thought that was an accusation, the dog's way of telling what she knew. Some people even suggested the big dog take the stand.

But why had the dog failed to protect the victims?

She had the motive—she clearly loved her mistress. She had the means, didn't she? She was a powerful animal with big teeth. And as far as anyone knew, she had the opportunity. She was out, not locked up in the house.

But the man accused of the double murder had been powerful, too. And he had a knife. In next to no time he slaughtered not one young, healthy person but two, nearly decapitating one of them, the woman with whom he was obsessed, the woman who thought, for one heady moment, that she had finally broken free of him.

Any dog worth its feed would know its owner's feelings toward another person, would feel the fear. Moreover, if accusations and suppositions were correct, in line with the second trial rather than the first, the killer had not been a stranger to the dog, someone to back down, an enemy to be dispatched without hesitation. Just a short while before, he had been the dog's master. So long before the night of the murder, she had seen him enraged, perhaps starting when she'd been a pup and no one had remembered to take her out on time. She'd been there when Nicole was beaten. Perhaps she'd been beaten, too. If Akitas were half as smart as their owners claim, perhaps she kept away to protect *herself*.

Two cases in which an Akita failed to stop a crime. Yet in both instances, the Akita people could only sing praises for the breed that bores so deeply into the human heart that all the dogs have to do to win the boundless love of their people is be themselves. And this the Akita can do with remarkable self-assurance.

Now there was a third case involving an Akita. Hadn't Lisa's dog been present when her owner had been murdered? Had the dog been complacent because she knew the killer? Someone who had the keys.

Be not afraid.

Had Lisa been writing when the killer arrived?

I'm sorry. Lisa. Not a suicide note.

Was it an apology to someone whose feelings she was about to hurt? Someone who was coming to hear the news of her departure? She'd told Avi she wanted to tell the others herself. One at a time. Had one of them been here?

If so, which one?

As of now, only the killer was privy to that information. And once again, the Akita knew. But sadly, she had no way of telling the rest of us the answer we so desperately sought.

27

His Eyes Were
Pinched and Small

WHEN I GOT back to school, he was sitting on one of the couches, his eyebrows pitched with worry. Ch'an didn't greet him. Instead, she quickly disappeared into the office. I heard her at her water bowl, heard her lie down with a sigh.

"I'm s-sorry about yesterday," he said. "Really s-sorry. I j-just forg-g-got about your—"

"Bullshit," I said, taking a seat across from him. "I've had enough lies, and I'm ready for the truth now. The appointment was in your book, your book was open, you didn't forget. And you didn't go shopping for Mother Teresa either. So where were you?"

He had his mother's eyes, washed out and saggy, and her fleshy cheeks, already losing their battle with gravity. They were trembling now, as if he were frightened. Good, I thought, exactly the effect I'd been looking for.

"I f-forgot," he said, petulant as a child. "Is th-that a c-crime?" His eyes were pinched and small, like a pig's.

"It's not a crime. It's a lie."

"What m-makes you—"

"You can tell me, Howie," I said, my voice now soft and nurturing, the voice he'd never heard at home. I didn't live that far away from the HB Acting Studio myself.

I pushed the t'ai chi magazines aside and put the bag of food on the low table between us, opening the bag and taking out the juicy hamburgers and fries, then the sodas, and putting one portion in front of Howie.

"You can tell me anything. You know you can. What happened yesterday?"

"I w-went for a walk. And I l-lost track of time. Th-that's all."

"Doesn't sound right to me, Howie. I'm trying to believe you. Honestly, I am. Hell, I *want* to believe you. But it just doesn't come together for me, Howie. It doesn't jive, does it, that you lost track of time and missed *two* appointments. Doesn't sound like you, Howie, a responsible man who cares for his mother in her old age."

Howie, who'd talked to me about a low-fat diet, always a dead giveaway, eyed his burger like a hungry wolf.

"Howie, you know you'll feel better if you're honest, if you tell me."

"It was my m-mother," he shouted. "Ha-happy now?"

And then it happened, the tears, first one, rolling down his doughy cheek, then a double. Thin-skinned, she'd said. Mother knows best.

"She was after me a-a-again."

"About money?"

"About everything, how inadequate I am, how insufficient a human being I t-turned out to be, how I d-d-disappoint her, in every way. 'You have a f-fine

mind, Howie,' she said yesterday. That's how it started.
She was st-standing in the doorway of my office with a
ci-ci-cigarette even though I told her not to smoke there
because it's not fair to the pa-patients. 'You have a fine
m-mind, Howie,' she said, 'so how come you n-never
use it?' That's what I li-live with, Rachel, and sometimes, every once in a while, I can't st-st-st take it, and I
just have to get away from her. But I am so sorry that I
had you come for no-nothing. There's no excuse for me
not calling you. None wh-whatsoever."

"It's no big thing, Howie."

"But it is. You're being so k-kind to me, and I *lied* to
you," he said, picking up his napkin and starting to
shred it.

"About forgetting the appointment? Forget it,
Howie. It's no big thing." I took a bite of my hamburger and salted my fries. Like an Akita, I knew how
to pay attention without seeming to do so.

"No. About Lisa. About, you know, us n-not having
a relationship." He opened one of the sodas and drank
as if he were at the twenty-mile marker of a marathon.

"You had a relationship?" I asked, incredulous, but
using the same neutral look I'd used as a dog trainer
when someone told me about the "little game" they
played with their dog that had "gone wrong." "You
were lovers?" I asked, as if it were the only obvious
conclusion an intelligent observer could draw, as if I'd
known it all along.

"No. N-not l-l-like that," he said, his neck all red and
splotchy, color flaring in his cheeks and chin. "We were
friends."

"Friends? Your mother said Lisa was going to *fire*
you."

Howie looked down at his shoes.

"Talk to me, Howie. The bitch was going to fire you. That's what your mother told me. So you tell me, Howie, what kind of a person fires a friend?"

"That's not what happened," he said, looking sadly at his hamburger, as if he thought I'd take it away once he spoke.

"That's what your mother said happened. Why did she tell me that, Howie? What's going on here?"

"Sh-she was m-misinformed," he said.

"Yeah? By whom?"

"She saw me," he wiped at his eyes with his hand, "crying," he said, almost inaudibly. "I mean, she heard me, pushed into my room, the way she always d-does, put on the light, almost blinding me, stood there making f-fun of me, why was I crying, what the hell was wrong with me, like she always does. I couldn't tell her the truth, so I told her, you know, what she told you, that L-Lisa said she'd fire me."

"You must have been pretty mad at Lisa to say that, Howie."

"No, I—"

"I guess, given the circumstances, anyone would be upset. Here you thought you had a true friend, and she was going to desert you, wasn't she?"

Howie shrugged.

"You told Lisa everything, Howie, didn't you? Then you can talk to me, Howie. I'm her cousin. Howie?"

"I guess," he said. Four years old.

"So you were crying because Lisa was going away?"

Howie nodded.

"And when your mother got after you, you gave her a good reason for the tears, one that would shut her up."

He nodded again. "She didn't know about Lisa and

me being friends. She wouldn't have much liked it, so I never told her."

"What would her objection have been?"

"She says I don't do enough for *her*," he said. "She doesn't want me wasting my time on other people when my own mother is sitting alone all day, rotting out, as if she didn't have a son to take care of her in her old age. She's not even that *old*," he said. "People still work, they live alone, at her age."

"Oh, Howie. No son could do more than you do."

He looked surprised, then pleased. "You look so much like her," he said, "it's almost like she's s-sitting here with me."

"Lisa?"

He nodded.

"I used to talk to her here, just like this." Howie ate some fries, then picked up his hamburger and just held it in his hand.

"When no one else was around?"

He nodded.

"Yeah. Lisa worked late a lot. Sometimes I'd come over and help her out, and then she'd let me"—he stopped and looked around—"unload. That's what she used to say to me, Rachel. Howie, you're carrying a building on your shoulders, you need to unload. Sit here and tell me your troubles." The tears began in earnest, but Howie didn't seem to notice. "When I'd talk to Lisa about my mother, it wouldn't seem so b-bad. She'd tell me, like you did, how good I was to take care of her, and I'd feel better, feel I could d-do it. But now, now with Lisa gone, sometimes I can't stand it, and I don't know what to do. There's no one else to d-do it but me. What choice do I have? And I do it, I do the best I can, but nothing s-satisfies her. The b-b-bitch won't let me breathe, she's on me day and night."

"How'd you get stuck with her, Howie? What happened to your father? Where's he?"

Howie stood so quickly, the couch moved back and hit the wall with a thud. His eyes were burning holes in me, his face a tapestry of rage.

I heard another noise, coming from the direction of Avi's office.

Then Howie began to come around the table toward me.

Ch'an came slowly toward us, her head down, her small, triangular ears alert, staring at Howie.

"Sit down, Howie," I whispered. *"Now."*

Howie sat trembling on the couch, unable to take his eyes off the Akita.

"N-never l-liked me," he said.

Did he mean Ch'an? Or his father?

Ch'an lifted her nose in the air, then headed straight for the hamburger in Howie's hand.

"Tell me about it," I said, breaking off a piece of my burger, taking a bite, and offering the rest to Ch'an. For a moment, my whole hand disappeared into her mouth, but she took the food gently, releasing my hand unharmed. "Come on, Howie, talk to me. You know you want to."

He took a wad of tissues out of his pocket and wiped his eyes. "He left when I was s-seven. Just w-walked out."

"And you never saw him again?"

Howie flushed.

"Did you ever see him again after that, Howie?"

"Once," he said. "He came b-back a year later, just showed up at the d-door. 'Tell your m-mother I'm here, son,' he said. So I left him there, in the doorway, and went to tell my m-mother. She said, 'You go tell that b-bum we're not interested. Tell him to go away and this time, don't come b-back.' "

"And what did you do?"

"What she said. I always do what sh-she says," he shouted at me. "You met her!"

"So you did what she said?"

"I d-did. I told him to go away. And not come b-back. Only now," he said, tears falling from his bas- set hound eyes, "now she says to me, 'Who's to take care of me but you, Howie? You're all I've got, son. Thanks to you!' "

I was going to ask why his sister wasn't sharing the responsibility of taking care of Dora. But hadn't I been too busy with work when my own mother had needed care? Doesn't the burden of a sick or aging parent often, for one reason or another, fall to one person in- stead of being shared?

"Then yesterday," Howie shouted, before I had the chance to ask him anything, "I couldn't take it any- more. It was too much pressure. I ran out of the house. I didn't even take my jacket. I walked all the way up to Forty-eighth Street before I noticed where I was. I went into some bar, a real dive, McCann's or McKay's, and sat there drinking beer until it was dark out. Then I felt so bad, I walked over to the Winter Garden and got tickets to *Cats*. She loves that show, my mother. She's seen it three t-times already. No, that's another lie. I got the tickets not to please her, but so that I could get into my own fucking apartment without her savaging me all night. I got the tickets to *shut her up,* and now I have to see fucking *Cats* again." He reached into his back pocket, took out his wallet, and held out the tickets for me to see. Two balcony tickets for *Cats*. "The old b-bat won't walk a step outside alone, even though the doctor says there's no reason on earth for her to stay inside the way she does. She says she's afraid, unless I'm with her. I bought her a d-damn walker, to steady her. But does she ever use it? No, she d-doesn't. She waits for me. I'm not a nice person, Rachel, you can see that. She's right about that. Only Lisa, she didn't care about the horrible stuff I said. She l-liked me anyway. I used to c-confide in her, tell her things I couldn't tell anyone else. I n-never had a f-friend like L-Lisa. I probably n-never will again."

"Of course you will," I said, reaching over and stroking his hand. "Anyone would be lucky to have you for a friend, Howie."

"Do you really think so?" he asked. Looking at nothing in particular, he began ferrying pickle chips and cold fries into his mouth, one after the other. I doubt he would have noticed if the place caught on fire. I watched his big, strong hands, delicately lifting each morsel and moving slowly and steadily between the paper plate and his mouth, as if he were performing a religious ritual.

"Howie," I said, after he'd finished the last of his food, "what did you make of the note Lisa left? The suicide note?"

"At first I thought she'd written it to me, because of the way I cried when she told me she was leaving." Howie took the wet tissues and blew his red nose. "But I know that's stupid." He ran his finger across his empty plate and licked it off. "It couldn't have been to me," he said softly.

"Why not?"

"Because I'm not that important to anyone," he said. He took a swig of soda and just looked down into his lap for a moment. "Except, of course, my mother."

28

I Tried to Imagine It

I COULD HEAR the music out on the street, the pounding beat that apparently helped people do enough reps to tear their muscle tissue so that, during the repair process, the muscle would grow larger. I could see Janet through the window, doing her own workout, her mouth twisted in agony as she hoisted her own weight with the strength of only one arm. I stopped at the desk and asked for her, and the guardian of the lobby, a budding bodybuilder who introduced himself as Skip, told me to wait while he went to find her. Perfect, I thought, because what I was after was not Janet. It was her appointment schedule.

As soon as the door to the gym closed, I leaned over the desk and did some hoisting of my own. I hoisted the trainers' schedules, kept in a three-ring binder, turning to yesterday and checking Janet's appointments between four and six. According to the book, Janet had been working when Paul was killed. I wrote down the names of her clients—Barb Lefrack at four, Sandy

Stiller at five, Mike Farley at six. Each name had a phone number beneath it, in case the trainer needed to cancel or reschedule. I copied those down, too.

When I'd come for my session, Janet had been busy on the phone. That's how I'd led three lives for ten minutes, one as myself, Rachel Alexander, private investigator, a second as Lisa Jacob's smart-mouthed cousin, and a third as Chippy the hamster, working out on the treadmill and hating it, thank you.

She could have easily disappeared while I was warming up, couldn't she? Suppose she'd had to answer a call of nature or run out and take care of some urgent business?

Paul had been killed only blocks away, and the murder itself probably took less than a minute, maybe a full minute if you left time for a quick "hi" before the deed got done and a hand slipping into his pocket to remove his cash afterward, so that the murder would look like a mugging that had gone too far.

Had the killer in fact approached from the front or the back? I couldn't recall Marty specifying that.

I tried to imagine it, a strong arm coming from behind, circling around the front, the other hand snapping the neck. I pictured his hands reaching up to pull the arm away, but it wouldn't have happened like that. There wouldn't have been time for Paul's face to register surprise. At least that was a merciful thought.

For a moment my mouth tasted sour, and I thought that one small piece of burger I'd eaten was coming back up my throat. Then young Skip returned to the desk, catching me with my nose in the appointment book.

"She's booked solid, huh?" I said, looking disappointed. "I was hoping she could squeeze me in."

"She said if you could wait," he said, turning the

book around so that it faced him, "her six canceled. But what she wanted to know was if you wanted to go get something to eat maybe, instead of working out?"

I looked at the clock on the wall behind him. It was only four forty-five.

"Great idea. Tell her I'll wait for her at her desk," I said, picking up a fitness magazine and looking toward the corner where Janet's desk sat, partly hidden behind a screen. From where I was standing, I could see Janet's chair, her jacket draped over the back.

"You got it," he said, heading back into the gym.

"Thanks," I said, hightailing it to the desk and picking Janet's jacket pocket before he could return to say, "She said, 'Cool.'" A moment later, Janet's keys in my hot little hand, I was at the front door before Skip had skipped back to the front desk to notice I had changed my mind. But when I opened the door, the buzzer sounded, and I heard him behind me.

"Aren't you staying?" he asked. "I told her you'd wait."

"I thought I'd take a walk. I'll be back by six."

He nodded and started fiddling with the tape deck, probably turning up the volume; there were still two or three people in the gym who hadn't suffered significant hearing loss from the music yet.

Janet lived on Grove Street. On the way there, I was hoping she didn't have a roommate.

She was on the top floor of what had once been a glorious town house, and now, like so many others, had been divided into small apartments and treated with not so benign neglect, inside and out.

Janet's apartment was in the rear. Keys in my hand, I knocked first, just in case, then waited and listened. I thought I heard something inside. I knocked again. This time I waited longer but heard nothing. I slipped the key into the lock and gave it a turn. Then what I saw gave me a turn.

Standing a few feet in front of me, square in the middle of a pretty, colorful handwoven carpet, her pretty, feminine head cocked to one side, her dark eyes curious and cautious, was a large white Akita.

I stood completely still. Even the sort of dog who wouldn't alert its owner when his Lincoln was being stolen might, at some given moment, feel it was her turn to save the day.

But once I'd had a moment to look at the Akita, I could see that she was just a big puppy, six or seven months old. She wagged her curled tail in slow motion, first to one side, sweeping over her back and leaning over her flank, and then, ever so slowly, to the other.

"Who's my good girl?" I said, kneeling down, arms to the side, my voice animated.

Head down, eyes squinchy, forehead wrinkled, the Akita came into my arms to be hugged. I confirmed her gender with one hand, using the other to scratch her neck. I kissed her small, triangular ears and read the tag on her collar, "Pola Bear." Then I checked my watch and got to work.

I started with Janet's desk, going through her receipts and bills, looking for something, I didn't know what. I didn't think Janet was sending those roses, but hey, this was the Village, anything was possible. Still, I didn't find receipts from a florist. Janet's receipts were all from the Foot Locker, Paragon Sporting Goods, or the Athletic Attic. But before I left the desk, I did find something interesting. Apparently Janet, like most other trainers, spread her services around in order to make more money. What I found was a 1099 from the Club. The world was rapidly becoming a smaller place.

I walked through Janet's apartment, looking at her

stuff. Stewie had said Janet lived in the gym, but her place was warm and homey, particularly for me, since it had the two things I needed to call a place home, a dog and plenty of sunlight. I looked in the closets and found exactly what I would have expected—workout clothes, running clothes, cross-trainers, running shoes, and sweats, nothing much in the way of taffeta dresses, no sexy lace teddies in the dresser drawers.

There was lots of food in the small kitchen, mostly gross-tasting stuff that was supposed to be good for you—millet, apricot butter, and tofu mayonnaise. There was a juicer on the counter, the same kind that Paul was using at the Club the first time I'd met him. Instead of finding parts of dead animals wrapped in aluminum foil in the freezer, I found a twenty-five-pound bag of organic carrots in the fridge, just waiting for the juicer to turn them into sludge.

I refilled Pola's water dish and gave her a couple of biscuits for being such a decent hostess, checked my watch, and quickly locked up and headed back to the gym to get Janet's keys back into her pocket before she noticed they were gone.

"Oops. She's still busy," Skip sang out as I passed the desk. "Someone came in for a makeup session. You got to squeeze those in," he said, rolling his eyes. "House rules. She said if you would stay, she would *treat* you to dinner, you know, for making you wait so long. Or you could work out meanwhile, if you want."

"I don't know."

"She said to tell you your abs needed work. And there wouldn't be no charge," he added in a stage whisper, even though no one else was within earshot.

"I'll leave her a note," I said. "I have to go home and walk my dog."

"Tell me about it," he said, rolling his eyes. "She's so

busy, busy, busy, but sometimes she's got to sneak out
and do the same thing. You gotta go, you gotta go, am I
right?"

I nodded.

"Too bad you can't stay. She'll be very disappointed," he said. "But even if you did, another person
might show up with an aerobic emergency, who knows,
right? She's very in demand," he whispered. "She's the
favorite. It's a lot of pressure on her."

Not as much pressure as *not* being the favorite, I
thought. I went back to Janet's desk to return her keys
and write her a little note, but when I slipped my hand
into her pocket, I felt something else, her wallet. I'd
been so anxious to get my hands on her keys, it hadn't
occurred to me the first time around that a wallet can
be rich with things other than money.

Don't stop digging until you know *for sure,* Frank
used to say when I'd come running to tell him I knew
who did it before I'd checked out everything.

But it's so *ob*vious, I'd said, two days into my second
case.

He'd looked down at his paperwork and smiled.
Ring a few doorbells, he told me. Ask a few questions.
Stick your hands in people's pockets. Snoop some
more, kid. *Then* come back and tell me who did it.

Who did it? he'd said, shaking his head. Who did it is
only the tip of the iceberg. You gotta know why. You
gotta know how. You gotta have proof, Rachel, he'd
said, because there's too many lawyers and not enough
people out there willing to serve time for killing them.
You get my meaning?

I had. So I angled myself away from the front desk
and slipped the wallet out of her pocket and onto my
lap. And in it, behind a picture of Pola, I found two
very surprising things.

I slid the wallet back into Janet's pocket, wrote her a note saying I'd see her on Monday, and rolled my sore shoulders a few times before heading home. Dashiell did need a walk. And I needed sleep. There was no way to fight the exhaustion any longer, and all I could think of all the way home was how safe and wonderful it would feel to get home, take off my clothes, floss, and crawl into bed with my dog.

As my eyes were closing, I thought I could smell those yellow roses, dying under the bushes, returning to the earth from whence they came, but it was probably just a trick of what my mother used to call my overactive imagination.

You ought to be a writer, she'd said once. Like your cousin Richie.

Yeah, right.

I closed my eyes and pictured the photos Ceil had shown me of Richie in drag. But then I was thinking of other pictures, the ones in Janet's wallet.

The first one behind the plastic window was Pola. She was lying on that handwoven carpet, a rawhide bone between her big white paws. She wasn't looking at the camera, the way Dashiell would have. She was looking off toward the windows, the sun filling her dark eyes with light.

Behind the picture of Pola, there was a photo of Lisa Jacobs, her curly hair loose about her face, her cheeks flushed, as if she'd just been running, or working out. She too was not looking at the camera. It looked as though she didn't know her picture was being taken. She was laughing, looking beautiful and full of life.

And behind the snapshot of Lisa, there was another familiar face. This picture wasn't a drugstore print. It had been cut from a magazine or glossy newsletter, the kind a gym might send to prospective members to entice them to join up.

His dark hair was wet and spiky. He was smiling. Thinking about him now, I could almost smell the faint odor of chlorine that used to linger in his hair and on his skin.

I buried my face in Dashiell's neck and, for the longest time, tried in vain to sleep.

29

Feeling As If My Heart
Were Breaking

EVEN THE SUNLIGHT slipping between the slats of
the shutters didn't wake me until two in the afternoon.
Feeling drugged instead of rested, I got dressed in whatever of Lisa's I found thrown on the rocking chair and
headed over to the waterfront.

I passed the Christopher Street pier where there were
dogs playing *hey, it's spring, let's chase the bitch and
maybe we'll get lucky* and where some of the most
gorgeous guys in the world were catching rays on the
narrow strip of pier beyond the fencing, some of them
naked, all of them gay, and headed south to the deserted Morton Street pier, where I could be alone and
think.

The Morton Street pier was in such disrepair that it
had been fenced off to keep people from using it. But
this was New York, so there was a place where the
chain link had been cut. I held it open for Dashiell,
stepping through the opening and walking down
toward the end of the pier. Standing there, watching the

Hudson flow south toward the Atlantic Ocean, I thought about Paul Wilcox and played with the silver bracelet he'd sent to Lisa after they'd broken up.

Be My Love.

Or had he?

Wasn't the lovesick stalker someone else? And whoever it had been, sending presents and posies and watching her window, wasn't he now watching me? After all, the last bouquet had been left not at Lisa's but in the gate on Tenth Street, where no one was supposed to know I lived. And wasn't Paul killed after I'd been seeing him?

I turned north and breathed in the fishy air that wafted over the Hudson and across the old pier, then began the form. Dashiell, who had been scrutinizing the weeds that grew between the broken paving stones that covered the pier, came close and sat.

When my hands formed the Tiger's Eyes, once again I felt the presence of something I needed to remember but couldn't grasp. Twice I backed up and started again, but still, nothing.

Still tired, and feeling as if my heart were breaking, I climbed back through the space in the fence, held it for Dashiell, and together we headed home.

30

And Then It Came to Me

SUNDAY NIGHT DASHIELL and I slept for twelve hours, waking up with barely enough time to get to the noon class at Bank Street T'ai Chi, a class I couldn't afford to miss because I had plans other than practicing the form.

Class had already started. Stewie's jacket was tossed over the back of one of the couches. You know, I thought to myself, throw your jacket around like that instead of hanging it up and your damn wallet could fall out of your pocket.

Or worse, your keys.

So I picked up Lisa's black practice shoes and sat on the couch next to Stewie's jacket to change my shoes, sliding my hand into the pocket, hooking his key ring on one finger, and slipping the keys into my pocket before I got up. Then I went to join the class in progress.

Moving slowly, as if in water, rooted to the ground, as if I were the great oak that stretched its arms heavenward from its place in the center of my garden, thinking now of nothing but what I was doing at the moment, I stepped into Single Whip and, following Stewie's lead and direction, continued along with the rest of the students.

Janet was there. After Stewie spoke, she took over, asking us all to stop so that she and Stewie could come around and make corrections. We froze, waiting, our legs burning, and after each of us had been checked, we continued with the form. We moved backward, doing Repulse the Monkey. We walked sideways, doing Cloud Hands. We opened our hips to do Fair Lady Weaves at the Shuttle. We stepped forward, folding our wrists before our chests, our hands closing into loose fists, the Tiger's Eyes.

Suddenly I was not seeing the polished studio floor beneath the circles formed by my hands, I was seeing Dashiell, days earlier, lying at the base of the oak tree, giving his full attention to the ground beneath his paws. I froze in place, my mind spinning, struggling again for whatever was just beneath my consciousness, looking through the Tiger's Eyes at the ground beneath me, giving it my full attention, as Dashiell had.

And then it came to me.

And when it did, it seemed so obvious, I couldn't believe I hadn't thought of it before.

After class Janet invited me to come to sword class at seven. I told her yes, I'd come. I thanked her, nodded to Stewie, changed shoes, signaled to Dashiell, and, feeling Stewie's keys in my jacket pocket, headed out the door.

I went first to the Sixth, asking for Marty at the desk.

"What's up, kid? You think of something?"

"Sort of. Marty, can I see the photos of Lisa Jacobs?"

Marty raised his eyebrows. "At the scene?" he asked.

I nodded.

He looked at me for a moment without saying anything, then told me to follow him. We passed the maps in back, near the arrest processing room. One had the locations of robberies, each marked with a pushpin. These fanned out all over the Village. The second map was for narcotics arrests. All those pushpins, sixty or seventy of them, were jammed into one small space, Washington Square Park.

I followed Marty up the stairs to the detectives' squad room, where he sat me down at one of the empty desks. Two detectives were working at desks over near the windows, and Marty went over to talk to one of them. I saw him hook his thumb in my direction twice, and when the detective he was talking to leaned back so that he could look past Marty and see me, I decided to skip being a wiseass and just looked away instead. When Marty came back, he had a folder in his hand.

"Is this going to jog your memory, so you'll have something to share with us?" he asked, just a tinge of sarcasm in his voice.

"It might," I said. "I had a thought this morning."

"Congratulations," he said.

The other detective—mid-thirties, thin, red hair, freckles—was doing the looking now.

"Well, more of a question than a thought," I said, deciding to ignore both Howdy Doody and Marty's tone. "I need to see the photos of Lisa. Okay?"

"Since you're in the middle of this now, and you're doing this to help out, as any good citizen would, why not?"

He laid the file on the desk and opened it. I leaned over the desk, took a good look, and winced. At first glance, except for the odd position of her legs and the fact that she was lying on the sidewalk and not in bed, Lisa Jacobs might have been asleep.

But of course, she was not asleep. A small dark stain had seeped out on one side of her head. The way her hair fanned out, you could hardly see it.

Her arms looked relaxed. One hand, as Avi had mentioned, was turned up toward the sky, as if to see if it were raining. The other arm lay still, palm down, across her chest, as if she were thinking of turning over.

She'd been wearing black leggings and a plain black sweater. You could see an inch of her white socks at her ankles. And beneath that, what I came to find out—whether or not she was wearing shoes. And she was—soft, low black suede oxfords with a leather sole, the sort of shoe Lisa Jacobs never would have worn walking, or running, across the pristine floor of the t'ai chi studio.

Unless, perhaps, there were some emergency, some reason to get to the window as fast as she could, without a thought to anything else, even a custom she had abided by faithfully for all the years she'd worked at Bank Street T'ai Chi.

"Lisa never would have walked across the studio with her street shoes on," I said to Marty.

"Rachel," he said, as patient as if I were more than a little bit slow, "when someone decides to end it all, they don't care about shit like that. You wanna tell me she was religiously neat, too, she never would have littered Bank Street? You're grasping at straws here. None of the rules count at this stage of the game," he said, pointing to the picture of Lisa dead on the sidewalk beneath where she'd taught and studied.

But I thought the rules you lived by *did* count up until the end. People folded their clothes neatly before a suicide. Or carefully buttoned up their uniforms and made sure their shoes were shined before eating their guns. What was the point of living your life with certain standards if you were just going to abandon them all at the last minute? And anyway, whether Marty believed it or not, I was still sure Lisa's death hadn't been a suicide, any more than Paul's had happened during a random mugging.

I took one last look and closed the folder, turning my attention to the big windows that looked out over Tenth Street. Had I walked over to them and looked out, I would have seen the wrought-iron gate that led to my garden, just across the street and a few doors west of the precinct.

"Is that it?"

I nodded. "I thought—"

"Suppose someone killed her," he said, his voice low, his back turned to the detectives so that neither of them would hear what he was about to say.

"Okay," I told him. On second thought, I might not have been able to see my gate, had I walked over to the windows. The precinct had moved here from Charles Street in the late sixties, and it appeared that no one had had the time to get the windows washed since then. They were practically opaque.

"Might you then suppose the ex-boyfriend, Wilcox, was killed by the same individual, not by a mugger?"

"I might," I said, turning back toward Marty.

"And is there any particular individual you have in mind? Is there someone you suppose it might be, or haven't you gotten that far yet?" Sounding just like my brother-in-law, the *mamzer*.

"Look," I said, but Marty held up a hand to stop me.

"In order to make an arrest," he said, "we need more than suppositions. We need—"

"Yeah," I told him. "I get it. Evidence. Not hunches. Something concrete, airtight. A bloody glove. Particularly helpful if it actually fits the suspect. Bloody footprints leading away from the scene, preferably right to the suspect's house. Or a signed confession. Something of that sort."

"We don't need a signed confession. It could be videotaped. That would be acceptable, too."

Okay, I thought, so we were both having a bad day. It happens. "I'll get back to you," I said.

"You do that," he told me.

How much pressure was the precinct under, I wondered, with an unsolved murder in the area? Like Marty really wanted to up it to two, go tell the detectives they'd made a little mistake about Lisa Jacobs's death, tell the press, inform her parents. That sure sounded like a half an hour alone with a box of Twinkies and a quart of chocolate milk.

"Look, I know you're busy. Thanks a million for showing me the photos."

"No problem, kid," he said. "Sorry I jumped all over you."

I shrugged my shoulders to tell him it was no big deal, water off a Labrador retriever's back. He picked up the folder and turned to go.

I almost stopped him, but decided against it. He was right. I didn't have evidence. I only had a hunch. And the terrible feeling that time was running out.

31

He Couldn't Get In,
Could He?

I GOT TO Stewie's apartment much later than I'd hoped I would, wondering as I knocked and waited exactly how early he left work. The welfare system was corrupt on both sides: people who should have been taxpaying, productive citizens getting checks, sometimes in more than one location, and employees signing out to the field and going to the Bronx Zoo, teaching t'ai chi, or merely going home.

Someone was playing with me now, letting me know he knew where I really lived, sending me flowers, calling up to see if I was home. I had to move fast, I thought, slipping the first of three keys into the first of the three locks on Stewie Fleck's apartment door, because whoever had killed Lisa and Paul was clearly playing for keeps, and it wouldn't take a genius to guess who might be next on his list.

I opened the door and quickly followed Dashiell in, closing the door behind us and locking the middle of the three Medeco locks. Then I waited, letting my eyes acclimate to the dark before feeling around for the light switch.

Stewie's studio apartment was on the first floor in the rear of a six-story tenement building on Bedford Street, a block and a half from Chumley's, where we'd had a couple of beers while he'd told me the story of how he found t'ai chi. Stewie was apparently one of those people who straightened up but didn't clean, as in, "I'll straighten up the bathroom." Whose husband hasn't said that? But there was no exasperated wife in Stewie Fleck's life to utter sarcastic epithets under her breath while handing him the Comet, Fantastic, Soft Scrub, and toilet brush. Everything was in order and covered with dust, to say the least.

Stewie didn't have a desk in the small room. There was a Murphy bed, and it was closed, locked up against the wall. There was a small Formica table with wrought-iron legs and one chair near the pint-size kitchen appliances in what was called a Pullman kitchen, maybe because it could fit in one of those miniature rooms you could get on a train. Stewie's breakfast coffee cup was in the sink, but the rest of the dishes were in the drainer. I'm sure if Beatrice were here she'd rewash them, but I had more urgent things to do.

It was after four, and Stewie could be home at any moment. I was hoping not to be here when he discovered his keys were missing, just in case the super had a set for emergencies such as this one.

I poked through Stewie's closet, checking out his inexpensive and tasteless wardrobe, finding nothing but small change and used tissues in his linty pockets. I looked at the vegetables in his refrigerator, feeling that sour taste in my throat as I did. Perhaps I should have left the Fantastic out, to give him a hint, but there probably wasn't any. Maybe it was made with animal products and he couldn't use it, for political or moral reasons.

I looked through a pile of magazines on the floor near Stewie's ratty couch, wondering why *he* wasn't on the dole. Surely he lived as if he were hovering at the poverty line. But the magazines were expensive ones, all photography journals, and his books were mostly photography books. The expensive Nikon' I'd seen at t'ai chi school was nowhere around. Maybe, like Diane Arbus, he liked to photograph life's losers, so he took it to work with him. Maybe not. I wondered now if the wonderful photos I'd seen of Lisa had been his, or the one of Howie doing t'ai chi. No way those were drugstore prints. Anyone who did work like that had to have a darkroom, but dark as the apartment was, he wasn't using the kitchen. There were no chemicals under the sink, no stores of paper, no enlarger in the small closet. And even if Stewie could have made do in the tiny bathroom, covering the window with thick black paper and laying a board over the tub to have a surface for the chemical baths and enlarger, still, the equipment just wasn't there.

I went back to the books. Sure enough, several were about developing and printing black-and-white film. I looked around again to see if I had missed a place where Stewie could have stashed an enlarger, trays, and chemicals, but the place was small, and the storage practically nil.

I can't recall who started sneezing first, me or Dashiell, but once I started, I kept going until there were tears coming out of my eyes.

I never heard the first few pops. I was probably still sneezing. By the time I realized what was happening, there were tissues everywhere. Like an idiot, I began to pick them up before separating Dashiell from the box, but no matter, he'd destroyed it already. One side had been mashed down by his big paw to anchor the box so that he could pull the tissues out. Now he was shaking the empty box violently from side to side, having the time of his life. I'd have no choice but to take the thing with me, ditch it in a garbage can on the street, and let Stewie figure he forgot he used his last Kleenex.

That's when I heard it, the ping of something metallic and small hitting the dull parquet floor.

"Take it," I told him, not seeing what it was, a coin perhaps. Or the rabies tag falling off his collar. I knew I had to find out what it was before leaving.

Dashiell's mouth was right on the floor for a moment, which meant he was scooping something up with his tongue, something too small to get his teeth around. Then I heard it against his teeth as he chewed on it, trying to determine if luck were on his side and he'd picked up something edible, because don't all dogs believe in their hearts that they aren't fed nearly often enough?

I called him over, whispering in case someone were in the hall. It was a quarter to five now, time to get out of here.

I heard someone outside and froze in place. Dashiell was approaching me, and the sound of his nails click-clacking on the wooden floor seemed as loud as hail-stones on the roof of a car. I signaled him to lie down by raising my arm over my head, then crept up to him and cupped my hand under his jaw.

"Out," I whispered, hearing the footsteps in the hall stop just outside Stewie Fleck's door.

But he couldn't get in, could he?

Unless the super had his keys.

Or he had an extra set over the jamb or under his ratty welcome mat.

Could he see light coming from under the door?

Crouched next to Dashiell, whose breathing seemed as loud as a respirator, I looked down into my hand at the saliva-covered key Dashiell had dropped there. It must have fallen out of the tissue box as he was annihilating it.

When the doorknob turned and rattled, my heart jumped, and while I was nowhere near as paranoid as Stewie, having only one lock on my cottage door, I was grateful I'd been paranoid enough to lock Stewie's door behind me.

He rattled the knob again, which was about as effective as kicking the flat tire you found on your car. I heard his footsteps as he walked away, then the click of the front door closing.

I opened my hand again and looked at the key that Stewie had hidden in his own home. What did he think, that just because he lived in New York City someone would break in and paw through all his worldly possessions?

I stuffed the torn tissue box and all the tissues into a dog pickup bag, waited an extra minute, heart still pounding, shut off the light, and let Dashiell into the hall, slipping out after him and locking all three locks, the key Dashiell had found in my other sweating hand. Then I looked for the stairs, because his darkroom would be in the basement, wouldn't it?

We didn't meet anyone downstairs. The building probably only had a part-time super. I tried to keep my eyes up; this was water bug territory if ever I'd seen it, and while I'd face a snarling dog or walk into a lion's den, so to speak, bugs were a horse of another color.

There were eight doors in the basement, all but one locked. I dumped the remains of Stewie's tissue box in the compactor room and went back to try the key Dashiell had found in each of the other locks, hoping one was a utility closet, with water, that Stewie used as a darkroom. At the fifth door the key moved and the tumbler turned over. I felt my heart start to pound again.

I found a light switch on the left, and as soon as the light went on, I inhaled hard enough to pull the whole room down into my lungs. There on the wall, over the sink and shelf full of trays for chemicals, and hanging on a wire, pinned up to dry, looking eerie in the glow of the red safety light, were photos of *me*.

Dashiell and I squeezed into the small room and, not knowing how Stewie would react to having lost his keys, or how soon after the locksmith let him in he'd notice his tissue box was missing, I locked this door behind me too.

Dashiell sat, and I began to look at the photos, one hand leaning on the counter for support.

I had been captured doing t'ai chi on the Morton Street pier, then holding the fence open for Dashiell as we were leaving.

There was a shot of me walking on Hudson Street, Dashiell heeling at my side. And several shots of me entering and leaving Lisa's building, even one of me looking out the window, at night. It seemed Stewie had more than just a Nikon with a telephoto lens.

There were close-ups, too. And shots at the dog run, most of me practicing the form, but some of me sitting on the bench and watching the dogs play. And one of me holding someone's cute Jack Russell puppy on my lap. There were even shots of Dashiell, but those were off on the little piece of wall to the right, opposite the side where Stewie kept his enlarger.

Then I noticed something else. The pictures of me all over the wall seemed to be tacked over other photos. In several places, I could see the edges of other pictures sticking out.

I leaned forward and pulled out some pushpins, carefully taking down a photo of me frozen in the middle of Cloud Hands, my arms moving from one side to the other in front of my chest, eyes on the horizon, knees bent, in Lisa's black leggings and sweater, her heart necklace dangling from around my neck. Under it, there was a similar photo. At first glance, it looked identical. But it wasn't.

There was a pull chain hanging down in the center of the tiny room. I gave it a tug and turned off the safety light. Then I leaned over the counter and looked at the picture again. Not me. It was Lisa.

I took out the rest of the tacks, exposing the prints underneath. There was Lisa dressed in black, doing Cloud Hands, wearing the same black shoes that I now practiced in, her hands moving like nimbi across the afternoon sky.

Under each picture of me, there was one of Lisa, sometimes two or three—Lisa walking in the Village, talking on the phone, walking her Akita, at her window late at night. Lisa, that little braid in her long curly hair, a smile on her pretty face, walking arm in arm with Paul. And in the pile of prints near the enlarger, me with Paul and Dashiell, and Paul leaving the Printing House alone.

The last two photos in the pile were pictures of me. In one I was leaving Lisa's building, Dash at my side, carrying a bunch of roses, twelve of them to be exact. And in the last, I was tossing those same roses into the trash basket on the corner. He must have used high-speed, professional film; every petal was in focus.

T'ai chi had certainly taught Stewie Fleck patience. No hunter had more successfully captured his prey.

I listened for a moment and, hearing nothing, opened the door and looked out into the dimly lit hallway. I shut the light, locked the door, and dropped the key in front of it, pushing it as close to the sill as possible with my foot. Then Dashiell and I moved quickly and quietly out of the basement and out of Stewie Fleck's building, blinking when we emerged into the comparatively fresh, clean, bright air of Bedford Street.

Unused to the light, I didn't see him leaning against the building, just to the side of the door, until he'd actually grabbed my arm.

32

"Rachel," He Said

"RACHEL," HE SAID, surprised, but not half as surprised as I was, "what are *you* doing here?"

He looked pleased, the fool.

"I came to see you," I said, "to see if you were here, you know, if you felt like a beer or something." God bless adrenaline. "I didn't even see you standing here. I must have passed right by you," I said, thinking no one, not even a vegetarian, could be stupid enough to believe *that* lie.

"I didn't see you either," he said, frowning. "I must have been looking the other way."

"So, how about it?"

Stewie looked lost in thought.

"A beer? My treat."

"A beer? Oh, no, I can't. I'm waiting for the locksmith. I lost my keys somewhere. I'm locked out."

"Bummer," I said, his keys as heavy as an anvil in my jacket pocket. Dashiell was sitting now, and I reached down to touch his head, for my own comfort as much as his.

"You're wearing it," Stewie said suddenly.

I looked at him and followed his eyes down to my wrist. Then I lifted my arm, as if I were about to do Push Hands, or defend myself from a blow, and Stewie's hand closed around the silver heart.

"It was Lisa's," I said.

"But I never saw her wear it," Stewie said.

"No," I told him, "I don't think she ever did. It was still in the little bag from Tiffany's, brand-new, not a scratch on it. It's so beautiful," I said, "such an extravagant gift. I thought someone should wear it."

Stewie beamed at me. "Yes," he said.

And that's when I thought of a Chinese proverb I'd found in one of Lisa's books. He who asks a question is a fool for five minutes; he who doesn't ask a question remains a fool forever.

So I asked.

"Did she write that note to you, Stewie?"

He dropped the heart and I dropped my arm, putting my hand back on Dashiell's head. Stewie took a step to the side, away from me. "What do you mean?"

"What happened, Stew? Did you tell her you loved her, that it was you sending the flowers, not Paul, that you'd sent the bracelet, hoping that since Paul was no longer in the picture—"

"No!"

"What did she say, Stewie? Did she laugh at you?"

"I don't know what you're talking about."

"I think you do, Stewie. I think you know exactly what I'm talking about."

"I don't. I don't know."

"There's something you want to tell me now, isn't there?"

"You're out of your mind," he said, a little on the loud side.

I felt Dashiell's head move. He was looking at Stew now, too.

"You don't know what you're saying. I never—"

But he didn't get the chance to finish, because that's when the locksmith arrived, and I wasn't sure if I should be annoyed or grateful, because it was pretty quiet on Bedford Street and Stewie Fleck was looking more than a little bit crazy.

"Mr. Fleck?" He was carrying a metal toolbox, and the patch on his navy blue work shirt said "Hudson Hardware."

"That's me," Stewie told him.

"Too bad we couldn't have that beer," I said. "I think we need to continue this."

But Stewie just turned, and he and the locksmith headed inside.

"Catch you later," I said. But the door had already closed, and at that point, I didn't know if Stewie Fleck would have heard me if it hadn't.

33

Better Safe Than Sorry

BACK AT MY cottage, sitting on the steps that led upstairs, just staring at the front door, I decided to add another lock or two. Better safe than sorry, as the condom ads say.

Not wanting to move, or unable to, I took the names and numbers I needed from my pocket and sent Dashiell for the cordless phone.

"Barb? Hi. This is Michelle, from the gym? Fine. Just great. Okay, I'm wondering if you can help me out here," I said, lowering my voice to a hoarse whisper. "Yeah. I spilled my Coke. . . . Right. She told me exactly the same thing. And I'm trying like hell to get off it, drink Water Joe instead, yeah, springwater with caffeine in it. Right. She told me that very same thing. Carrot juice. And make sure the carrots were grown without pesticides. So, Barb, here's the thing, I spilled my Coke on the appointment book, and we can't do Janet's check, so I'm calling to verify, it looks like your name here in the book, but I can't see if it's checked off or what, so did you make that training session with Janet last Friday? Four? Great. Thanks a bunch."

I dialed the next number.

"Sandy? Hi. This is Michelle from the gym. How are you? Yeah, me, too. Listen, Sandy, I wonder if you could help me out here. There's been a little mix-up at the gym. Well, the truth is, I spilled my coffee on the appointment book. Yeah. That's what *my* mother used to say, too. Anyway, we're doing payroll, you know, and I need to verify if you were in for your five o'clock with Janet on Friday, because the place where she'd check it off is like rotted out from the coffee. You were? Great. Oh? Oh? No, of course she'll still get paid. Twenty minutes late? Because she had to what? Oh, right. Take her puppy out. Tell me about it. Half the time she sends me. So was she like all sweaty when she came back? She likes to run with Pola, get her tired fast so she can get back to work. Yeah, right," I said. "No, no problem. We don't dock the trainers for lateness. Yeah, she is the best, isn't she?"

But, of course, she *could* have run home to walk the dog. Just because she had the opportunity to do the killing didn't mean she did it.

Did it?

And just because Howie had tickets to *Cats*, that didn't mean he bought them on Friday afternoon.

And just because Stewie Fleck was stalking Lisa—Jesus, and now me—that didn't mean *he* had killed Lisa and Paul.

Did it?

After all, hadn't O. J. Simpson stalked his wife? Yet at his first trial, he got off. Apparently those jurors didn't think there was much of a connection between stalking and murder. Even though lots of other people did.

And when push came to shove—and I had every intention of pushing and shoving Stewie Fleck again—wouldn't he vehemently claim that what he'd done had been perfectly harmless? Whom, after all, had he hurt, taking pictures and sending presents?

But just the thought of that revolting little creep watching me, photographing me, following me, made me feel sick.

When I checked my watch, I saw it was almost time to go. Sword class was at seven, and I had to get there before any of the others arrived.

Climbing the stairs, I couldn't see light coming out into the hall from an open door, nor could I hear anyone talking. There were no jackets hanging on the hooks in the hall, no street shoes in the little cubbies that, except during class, held people's t'ai chi shoes.

The door was locked. So far, so good. I opened it, turned on the lights, and, out of habit by now, changed to Lisa's black shoes. I went to see if Avi was in the office, because sometimes he'd be holed up in there with the door locked and the rest of the lights off. But not this evening.

I dropped Stewie's keys next to the couch where he had tossed his jacket before the lunchtime class and pushed them with my foot so that they were half under the couch and half sticking out. Then I sat on the floor against the wall with Dashiell at my side, wondering how a nice girl like Lisa got herself mixed up with so many people who had the motive, means, and opportunity to do her in, wondering which one had, wondering whether—no, not wondering, fairly sure that—whoever the killer was, was already looking hard in my direction. It was only a matter of time now until the cousin shtick was going to wear thin, thin enough to see through, if it hadn't already. At least one of them already knew where I lived.

Janet came first. I could hear her on the stairs. I could smell the organic chamomile and aloe shampoo I'd seen in her bathroom, and anyway, by now I knew her footfall. I heard her plunk down a heavy backpack and put one shoe up on the top of the shelves where the shoes were to unlace it, then the other, and then she walked into the studio and called Dashiell for a head scratch.

"Sorry you couldn't wait," she said. "I was going to treat you at Charlie Mom's again."

"Did you go already?" I asked.

"Uh-uh. Truth is, it would have been a bust anyway. People show up," she drawled, "they don't even call, and the policy is"—Janet sighed—"the policy is never to let a dime walk out the door. I might look elsewhere soon, you know."

"Where else have you worked?" I asked, pulling my socks up tight and smoothing my leggings over them.

"Oh, I was at the World Gym two years ago, and last year I worked on Christopher Street, where I am now, but I also taught classes at the Club, on Varick."

"Where Lisa's boyfriend worked?"

"I heard about that," she whispered. "It was on the news. Jesus," she said, shaking her head. "You know, when I moved here from Texas, everyone I met said the Village was the safest neighborhood in New York City. I don't know. What is this world coming to, you can't walk around the neighborhood anymore without getting killed? Is that hers, too?" she asked.

"Excuse me?"

"That silver bracelet you're wearing. Was that Lisa's, too?"

I picked up the heart and let it drop.

"Yeah. I found it with her stuff. But I don't think she ever wore it. It looks brand-new."

Janet held the heart and read it.

"I don't know why not. I sure would have. It's nice. Don't you think so?"

I nodded.

"I guess Paul got it for her," she said.

"I guess."

I watched the muscles in her cheeks jump.

"Are you staying for class?" she asked.

"I think I'll just watch. I don't think I'm ready for this."

"Sure you are. You can do it. You can do anything you set your mind to, don't you know that, woman?"

"I'm going to pass," I said.

Janet shrugged. "Suit yourself. But we can still have dinner if you want. Charlie Mom's, after class?"

"Sure. Sounds great."

Then she turned, because we heard someone on the stairs, someone walking slowly. "Howie," she called out.

"It's m-m-me," he answered.

A moment later Howie and Avi walked into the studio. Avi had a bag from Staples with him. Howie looked at me and smiled, then sat across from me. Avi put his package down on the couch and joined us all on the floor, sitting in a circle around Dashiell. Then three other advanced students arrived and greeted us, a really skinny guy with a ponytail like Avi's, a short, muscular black man whose biceps rivaled Janet's, and a woman of seventy or seventy-five, thin and lithe, there perhaps to prove the point that t'ai chi helps you to live longer.

Avi stood, and everyone went to the supply closet and got swords. I sat with Dashiell watching the ritual-ized movements, the sword as an extension of the hand, an extension of one's *chi*. And while I was watching, I heard Stewie Fleck on the stairs, heard the squeak of his sneakers, heard him changing his shoes, and then he was there, a few feet away, looking around the couch. I turned to watch the class, hearing the jingle of Stewie's keys being scooped up from the floor and dropped into his pants pocket, waited while he got his sword from the closet, then turned to look at him as he passed where I was sitting to join the class, making a point, it seemed to me, not to look at me.

But then he didn't join the class. He came back to where I was sitting and squatted, sitting on his haunches the way Avi always tells us to.

"I know what you did," he said, his eyes hard.

"And I know what *you* did," I said back to him.

He glared at me. "I don't have time for this now," he whispered, standing up quickly and going to join the class.

The moment class ended, Janet pulled on my sleeve and nodded toward the door. I changed my shoes, grabbed my jacket, and picked up Dashiell's leash. Out in the hall, I noticed a baseball cap hanging on one of the hooks, but Janet didn't take it, and now I wouldn't be there to see who would.

Good thinking, I told myself. Like it would be terrifically significant to see who took the cap, like it was even legal to live downtown and not have at least a few of them. Besides, no matter who owned this one, I already knew who stood across from Lisa's in the weeks before she died.

Walking over to Charlie Mom's, Janet was quiet.

"When did you get Pola?" I asked her, wanting to get something going.

She turned and looked at me.

"Skip," I said, watching her face harden. "He said

you sometimes had to run home to walk her. I was surprised you never mentioned her."

Janet shrugged. "I missed Ch'an. After Lisa"—she paused, as if looking for the right word—"well, Avi doesn't bring her in all that often. Not the way Lisa did. There's something about Akitas, I don't know, but I just missed being around one. I was able to find one, a female like Ch'an, only white, that a breeder in Jersey had held on to and then decided to sell. She's seven months old, a real peach of a dog. I've only had her since, well, just a few weeks. That's why I sometimes run out to give her an extra walk. She'd been a kennel dog, so I wasn't sure about her housebreaking, but she's doing real good, she's real clean in the house."

I nodded.

"They're pretty popular," I said, "Akitas."

Janet nodded.

"Paul said he liked them, too."

I felt her tense, the way I could always feel the tension surge in some male dogs when there was the perceived threat of another intact male approaching.

"So did you know him before Lisa?" I asked. "I mean, since you worked in the same gym with him. Or had Lisa met him before?"

"I introduced them."

Bummer, I thought.

"Lisa came over to train with me, and Paul came into the gym to ask me something, so I introduced them."

"And what? Rockets went off? Soft music started playing, you know, like in the movies, to indicate two people are falling in love?"

"Something like that," she said.

"Did they start dating right away, or what?"

"Lisa started swimming again."

"What do you mean?" As if I didn't know.

"She hadn't been swimming for a long time, except in the summer, when she'd visit her parents. And after she met Paul, she began swimming regularly again. He used to call her *xiao yue*."

We stopped on the corner, neither of us speaking as we waited for the light to turn green.

"It means *little fish*," she said as we crossed Seventh Avenue.

The waiter at Hunan Pan had looked away when he'd told me, not wanting to embarrass me by paying attention to how I might react. Such a nickname is given in great affection, he'd said, looking toward the other side of the restaurant, to family members.

"Did Lisa stop training with you after she met Paul?" I asked Janet when we'd reached the safety of the other side of the street. She didn't respond. "I don't guess she had the time to do both."

We'd arrived at the restaurant. Janet stopped and turned to face me. "You know, I'm going to beg off, Rachel. I wasn't thinking. It's late, and Pola's been alone all day. I'd feel like such a bitch, staying out even later. I'll catch you another night," she said and, not waiting for a response, turned and headed in the direction of home.

It was quiet for the Village. Even weekday nights, there are people everywhere, going to plays and clubs, going to or coming from restaurants, walking their dogs, or just hanging out at the coffee bars that have suddenly cropped up like weeds, one to a block. Some sit inside, reading the newspaper or a magazine. Others sit outside, on a bench, watching the passing parade, as if they were in Rome or Paris. But tonight was sort of peaceful, and Dashiell and I walked slowly, enjoying the quiet.

How should I feel, I wondered, about Paul using the same term of endearment for Lisa and me?

He'd loved her. That I knew. What harm would it cause to think the obvious, that in the short time I knew him, he had come to love me, too? What difference could it make anyway, I thought, now that he was dead?

Suddenly a hand grabbed my arm, and someone was in my face.

"You were seen," he said, his seething rage barely under control. "What the fuck is going on, that's what I want to know."

"You were seen, too, you little creep," I told him, turning slightly so that I all but disappeared. Stewie stumbled forward.

"What are you talking about?" he said, catching himself, trying to act as if nothing had happened.

"You were seen standing across from Lisa's every night, skulking around in the dark, staring at her window, watching to see who came and went," I said, stepping forward. "What the fuck was that all about?"

Stewie Fleck looked off to the side, took off his baseball cap, and smoothed his hair forward.

"I . . ."

"What? You what?"

I grabbed the front of his jacket and pulled him back toward me.

"Quit that," he said. "Get your hands off me *now*."

And with that, he pushed back. Hard.

As I caught my footing, I felt Dashiell brush my leg as he stepped between us. We both looked down at him, his tail, rigid now, level with his back, moving ever so slightly from side to side, just stirring the air. He was facing Stewie, who this time stepped back without being pushed.

"What were those pictures all about, pictures of Lisa, now pictures of me?" I said, my voice much too loud.

"You were in my darkroom?" he said, seething, but trying not to shout, trying not to inspire Dashiell to anything more than what he was doing, watching to see what would happen next, as if he had all the time in the world and absolutely nothing better to do.

"I was," I said. "So are you going to tell me what this is all about, Stewie? Or would you rather just cross the street"—I indicated the Sixth Precinct with a tilt of my head—"and tell them what the hell you had in mind when you decided to stalk Lisa? And Paul. Both of whom are dead."

"You bitch," he said, forgetting Dashiell and shoving me back.

Then several things happened nearly at once.

I heard Dashiell's growl as I caught myself, one foot behind me, and as Stewie Fleck slipped between two parked cars and ran for his life, crossing the street on an angle so that he'd get to the other side as far away from the police station as possible.

And Dashiell, never one for wasted action and clearly understanding that the shortest distance between him and Stewie Fleck was not around the car but over it, in one move landed on the roof of the Mercedes-Benz parked just to our left, setting off its alarm.

"Leave it," I told him.

So instead of leaping into the middle of the street and chasing down his prey, my designer wolf stayed just where he was, the car's horn blaring on and off, the headlights flashing, while across the street, heading for the corner, was Stewie Fleck, moving as fast as the designated dinner in the middle of a caribou hunt.

34

I Listened to the Dial Tone

INSIDE THE COTTAGE, Dashiell asleep on the couch, I could hear the car alarm, still going off. No matter that it was a few steps away from the Sixth Precinct, no one would do anything about it until the owner showed up. And that might not be until tomorrow.

I began to pace around. It was too noisy to sleep. Unless you were a pit bull. And I was too unhappy with the way my case was going to sleep, even if it had been quiet. The more I learned, the less I knew.

Talking it out sometimes helped, I thought as I picked up the phone. I was just thinking about you, she'd say. I listened to the dial tone, but I never dialed. What had I been thinking? I had so successfully filled myself up with Lisa Jacobs that I had all but forgotten about Lili and Ted. For just a moment I thought about him, my brother-in-law, kissing the blond, and then I consciously withdrew myself from the problem. It was theirs to solve. I didn't call. Instead, I closed my eyes and pictured the bouquets of roses that Lisa had hung over her dining room table. I thought about the sound of her earrings, the smell of her perfume, the soft feel of her sheets, and the gentle touch of her lover, when he became my lover. And I put down the phone, because I was back where I belonged.

Avi had been telling me to rely on myself. That was exactly what I needed to do. Leaving Dashiell sleeping on the couch, I grabbed Lisa's jacket and headed for someplace where I could be alone and think, someplace far away from the noise of the car alarm.

Walking toward the waterfront, I began to think about how weird it was that nearly everyone in Lisa's life had a motive to kill her. It was more like a made-for-television movie or a novel than real life.

Real life, it's the husband, the boyfriend, the business partner, ba-da-boom, the cops go after one person, the schmuck usually ignores the Miranda warning, places himself at the scene, changes his story five times, then confesses.

Or no one seems to be guilty. The person was wonderful, his friends were wonderful, everything was wonderful. Until you start to turn over the rocks and watch the worms crawl out.

This case was driving me crazy. There was no one I *didn't* suspect. Maybe it was because she had so much. Everyone who knew her had reason to be envious.

It would be only human, wouldn't it?

Lisa did everything well. She was beautiful. She had money. Her father bought her this gorgeous apartment, full service, great light, all paid for.

But that wasn't half of it. She was smart, I thought, now heading north along the waterfront area, the Hudson dark and forbidding to my left, the wind going through Lisa's thin jacket. She was talented, focused, and lucky too, I thought, but then I began to shake my head. Lucky? Well, she was lucky until the end. Then she got very unlucky.

I thought about the people in her life, all of them in *my* life now. Any of them could have done it.

The only one I really *liked* in all this was Avi. So I began to wonder if I was being blind, no one to shout from the shore and head me in the right direction, blind because I liked him so much, admired him, as if that meant he weren't capable of murder.

I had been sort of skipping over him because I thought he was so special. But all kinds of people commit crimes, and he *could* have done it. I thought about how sweet he'd been to me. Not sweet, really—generous would be more to the point. I guess I'd prefer it if it were one of the others. And then I found myself talking out loud, a typical New Yorker. Is this pathetic, I said, or what? I'm supposed to be a fucking detective.

Jesus, I was cold. I crossed West Street again, but instead of getting out of the wind, I walked along the other side of the traffic, finding myself headed toward Bank Street. I crossed the street and walked into the Westbeth courtyard, across the street from the studio, the place where Paul was killed, and sat facing the school and looking up.

It was late now, very late, but the studio lights were on, the only ones on in the whole building. I wondered who was there. For a moment I had the eerie feeling that if I went upstairs, it would be Lisa, sitting at Avi's desk, the way she used to, doing the paperwork, Ch'an at her side. I shivered at the thought.

It was probably Avi, catching up on the work Lisa used to do for him.

From the very beginning, I didn't want it to be him, so I kept looking for ways it could be the others. But now that I was thinking about it, it occurred to me that the tradition in t'ai chi—no, not just t'ai chi, all the martial arts—is for serious students to remain with their master for years and years, and not go off on their own, not leave or anything, until the master dies. And Lisa had told him she was leaving, she was going to break with tradition and go off to study in China.

Of course, I thought, standing up, then sitting down again. Her note. It was on *his* desk. What was that they said in real estate? Location, location, location. How could I have missed this?

I could go upstairs, I thought. We need to talk, I could say. Of course, he'd say, looking at me the way he always did, as if there weren't anything that might happen that could be more important than whatever it was I had come to say, as if there were no tomorrow and nothing existed but now.

He'd wait. All I would hear would be the sound of my own breathing.

It's not going well, he might ask, your search for answers? You haven't learned anything? And I could shrug and say, oh, I've learned a lot, just not enough.

I've made a big decision, I could say, just to make sure I had his complete attention. What is that, Rachel? he'd say, and then I'd tell him that my intention had been to learn about Lisa, to understand her life so that I might understand her death. I could tell him how arrogant a notion that was, to think I might become privy to the complexity of another human being by meeting her colleagues, her mentor, her sweetheart, as if, by looking through her books, wearing her clothes, or sleeping in her bed, I would suddenly know who she was, how she felt. What happened, I could say, is that I only learned more about me, who I am, how I feel.

Rachel, he'd say. But I'd hold up my hand. Let me finish, I'd tell him. Something happened to me, something got started that I need to finish. So I've decided to leave here. I've decided to continue my studies in China.

What are you saying? he'd ask, shocked. Lisa's dead, I could say. What difference does it make why she killed herself, when you think about it? But walking in her shoes, reading her books, studying t'ai chi, that's what became important to me. And if Lisa felt the way to do that was to do it in China, then that's what I'm going to do.

But why not stay here and study? I can teach you, he'd tell me, not wanting to let me go. And I'd just say, I can't. I have to follow through with this.

Would he look away? Would there be tears?

I never meant . . . , he might say. And I'd tell him, it doesn't matter what you meant. Or what I meant. It's just something that has to be now. My aunt and uncle are letting me use Lisa's ticket, so I can take Dashiell with me. Everything is paid for. And there's nothing to keep me here, no husband, no job. This was meant to be, Avi. It was fate that brought me here, so that this could happen. Do you believe in fate? I'd ask him.

Now that I was letting in the dark thoughts I'd been avoiding, something else occurred to me. I'd assumed Paul was on his way to see me at the studio. What if he'd been on his way *from* the studio, after being told by Avi that I wasn't there? What if Avi had followed him out?

But why? I searched my mind and couldn't think of a time I'd mentioned him to Avi. If he'd view Paul as a threat to our master/slave relationship, how did he know? And then I remembered the first time we'd met. Avi had picked up the scent of Lisa's perfume from her scarf. Surely he'd noticed the stronger scent of chlorine. Surely he'd understood its significance.

Did he want to make sure that this time nothing

would distract his new apprentice from her studies? Like Lisa's father, was he able to give Lisa anything under the sun, except her freedom?

Zen, I'd read in one of Lisa's books, is simply a voice crying, Wake up, wake up. That was exactly what I had to do, before it was too late.

If I had something to ask Avi, there was no time like the present. I looked up at the studio windows. The lights were still on. I got up, walked across the street, and, taking a couple of deep breaths, prepared to take the stairs, as Lisa always had.

35

I Could See His Aura

SHE WAS STANDING in the doorway, a thin woman in a worn-out coat. "You going in?" she said, pushing her brown bangs off her sallow face.

I nodded.

"I usually clean of a Sunday, when no one's here," she said, the keys in her hand, "but my sister's daughter is getting married, thank God." She opened the door for me. "You people work so late," she said, "no one else in the building. The old man was just leaving when I got here," she said, ringing for the elevator.

I walked in but didn't turn on the lights. Instead, out of habit I guess, I took off Lisa's jacket and changed to her shoes, then, standing in the center of the studio floor, slowly began to do the form. Stepping into White Stork Spreads Its Wings, my right arm bent, my wrist above my eyes, so that I would be able to see the enemy, all I could see was myself reflected in the mirror, wearing Lisa's shoes, Lisa's black workout clothes, and Lisa's bracelet. It dangled heavily from my wrist, reminding me of the weight I had taken on, the obligation to see this through and find out why Lisa, and now Paul, were dead.

Instead of paying attention to what I was doing, I thought about Stewie Fleck, of how guilty he'd acted.

But then I remembered three dogs I was training years ago. When the owner came home and found something wrong, he'd shout, Which of you hoodlums did this? One never looked guilty even if she was. One only looked guilty if he'd done it. And one always looked guilty, no matter who tore the pillow, ate the defrosting chicken, or left a dump on the rug.

Hadn't Janet managed to keep alive the resentment she'd felt for Lisa when she'd come to the school and immediately become Avi's favorite? Lisa had stolen not one but two treasures from Janet. Then she'd tossed them both away, the way the alpha dog might take the best bone, only to drop it a moment later, having taken it as an object lesson, just to prove he could.

Push, push, that's a dog's world, a way of finding out who's who and what's what. Is that what Janet thought Lisa had done, taking Paul and then throwing him away? And did Janet change her rationale with the second killing, leaving the person who stole from her alive to suffer the sting of loss, as she had?

I heard the whine of the elevator. My spine straight, my eyes forward, I moved from my center, continuing the form as the door opened and a moment later closed again. I saw him out of the corner of my eye, just standing there watching me. I finished the form, slowly lowering my arms as I came back to my full height, then turned to face him.

"What are you doing here so late?" I asked. "Couldn't you sleep?"

He shook his head.

"Me neither," I told him.

He looked awful, pale and tired. His shirt looked as if he'd slept in it. His hair hadn't been combed.

"Do you come here often, this late?" I asked, thinking about what the cleaning lady had told me.

"No," he said. "I saw you."

"You saw me?"

"In the courtyard. I often s-sit there. It's so peaceful," he said, his voice flat, his arms hanging down at his sides. "I saw you sitting there. Then I saw you c-come up here. So I f-followed you."

A chill passed through me, as if maybe a window had blown open, letting in the cold night air. But I could see them in the mirror, and they were all closed and latched. Still, I was so cold I thought if I didn't do something fast, I might start shaking. So I did something. Like a dog, I pushed.

"It must be hard for you," I said. "You must get so frustrated. And so lonely."

"It's not so bad when I have someone to talk to," he said, no emotion showing on his face. Or was it just too dark to see?

"Too bad there's no one else to share the load?" I said, picturing the little girl with a round face, like Howie's, the pretty little girl who was clearly her mother's favorite. "No other siblings?"

Howie blinked.

"What about your sister?" I asked, hackles up, teeing up on him now.

"What do you m-m-mean?" he said.

"Your mother said—"

"No. She told you about *that*? She's a liar," he shouted. "It was *her* fault, not m-mine."

"Tell me about it."

"Didn't *she* tell you already?"

"Do you think I'd believe *her*? Come on, Howie, Talk to me."

"I was only seven," he said. "She can't hold me responsible. It was *her* job to watch her, not *mine*."

"But she'd been drinking?"

"A lot," he said, taking a step closer.

"Had she passed out?"

"I don't *know*. I was playing with my miniature cars, on the floor. I had my *back* to them. I didn't s-see. I was only a kid, for chrissake."

"And your mother? What did she say happened?"

"*She* was the one should have been watching. But she blamed *me*. She said I could have prevented it, if I wasn't such a d-dummy. That's what she told the p-p-police. 'My son was supposed to be watching her.' She'd never told *me* that. She never."

"And exactly what was it that happened when no one was watching?" I asked, even though part of me didn't want to hear the answer.

Howie took another step toward me.

"She must have climbed up on the s-sill," he whispered, his face alive now, "and somehow the cord of the venetian blind must have gotten wrapped around her neck. And then she lost her b-balance and fell out. At least th-that's what the p-police said happened. It was very tragic."

In the dark, I thought I saw him smiling.

Was it after that tragic accident that his father had left the first time?

"I guess that's why we live on the ground floor now."

Had little Howie stopped playing with his miniature cars long enough to speed his baby sister on her short flight to nowhere?

Had he done the same for Lisa? Surely it wouldn't have been the first time a man killed a woman because if he couldn't have her, he'd make damn sure no one else would either.

With Lisa gone, he'd latched on to me.

And sitting in the courtyard one afternoon, he'd seen Paul on his way to the studio. Surely Howie would have understood the significance of that, and the threat implied in it. Wouldn't the thought of losing me make him beside himself with rage? Mightn't it even make him furious enough to kill?

Don't ask me why, but even as I wondered if I'd be able to defuse the bomb that I myself had armed, I made things worse. Once set in motion, some things are impossible to stop.

"So, Howie, were you also present the night that Lisa lost her balance?"

"She had no right to do that to me. She had to be punished." He looked at the windows, then back at me. "How else would she learn?"

Had Lisa been writing to him, because he'd cried so when he'd heard her plans? Had he left and come right back, his tears turning to rage on his way down the stairs? Was it Howie, then, not Lisa, who had opened the window, Howie saying he couldn't go on without her friendship? And then what? Had he climbed up on the sill? Of course. And Lisa, her heart pounding, had run across the studio floor in her street shoes to stop him.

He was just standing there, between me and the door, so close I could feel the heat of his body, his eyes as glassy as if he were a dog with rage syndrome. In the dark I could see his aura, red and shooting out around him, like those telescopic photos of the sun. Howie Lish was looking like something that was about to explode.

36

"I Don't Believe You," He Said

SUDDENLY HOWIE CAME to life, grabbing both my wrists in one big paw and, with the other, slapping me hard in the face. "B-bitch," he said, "you're just like h-her, only pretending you care."

"You're wr-wrong, I *d-do* care," I said, desperation in my voice. Now I was the *hikavater*.

T'ai chi, Avi had said, teaches you who you are, and when you know yourself, you can understand others. But I've always known who I am, a person who sees the world through dog-colored glasses. Now I remembered those magazines under Howie's bed. And I knew who he was, too.

My cheek was on fire, and fear had risen in my throat like a bad meal. No one else here, I thought, pushing the fear away. Rely on yourself.

"Ooo, you like it rough," I said. "You have no idea how that turns me on."

"What did you say?"

"Holding me so that I can't get away, slapping me

around, it really turns me on," I told him, looking right into his eyes. I began to laugh. "I mean, it *really* turns me on."

He stopped moving.

I was standing in the middle of the studio, my hands numb from the pressure on my wrists, and the only sound was Howie Lish's heavy breathing.

"Couldn't we do this with less on?" I said, hoping he'd think I was trembling from desire and not fright.

"I don't b-believe you," he said.

"Try me," I told him.

I felt the grip on my wrists loosen a little. I could see the beads of sweat on his cheeks, and running down his neck.

"Let me take my clothes off, slowly, while you watch," I said, someone playing kick-the-can with my heart. "And then you can take yours off, Howie. And I'll watch."

He tightened his grip again.

"You've been thinking about it, haven't you?" I asked him. "I have. Ever since the massage."

Howie smiled. "Go ahead," he said. "Undress."

"I can't, with you holding me. Plenty of time for that later. We have all night, don't we?"

And then I was free, but Howie was so close and the door so far away.

As slowly as if I were doing t'ai chi, I pulled Lisa's black sweater over my head and dropped it onto the floor.

I could feel Howie's breath on my bare skin.

I unhooked my bra, holding it out to him on one finger and then letting it slip into his big hand.

"You, too," I said, stepping back one step and slipping off Lisa's leggings. "I want to see you, Howie."

And as a final sign of good faith, I slipped my under-pants down and stepped out of them.

Howie dropped the bra and began to undress, quickly unbuttoning his shirt and pulling it off. Then he opened his pants and let them drop and began to pull down his underwear. Looking in the mirror, I could see the big, white moon of Howie's ass shining back at me. I could see myself, too, no longer in black, naked now, except for Lisa's t'ai chi shoes and her heavy, silver bracelet hanging from one wrist like a handcuff.

Howie's erection had popped loose and was staring me in the face; his pants and shorts were around his ankles. As he lifted one foot to jettison them on the pristine oak floor of the studio, I remembered Avi telling me that in martial arts, unless doing something gives you a clear advantage, it's better to do nothing at all. For a moment, that's what I did—nothing. Then slowly I reached out for Howie, as if to embrace him, slipping my hands around his sweaty neck, and using a martial art even older than t'ai chi, I too lifted a foot, driving my knee as hard as I could into Howie's naked crotch. And when he'd doubled over, folding at the waist, his head coming forward, I lifted my knee a second time, even harder, and heard it crack against Howie Lish's forehead.

That's when the door opened and Avi walked in, Ch'an trailing behind him.

37

He Seemed to Be Smiling

HE LOOKED SLOWLY from my head to my feet. Too slowly, if you ask me.

"Ah," he said, focusing on Lisa's black cotton shoes. "You've been practicing. Excellent."

He seemed to be smiling, but it was too dark to be sure.

He turned away and headed for his office, Ch'an padding along at his side. "I forgot my keys," he said, "good, good, they're on the desk." I heard him dialing as I quickly got dressed.

I looked down at Howie. His eyes were still closed and there was a large red bruise on his brow. "Thinking," O. J. Simpson had once said, "is what gets you caught from behind." I'd say in his case, and Howie's, it was *not* thinking that had done them in.

After the police left, taking Howie with them, Avi and I sat on the couches and talked until the sun came up. Then I made a phone call and headed home to change to my own clothes, pick up Dashiell, and get the car.

A thin dusting of sand, carried by the wind, covered the street where I parked the Taurus. When I opened the car door, Dashiell headed straight for the ocean, and before I'd locked the car, he was out of sight.

I slipped off my shoes, rolled up my jeans, and swimming in the sea of now, stood in the surf with my dog, just listening to the roar of the waves. Then the yin and yang of private investigation went to see the Jacobs family one last time, to tell them that what had happened to their beautiful daughter had not been their fault.

Carol Lea Benjamin is a noted author about, and trainer of, dogs. She lives in New York City with her husband and two dogs. Her first Rachel and Dash mystery, <u>This Dog for Hire</u>, won a Shamus Award.